The London
Train

Also by Tessa Hadley

ACCIDENTS IN THE HOME
EVERYTHING WILL BE ALL RIGHT
SUNSTROKE AND OTHER STORIES
THE MASTER BEDROOM

The London Train

Tessa Hadley

JONATHAN CAPE
LONDON

Published by Jonathan Cape 2011

2 4 6 8 10 9 7 5 3 1

First published in Great Britain in 2011 by
Jonathan Cape
Random House, 20 Vauxhall Bridge Road,
London SW1V 2SA

www.rbooks.co.uk

Addresses for companies within The Random House Group Limited can be
found at: www.randomhouse.co.uk/offices.htm

The Random House Group Limited Reg. No. 954009

A CIP catalogue record for this book
is available from the British Library

ISBN 9780224090971

The Random House Group Limited supports The Forest Stewardship
Council (FSC), the leading international forest certification organisation.
All our titles that are printed on Greenpeace approved FSC certified paper
carry the FSC logo. Our paper procurement policy can be found at
www.rbooks.co.uk/environment

Mixed Sources
Product group from well-managed
forests and other controlled sources
www.fsc.org Cert no. TT-COC-2139
© 1996 Forest Stewardship Council

FSC

Typeset by Palimpsest Book Production Limited,
Falkirk, Stirlingshire

Printed and bound in Great Britain by
CPI Mackays, Chatham, Kent ME5 8TD

for Ed and Alice

Contents

The London Train

I

By the time Paul got to the Home, the under-takers had already removed his mother's body. He protested at this, it seemed done in indecent haste. He had set out as soon as they telephoned him; surely they could have waited the three or four hours it had taken him to get there (the traffic had been heavy on the M5). Mrs Phipps, the owner of the Home, guided him into her office, where whatever scene he might make wouldn't upset the other residents. She was petite, viva-cious, brown-skinned, with traces of a South African accent; he didn't dislike her, he thought she ran the Home to a good standard of care, his mother had seemed to resign herself gratefully to her efficiency and brisk baby-talk. Even at this moment, however, there was no sign that the taut, bright mask of Mrs Phipps's good humour, respectfully muted in the circumstances, ever gave way to any impulse of authentic feeling. Her room was pleasant; an open sash window let in the afternoon spring sunshine from the garden. On the wall behind her desk was pinned a colourful year planner, almost every square scribbled over with busyness and responsibility: he imagined a space on the planner where his mother's occupation of her room abutted abruptly onto blankness.

If he wanted to see his mother, Mrs Phipps said, putting the right nuance of sorrowful tact into her voice, she could telephone the undertakers, he could go to see her there. Paul was aware of the hours ahead as requiring scrupulous vigilance; he must be so careful to do the right thing, but it wasn't clear what the right thing might be. He said he would take the undertakers' address and number, and Mrs Phipps gave it to him.

– I ought to let you know, she added – because I wouldn't want you to find out in any roundabout way, that Evelyn made another of her bids for freedom last night.

– Bids for freedom?

He thought that she was using an odd euphemism for dying, but she went on to explain that his mother had got out of bed at some point in the evening, and gone into the garden in her nightdress. There was a place they always looked when they couldn't find her: Evelyn's little den in the shrubbery.

– I'm sorry that it happened. But I did warn you that we simply aren't able to provide twenty-four-hour supervision of residents when they fall ill. The girls were in and out of her room all evening, checking on her. That was how we realised she had got out. To be frank with you, she was so weak none of us had imagined she was even capable of getting out of bed. She can only have been out there for ten to fifteen minutes before we found her. Twenty at the most.

They had brought her inside and put her back to bed. She had had a good night; she only deteriorated after breakfast this morning.

Mrs Phipps was worrying that he might make a complaint, Paul realised.

– It's all right. If that's what she wanted to do, then I'm glad she was able to get out.

She was relieved, although she didn't understand his point. – Of course we were worried about her body temperature, these spring nights are treacherous. We wrapped her up warmly and made her a hot drink, we kept an eye on her all through the night.

Paul asked if he could sit in his mother's room for a while. They had already stripped her bed and pulled up over the mattress a clean counterpane in the standard flowered material that was everywhere in the Home: there were no signs he could see of what had taken place in here. Mrs Phipps had reassured him that his mother had 'gone very peacefully', but he took this as no more than a form of words. He sat for a while in his mother's armchair, looking round at her things: the last condensed residue of the possessions that had accompanied her from her home to her small flat in sheltered accommodation and then to this room. He recognised some of them only because he had moved them for her each time; others were familiar from his childhood and youth: a majolica fruit bowl, a blue glass girl who had once been fixed on

5

the side of a vase for flowers, the red Formica coffee table that always stood beside her chair, with its built-in ashtray on a chrome stem.

When Paul left the Home, he drove to the undertakers and sat in his car in their small forecourt car park. He had to go inside and talk to them about arrangements for the funeral; but there was also the issue of seeing his mother's body. He was his parents' only child. Evelyn had absorbed the brunt of his father's death twenty years ago, when Paul was in his twenties: now all the lines met in him. Of course his wife would be sorry, and his children too; however, because for the last few years Evelyn's mind had wandered farther and farther, she had become a distant figure to the girls, and he had only brought them to visit her every so often. She still recognised them, but if they went into the garden to play, or even if they went to the toilet, or moved round to the other side of her chair, she would forget she had already seen them; each time they returned she would greet them again, her face lighting up with the same delight.

His father had died in hospital after a heart attack; Evelyn was with him, Paul had been living in Paris at the time and had not arrived until the next day. The possibility of seeing the body had not arisen; in his concentration then on his mother's bereavement, it probably hadn't seemed important. Now he did not know whether this was important or not. He peered into the undertakers' shop window with its kitsch discretion, urns and pleated silks and artificial flowers. When eventually he got out of his car to go inside, he realised it was past six o'clock. There was a closed sign hanging on the shop door, with a number to contact in case of emergency, which he didn't write down. He would come back in the morning.

He had got into the habit of using the Travelodge, if ever he needed to stay overnight in Birmingham when he came to visit his mother; conveniently, there was one only ten minutes' drive from the Home. He unpacked his few things, a clean shirt and socks, toothbrush, a notebook, the two books of poetry he was reviewing – he had not known when he set out in the morning how long he would need to stay. Then he telephoned Elise.

– She'd gone by the time I got there, he said.

– Oh, poor Evelyn.

– Mrs Phipps said she went very peacefully.

– Oh, Paul. I'm so sorry. Are you all right? Where are you? Do you need me to come up? I'm sure I could get someone to have the girls.

He reassured her that he was all right. He didn't want to eat, but walked around the streets until he found a pub where he drank two pints, and browsed a copy of the *Birmingham Mail* that was lying on a table. His mind locked into the words, he read each page exhaustively, taking in without any inward commentary every least detail: crime, entertainment, *in memoriam*. He had a dread of being overtaken by some paroxysm of grief in a public place. Back in his room, he did not want to read either of the poetry books; when he had undressed he looked in the drawer of the bedside table for a Bible, but it was a New International Version, no good to him. He turned out the light and lay under the sheet, because the heating was stuffy and airless and you could not open the windows more than a crack. Through the crack the fine spring night sent its smells of greenness and growth, mingled with petrol fumes from the road outside that never stilled or grew quiet, however late it was. He was relieved, he thought. What had happened was merely the ordinary, expected, common thing: the death of an elderly parent, the release from a burden of care. He had not wanted her life prolonged, in the form it had taken recently. He had not visited her as often as he should. He had been bored, when he did visit.

When he closed his eyes there came an unwanted image of his mother out in the dark garden of the Home in her nightdress, so precise that he sat up in bed abruptly. She seemed so close at hand that he looked around for her: he had the confused but strong idea that this present moment could be folded closely enough to touch against a moment last night, that short time ago when she was still alive. He saw not the bent old lady she had become, but the mature woman of his teenage years: her dark hair in the plait she had long ago cut off, the thick-lensed black-rimmed glasses of those days, her awkward tall strength and limbs full of power. When she was still alive it had been difficult sometimes for him to remember her past selves, and he had been afraid he had lost them for ever, but this recall was vivid and total. He switched on the light, got out of bed, turned on the television and watched the news, images of the war in Iraq.

Lying stretched out again in the dark on his back, naked, covered with the sheet, he couldn't sleep. He wished he could remember better those passages in *The Aeneid* where Anchises in the Underworld explains to his son how the dead are gradually cleansed in the after-life of all the thick filth and encrusting shadows that have accumulated through their mortal involvement, their living; when after aeons they are restored to pure spirit, they long, they eagerly aspire, to return to life and the world and begin again. Paul thought that there was no contemporary language adequate to describe the blow of his mother's vanishing. A past in which a language of such dignity as Virgil's was possible seemed to him itself sometimes only a dream.

The next morning when he went back to the under-takers he told himself in advance that he must ask to see her body. However, once he was involved in making the arrangements for the funeral, he found it difficult to speak at all, even to give his minimal consent to what-ever was proposed: his dumbness did not come from deep emotion, but its opposite, a familiar frozen aver-sion that seized him whenever he had to transact these false relations with the external world. He imagined the young man he spoke with had been trained to watch for the slips and give-away confusions of grieving family members, and so he tried to make himself coldly impen-etrable. Elise should have been there to help him, she was gifted at managing this side of life. He could not bring himself to expose to the youth's solicitude any intimate need to touch his mother a last time; and perhaps anyway he didn't want to touch her.

Afterwards he went to the Home as he had arranged, to deal with paperwork and to clear his mother's belongings from her room, although Mrs Phipps had insisted there was no hurry, he was welcome to leave things as they were until after the funeral. He sat again in Evelyn's armchair. The room was really quite small; but on the occasion they had come here first to look at it, there had been someone playing a piano downstairs, and he had allowed this to convince him that the Home was a humane place, that it would be possible to have a full life here. He had not often heard the piano afterwards. When he had packed a few things into boxes he asked Mrs Phipps to dispose of the rest, and also to show him what she had called his mother's 'den' in the garden; he saw her wonder whether he was going to make difficulties after all.

In the garden the noise of traffic wasn't insistent. The sun was shining, the bland neat garden, designed for easy upkeep, was full of birdsong: chaffinch and blackbird, the broody rumble of the collared doves. Mrs Phipps's high-heeled beige suede shoes grew dark from the grass still wet with dew as they crossed the lawn, her heels sinking in the turf, and he saw that she was annoyed by this, but would not say anything. The Home had been a late-Victorian rectory, built on a small rise: at the far end of the garden she showed him that, if you pushed through the bushes to where the old stone wall curved round, there was a little trodden space of bare earth, a twiggy hollow, room enough in it to stand upright. The wall was too high for an old lady to sit on or climb over, but she could have leaned on it and looked over at the view, she could have watched for anyone coming. When Evelyn was a child, when there was still a rector in the rectory, everything beyond this point would have been fields and woods: now it was built up as far as the eye could see. Paul pushed inside the hollow himself and looked out, while Mrs Phipps waited, politely impatient to get back to her day's business. He could see from there the sprawling necropolis of the remains of Longbridge, where Evelyn's brothers had worked on the track in the Fifties and Sixties, building Austin Princesses and Rileys and Minis. At night this great post-industrial expanse of housing development and shopping complexes and scrapyards was mysterious behind its myriad lights; by day it looked vacant, as if the traffic flowed around nowhere.

He couldn't feel anything inside his mother's space, couldn't get back the sensation of her presence that had come to him the night before; there had been no point in bothering Mrs Phipps to bring him out here. But in the afternoon, driving back to where he lived in the Monnow Valley in Wales, he found himself at one point on the M50 quite unable to turn his head to look behind him, so sure was he that the boxes of Evelyn's bits and pieces on the back seat had transmogrified into her physical self. He seemed to hear her familiar rustle and exhalation as she settled herself, he tensed expectantly as if she might speak. His knowledge of the fact of her death seemed an embarrassment between them; he felt ashamed of it. He had driven her this way often enough, bringing her home for weekends before she grew too confused to want to come. She had liked the idea that her son was bringing up his family in the countryside: although all her own life had been spent in the city, she had had a cherished store of old-fashioned dreams of country life.

In Evelyn's room the miscellany of her possessions had seemed rich with implications; transposed here to Tre Rhiw, he was afraid it might only seem so much rubbish. He couldn't think where they would keep the ugly fruit bowl, or the Formica smoking table. There was no smoking in this house. His daughters were fanatical against it, at school they were indoctrinated to believe it was an evil comparable to knife crime or child molestation. Paul had given up anyway, but when his friend Gerald came round in the evenings the girls supervised him vigilantly, driving him out even in rain or wind to smoke at the bottom of the garden; in revenge Gerald fed his cigarette butts to their goats.

The girls were still at school; the bus didn't drop them off until half past four. Elise was in her workshop, but she came over to the kitchen as soon as she heard him. She was in her stockinged feet, with a tape measure round her neck, red and gold threads from whatever fabric she was working with clinging to her black T-shirt and leggings. She had a business with a friend, restoring and selling antiques. Paul called her a Kalmyk because of her wide cheek bones. Her skin was an opulent pale gold, she had flecked hazel eyes; her mouth was wide, with fine red lips that closed precisely. She was three years older than he was, the flesh was thickening into creases under her eyes. She had begun dyeing her hair the colour of dark honey, darker than the blonde she had been.

– You've brought back some of her things.

– There's more in the car. I told Mrs Phipps to get rid of the rest.

She picked items out of the box one by one and held them, considering intently a Bakelite dressing-table set, filled with scraps of jewellery. – Poor Evelyn, she said, and her eyes filled up with tears, although she hadn't been particularly close to his mother. She had used to get exasperated, when Evelyn was still *compos mentis*, about her panics, her fearful ideas of what went on in the world outside her own narrow experience of it. Evelyn's eagerness to spend time with them would always sour, after a couple of days, into spasms of resentment against her daughter-in-law, Elise's insouciant-seeming housekeeping, her unpunctuality. Evelyn had been bored in the country, she had feared the river, and the goats. They always ate too late, which gave her indigestion.

Elise put her arms around Paul, and kissed his neck. – It's so sad. I'm sorry, darling.

– I wish I could have been with her. It doesn't seem as if anything real has happened.

– Did you see her?

13

He shook his head. – They had already taken her away.

– That's awful. You should have seen her.

After she had hugged him for a while, she took the kettle to the sink, filled it from the noisy old tap that squealed and thundered, lifted the cover of the hotplate on the Rayburn.

– I don't know what to do with all this stuff, he said.

– Don't worry. Think about it later. It will be good to have her things around, to remind us of her.

Paul carried the boxes down into his study. This was at the opposite end of the kitchen to Elise's workroom, built into an old outhouse sunk so low into the steep hillside that the sloping front garden crossed his window halfway up; on the other side, he had a view of the river. The walls were eighteen inches thick; he liked the feeling that he was at work inside the earth.

When the girls came home they were briefly subdued and in awe of what had happened to their Nana; they cried real tears, Becky shyly hiding her face against her mother. She was nine, with a tender sensibility; shadows had always chased across her brown freckled face. Ten minutes later they had forgotten and were playing outside his window in the front garden. He could see their feet and legs, Becky jumping her skipping rope, Joni the six-year-old stamping and singing loudly: 'Bananas, in pyjamas, are coming down the stairs.'

II

At the end of all the other transactional calls he had to make the next day, Paul meant to telephone Annelies, his first wife. Before he could get round to it, Annelies telephoned him, which was not usual; often they did not speak for months at a time. She sounded as if she was offended with him, but he was used to that: it had been their mode together, the contest of hot offence and cold repudiation, ever since they first found themselves in this awkward relation, strangers bound together by the thread of their child – his oldest daughter, who was now almost twenty. He had not been much older than that himself when she was born.

– How long do you think it is since you last saw Pia? Annelies demanded as soon as he picked up the phone.

– I was going to telephone you, he said. – I have some news. Mum died yesterday.

He tried not to be glad that he cut her righteousness off in mid-flow.

– Ah, Paul. That's sad. How sad. I'm so sorry. Pia will be upset, she loved her Nana.

Paul had used to drive Pia to Birmingham, to visit her grandmother in the Home. It was one of the ways he filled the time he spent with his oldest daughter, and it was true that she had seemed genuinely attached to Evelyn. She had surprised him; he did not think of Pia as resourceful, but she had been full of patience, not minding the old lady's repetitions, having her hand squeezed in emotion, over and over.

– Should I talk to her?

– She isn't here. This is why I was telephoning you.

– You mean she's out?

– No. I mean she's gone. Taken her stuff and gone. Not all of it, of course. Her room's still one hell of a mess.

– Gone where?

– I don't know.

Pia had left home after an argument with her mother about a week ago. There was no point in raising any alarm, going to the police, because Pia had phoned Annelies twice, to tell her she was safe. She said she was staying with friends.

– Then I suppose she's all right. She's old enough. She's free to go where she likes.

– But which friends, Paul? Is it too much to want to know where she is?

Pia was supposed to be in the first year of a degree at Greenwich, in subjects he was never precisely sure of: media, culture and sociology? Paul had taken her

16

out for a meal when he was last up in London, a few weeks ago. He tried hard now to remember what they had talked about. Instead he remembered a new steel stud that she'd had fitted in her lower lip: she had sucked at this stud whenever their conversation dried up, which it often did, stretching her top lip down to pull at it in a way that was nervous and unattractive. He had tried to get out of her some spark of interest in what she was studying, but she spoke about it all with the same obedient flatness. Her mouth with its full, pale lips and strong shape was like his own, he knew that: Pia was supposed to look like him, she was tall and fair and thin as he was, her skin was susceptible to flares and rashes, like his when he was adolescent. In spirit she couldn't have seemed farther from how he was at her age: he had been consumed in the cold fire of politics and ideas, she was anxiously shy, wrapped up in the tiny world of her friends and their fads, devoid of intellectual curiosity.

– She'll soon be back, he reassured Annelies. – As soon as she realises she has to do her own washing and buy her own food.

Annelies came to the funeral, in a black suit that fitted too tightly. She was almost matronly these days; Elise beside her seemed light and elastic on her feet as a girl, even though she was the older of the two. Elise had said black didn't matter any more, she had let Becky and Joni wear their party dresses: the little girls scampered, vivid as sprites in the sunshine, among the ugly monuments of the crematorium. Elise and Annelies had never been rivals; Paul's first marriage had been over for several years when he met Elise. Elise had made a point of winning over his forthright, abrupt first wife. Now the two women borrowed tissues and whispered confidences, squeezing and touching one another in the way women did. He felt remote from Annelies. She was beginning to look like her mother, a stout, sensible Dutch primary-school teacher.

During the perfunctory service Paul couldn't take in what he ought to. The minister was a stranger who had been supplied with a few platitudes: Evelyn had worked hard all her life, much of it at Wimbush's bakery; she had devoted herself also to her family; in her retirement she had enjoyed travelling all over Britain and Ireland, and farther afield too. Paul had had no idea, when asked, which were his mother's favourite hymns. She had never been a churchgoer, although she had been coyly, almost flirtatiously, interested in religious ideas. He had guessed at a couple of things from his childhood: 'There Is a Green Hill' and 'To Be a Pilgrim'. At the end of the service net curtains were pulled jerkily on a rail around the coffin before it was shunted off.

Paul's cousin Christine had offered to have a little gathering after the funeral at her place, which wasn't too far from what she called, with ghoulish familiarity, 'the crem'. There were plenty of family at the service and the party, which touched him, although Evelyn had been the last of her generation, and there was probably no one here he would come back to visit once today was

18

over. Chris made a point of sitting squeezing his hands in a chair with her knees touching his. He liked her plain, long face with glasses, her grey hair cut tidily short, the silk scarf she hadn't quite got right, thrown over her shoulder; she was confident and funny. Most of the cohort of cousins in his generation had done well for themselves, they had made the archetypal baby-boomer move out of their parents' class, they were in local government or in hospitals, or worked in middle management. Chris was a school secretary, her husband a manager in a company servicing photocopiers. Their house was comfortable, lovingly done up.

Paul and Chris hadn't much else to talk about except to reminisce over the old days. Her memories of the family were much fuller than his, as if despite appearances she had only ever moved a step away from that world: she wasn't nostalgic for it, but she talked as if it was something she had not yet finished with, even though her own parents were long dead. She could remember sharing an outdoor toilet in the back yard, and eating off a table spread with newspaper. Her family had moved when she was nine out from the centre of town, in the slum clearances, as his parents had too, when he was a baby. In their council house on one of the new estates, Chris's mother had suddenly produced tablecloths, curtains, carpets: she had been saving them, wrapped in their polythene, because they were too good to use. Chris told the story in a kind of rage of amusement, even after all these years, at the waste of life, 'doing without', 'saving for later'.

* * *

19

In the days after the funeral, Paul sat fruitlessly in his study for hours, ostensibly working on his review, writing and then deleting, pretending to himself that he was making a breakthrough and then recognising each breakthrough in turn as another dead end. After a while he would cross the yard and go into Elise's workshop. She had converted the old tumbledown barn into a studio when they first moved in to Tre Rhiw; she could do bricklaying and plumbing and plastering, and had taken electricity into all their outhouses. She had been surprised, when they were first together, at his practical incompetence: hadn't his father been a manual worker? Her father had been a general in the army, then a military adviser in Washington. Paul had explained that his father, a tool-setter in a screw factory, had never done anything in the house, he wouldn't touch anybody else's job. A specialism so narrow as his – one machine, one product – didn't teach transferable skills. The Swiss machines he oversaw in his last years at work had been fully automated, in any case.

Huge glass doors were let into the side wall of the barn, to give the maximum light: beyond them a row of pliant, graceful aspen poplars ran up beside the house from the river to the road at the front, breaking up the glare of the sun – or, more usually, breaking the force of wind and rain against the house. In the barn, planes of yellow sunshine swam with motes of dust from the cloth Elise was using to cover an early Victorian chaise longue, a raspberry velvet with a fine pattern in it, like tiny leaves. Her business partner,

Ruth, scoured the sales and auction rooms for unusual pieces, found buyers for their finished products, and delivered them; Elise repaired and upholstered and French-polished as necessary. They had a genius for spotting derelict bits of junk and seeing how they could be made enchanting: the pieces always looked as if they were smuggled out from *Alice in Wonderland,* thick with mockery and magic. Tre Rhiw was full of treasures: after a while the plump-stuffed love-seats and misty mirrors and little spindly bureaux Paul had got used to disappeared, sold on to customers, and new oddities took their place.

Elise paused in her heaving of fabric through her sewing machine, taking off the glasses she was beginning to need for close work, smiling and wiping her face on her sleeve. – Why don't you make coffee? she suggested consolingly.

He didn't want to talk to her about how he felt, but heard it spilling out of him nonetheless. – I'm dry. I've dried up.

– Why don't you write about Evelyn? You know, about her life, all the stuff about how she nearly emigrated, and then working in the bakery, and so on. Isn't that all really interesting?

He hated the idea of turning his mother's life into material, garnering for himself the glamour of the proletarian hardship in his background, when the truth had been that he had left her determinedly behind, casting off her way of life. He wouldn't even argue with Elise. It wasn't the first time she had suggested this. He supposed the social milieu he came out of – the working class of a great manufacturing city – seemed as alien and exotic to his wife as her background did to him: show jumping and boarding school and a house in France. It had excited them, when they were first together, to play out their class roles as though they had been born in another century: he would have been her servant, she would have been his mistress, finding his accent and uncouthness an impassable divide, deeper than all the efforts of sympathy and imagination.

– No, I wouldn't, Elise had insisted. – I wouldn't have been like that. Not everyone was like that, there were always feelings that transgressed those boundaries.

The weather was hot and fine. He went out with his friend Gerald, for one of their usual walks in the countryside. They followed the Monnow downstream; it hurried noisily over the lip of boulders and pebbles washed smooth, bulging under the thick lens of water. The path first hugged its bank, then meandered away from it across small fields with hedgerows dense with birdsong, bee-drone; blossom was snowed over the stumpy bitter blackthorns, the beeches' slim buds were fine tan leather, the still-bare ash dangled its dead keys. One of the great patriarchal beeches had come down across the path in a high wind only a few weeks before, its roots nakedly upreared, the buds at its far extremity still glistening with deluded life, a woodpecker's neat secret hole exposed at eye level, a raw crack in the wood of the massive trunk where it had hit the earth. They had to climb over it, admiring the thick folds in the beige hide where the limbs pushed their way out.

Paul said he had been thinking about the old model of human time as a succession of declining ages, each approximating less and less to the intensity and quality of the original life-force. Cultures gained through time in technical sophistication, but in adopting increasingly complex forms, the primordial force expended and exhausted itself, lost density and beauty.

– And then what? Gerald said.

– The Stoics thought that, like growth from a seed, at the end of a phase all life dies back inside itself, the form is annihilated, the force remains alone. We're living at the end of something, using something up.

– It's more likely that life on earth will just ramble on and on farther ahead than we can see, inventing new kinds of messes, undergoing all sorts of horrors and then patching up again, changing the shape of things out of all recognition. Each generation insisting, this is it, we've really done for it, this really is it this time.

Gerald was delicately intelligent, sceptical, huge, with a craggy pockmarked face, massive jaw, long hair tucked behind his ears. He had a fractional post (all he wanted) teaching French literature at the University of Glamorgan, and he lived alone in a disordered flat in Cardiff, his carpet stained brown with tea from the huge pot he was always topping up. The place reeked of marijuana, he lived on hummus and pitta bread and Scotch eggs; utterly undomesticated, he was able to keep his own times and lose himself in whatever labyrinths of

23

reading or thought he strayed into. Paul and he were working together, fitfully, on translations of Guy Goffette, a Belgian poet. Sometimes Paul thought that Gerald's freedom was what he wanted most and was deprived of, because of the distractions of his family. But he shrank from it too; what bound him to the children seemed to him life-saving. He thought of them as his blessing, counterbalancing the heady instability of a life lived in the mind.

Paul lamented some of the renovations in the valley, ugly barn conversions for holiday lets. Cottages that were once the homes of agricultural labourers fetched stockbrokers' prices now, as if the countryside was under some sick enchantment, in which the substance of things was invisibly replaced with only a simulacrum of itself. Gerald told him his regret was romantic; he asked Paul if he wanted back the unsanitary homes of the rural poor.

– Did you and Gerald talk? Elise asked later. She was cleansing her face in front of the mirror in the bedroom, sitting in the long T-shirt she wore for bed.

– About what?

– About Evelyn, what you're feeling. I suppose that's improbable. You two never talk about real things.

– They are real.

She was pulling the faces she made to stretch the skin while she scoured it with greasy cotton-wool balls; her hair was scraped out of the way behind a band. When she was finished, she stood over him where he sat on the side of the bed, raking his hair with her fingers away from his brow, frowning into his frown, interrogating him.

– Tell me how you're feeling, she said. – Why don't you tell me?

– I'm all right.

In the night he woke, sure that his mother was close to him in the bedroom. The pale curtains at the window were inflating and blowing in the night wind; he had a confused idea that he was sick and had been brought in to sleep in her bed, as had happened sometimes when he was a child. Evelyn would wake him, moving around late at night in the room and undressing, quietly in charge. He seemed to smell the old paraffin heater. He struggled to sit up, clammy and guilty, breathless. Elise slept with her back turned, a mound under the duvet, corona of hair on the pillow. Light from the landing slipped through the crack where the catch was broken and the door never quite closed; the dressing-table mirror picked it up and shone like flat water.

When he was a teenager, he had thought his mother an exceptional, unique woman, thwarted only by her limited life and opportunities from becoming something more. She was physically clumsy, good-looking, but inept in her relations with other people, shyly superior. As if it explained something, she had always told the story of how she had been on the point of emigrating to Canada, after her parents died: she had been a dutiful daughter, nursing both of them through long illnesses. She had filled out all the papers, she said. Then instead, at the last minute, in her late thirties, she had married his father and had Paul, long after she had given up hope of having a child of her own. When he was a boy she used to hold his face between her hands, and he had read in her look the promise of himself, surprising and elating her, the giftedness she could not account for.

III

Pia didn't come home. She was still calling her mother, insisting she was all right, but when Annelies contacted the university, they said she had dropped out of all her classes. Paul went up to London, not knowing what he ought to do to help. Annelies had lived for years in a terraced street off Green Lanes road in Harringay: he could have believed himself in Istanbul or Ankara, the shop signs unintelligible to him, the heaped-up luscious excess of fruit and vegetables lit by electric lamps under green plastic awnings, the cafés with baklava and brass coffee-makers set out in their windows, everything still open for business at seven in the evening, rich with the smells of lamb and garlic from the restaurants. Annelies's little house was over-stuffed and airless, sweat glistened on the tanned, freckled skin across the top of her breasts. She wore a sleeveless flowered dress; the brassy glints in her curls were beginning to be mixed with grey. They sat in the kitchen and she opened a bottle of Gewürztraminer,

27

which he didn't like, but drank because there wasn't anything else. Hearts were stencilled on the kitchen walls and on the painted bench at the table. There were hearts everywhere he looked: fridge magnets, postcards, tea towels, even heart-shaped pebbles picked up from the beach. Annelies worked for the Refugee Council, helping asylum seekers appeal against deportation. Beside this, in her house, Paul's half-realised writing career seemed a shoddy equivocation.

– What are we going to do, Paul? Have you spoken to her?

– She won't answer her phone when she sees it's me. I asked Becky to text her; she texted back the same stuff – she'll be in touch soon, not to worry.

– But she's given up her college course: how can I not worry? How is she feeding herself, I'd like to know? How will she pay the rent, wherever she's living? When she telephones, she won't answer any of these questions! You should hear her, Paul, she doesn't sound like herself. Something's wrong, I know it. I beg her to tell me where she is; she cuts me off.

Privately Paul thought that Pia's giving up the course didn't matter much. It might even be good for her, to have a taste of the world outside the routines of education and the safety of her mother's house; she was one of those girls who got through school drawing perfect margins and underlining their headings in red biro, cutting and pasting projects from the Internet. But he felt sorry for Annelies, in her distress shaken out of the normal pattern of her relationship with him. Usually she would never appeal to him, or allow him to see she was afraid. She seemed disoriented, in this home where signs of Pia were everywhere around them: her childish drawings framed on the wall, photographs of her at every age on the pinboard, teenage jewellery hung over the cup-hooks, red high heels that could not possibly belong to Annelies in a corner. His daughter seemed to him to flavour the house more distinctively in her absence than she had when she lived here.

He asked about the argument they'd had.

– It was nothing. I came into her bedroom without knocking, that's all. What is she doing in there, that she needs to hide it? She was only playing with her make-up, I could see. I asked her, doesn't she have college work to get on with?

Annelies saw no need for locks on bathroom doors; when she was married to Paul she used to look over his shoulder when he was writing, hadn't understood why he raged at this. And at first it had been what he had loved, how she had stripped off for him fearlessly; holidaying in Sweden, she had dived without a qualm into freezing water off the stony islands they rowed out to, while he was still picking his way painfully across the rocks.

– I'm liberal, she said now, – you know that. But what about drugs, sexually transmitted diseases? There must be a boyfriend involved, I'm sure, someone Pia doesn't want me to meet.

– She's not stupid, she's a sensible, sound girl. We have to trust her, it's all we can do. I'll talk to student services at Greenwich, though I don't suppose they'll know anything. I'll see if I can find some of her friends.

In her absence, he felt he hardly knew Pia, although those hours they spent together in her childhood, when he had looked after her at weekends, had sometimes seemed to stretch out to a punitive length, so that he longed to get back to his work, his books. He would surely have stirred – even in those days, as a reluctant father, much too young – in response to a child who was spirited, suggestible, haunted: he had looked to see if any of this was in Pia, but he had not found it, or she had resisted his finding it. Determinedly she had made herself stolid, sulky, unyielding. She had dragged flat-footedly after him round the museums, the National Gallery, raising her eyes to the paintings when he told her to look, but refusing to see what was in them. She had not read the books he bought her. In the museum shops she had yearned over soft toys with cartoon animal faces: she had seemed to care more about buying things than seeing things or knowing them.

He stayed the night with friends and went to Greenwich the next day, thinking he might do better in person than on the telephone: but they weren't allowed to give him any information. Not even about her timetable, so that he could ask after her among her classmates? The young woman looked at him with patient hostility.

– I know it's difficult for parents, she said. – But the students are adults. If you were on a course here, you wouldn't want us giving out your personal data to anyone who asked.

– You told her mother, though, that Pia had dropped out of her classes.

– I don't know who gave out that information.

He was shocked to find himself closed out; he had counted on the power of his confident concern, and the charm he had turned on this doughy-faced girl in glasses. Talking to Annelies the night before, he had not taken her anxiety seriously. Now, making his way back to Paddington, the crowds pouring along the streets and into the entrances of the Underground station seemed an infinite stream: the mind, he thought, was not naturally equipped to conceive of the multiplication of all these lives heaped up together in a metropolis, mountain upon mountain of life-atoms. Slipped away from them into this, Pia was lost – if she chose to be. Her mobile was the only slender link they had to her: what if she stopped calling, or lost her phone? How could they hope to trace her then?

Shuffling in the crowd towards the exit from the Tube at Paddington, he glanced across to the opposite platform and suddenly, extraordinarily, was sure he saw Pia waiting there, standing out tall above the people in front of her, staring into the distance from where the train was coming, pale hair fastened into bunches on her shoulders, black jacket zipped to the neck. If he had not known her, he would have seen a serious and dreamy girl, not unattractive but old-fashioned, somehow vulnerable and raw. Paul shouted her name, disrupting the queue for the exit, forging towards the platform edge to attract her attention, waving his arm. He thought she turned and looked towards him – but then everyone looked, and at that moment the train roared in, swallowing up his sight of her, probably to carry her away; he was left cut off with his conspicuousness, the object of everyone's idling attention.

In case she had waited, for a different train or for him, he hurried over to the opposite platform, but of course by the time he got there the train was gone, and Pia with it, if she had ever been there. He began at once to doubt that he had seen her. It must have been some other girl, blonde and tall as Pia was, appearing at the right moment to collaborate with his fears. He was agitated by his exaggerated response and his disappointment, which translated as he recovered into a loop of worry, circling round and round. All the way home on the train, a woman in a seat nearby, not visible to him, talked into her mobile at full volume, filling up every crevice of his privacy, so that he couldn't concentrate on his book. – I think that's a beautiful feeling . . . you said before you wanted to move on . . . for any person growing emotionally . . . it's a different sort of painful, it's the healing kind . . .

When he arrived back at Tre Rhiw the last sunshine was still on the back garden, slanting obliquely, burnishing the grass and shrubs as if the light was yellow oil. The spell of fine spring weather was holding, everyone's pleasure in it tinctured with nervousness, because of climate change. The girls were playing with their goats in the field, feeding them leftover vegetables. Joni was fearlessly familiar with animals: she crooked her arm around the goats' necks and nuzzled their ears, kissing their pink grey-spotted lips, with a sense of the impudence and effect of her own performance. Becky was more circumspect, anxious for the goats' feelings, holding her hand out carefully flat to offer them food, as she had been taught. The animals tolerated them, businesslike they munched on, beards wagging, alien eyes cast backwards as if they were unwilling witnesses to visions. Elise was sitting out in her sunglasses, tinkling the ice in a Campari, on one of the deckchairs she had covered in leftovers from the fabrics she used in her work; a fantastical vine seemed to wind out of the top of her head, drooping with fruit. She waved her drink at Paul, told him to bring another deckchair from the house. When he said he thought he'd seen Pia at Paddington, Elise believed it was possible: she did wear a black jacket, she could have been on her way back from south Wales, she might have been visiting her friends in the village.

– Without letting us know she was here?

– Perhaps, if she doesn't want us to know what she's up to. She doesn't want you pressuring her to go back to college.

– What friends, anyway?

– She likes the Willis boy.

– How can she?

Paul didn't get on with the Willis family.

– They're rather alike, don't you think? Elise said. – Pia and James?

She reassured him that he didn't need to be anxious. – I'm sure Pia's OK. She needs some space to herself, I expect. Annelies can be a bit overwhelming, bless her.

Elise pulled up the skirt of her dress a few inches to give her thighs to the sun, liberating her feet from her flip-flops, stretching her strong brown toes, nails painted vermilion. – Aren't you worrying because you feel guilty, after all those years when I had to remind you even to phone Pia?

Paul went to make himself a drink. In the long, low stone-flagged kitchen, built like a fortress against the weather, the dark was thickening while light still blazed at the deep-recessed windows; an orange sliced on the table scented the air. He tried not to think about how he had neglected Pia: it was pointless, a self-indulgence, no use to her. In his study he poked around in the boxes he had brought from Evelyn's room. Certain objects as he lifted them out brought back the strong flavour of his childhood: a china biscuit barrel with a wicker handle, a varnished jewellery box that played a tune when the lid was opened. These had been set aside from use in their sitting room at home, almost like religious icons, in a cabinet with glass-fronted doors; packed together in the box, they still seemed to hold faintly the smell of the green felt that had lined the cabinet shelves, though the cabinet had been left behind years before, when Evelyn first moved.

At the bottom of one box were copies of his own books – the one on Hardy's novels, which had been his PhD thesis; the one on animals in children's stories; his last one, on zoos. He had given them to his mother as they were published, and she had displayed them proudly on her shelf, assuring him that she read them, although he could only imagine her processing the pages dutifully before her eyes, relieved when she reached the end as if she had completed some prescribed course of improvement, opaque to her.

The land behind Tre Rhiw sloped down to the river: first the garden, then the scrubby bit of meadow where the goats were fenced in and Elise kept her chickens and grew some vegetables. When they had first moved in, their property had bordered three small fields belonging to a couple who had grown too old for farming: they only kept a couple of superannuated horses and a donkey, to eat down the grass. Those old fields were mounded with the ancient hemispherical ant heaps found on land not broken by heavy machinery, their clumps of hazel scrub were cobwebbed with lichen, the tussocky grass blew with toadflax and cranesbill and cornflowers in spring and summer.

When the old man died, and the woman moved to live with her daughter in Pontypool, their house with its land was bought up by Willis, a farmer on the other side of the village, who ripped up whole lengths of ancient hedgerow to make the three fields into one, ploughing up the hazel scrub and the ant heaps. Paul had confronted him, ranting, threatening him with legal action, although there were probably no laws against what had been done. Elise said it was a fait accompli, they might as well let it go, there was no point in getting on the wrong side of Willis, they all had to live together. Nothing anyway could ever restore the hedges that had gone, which had probably been centuries in the growing. Since then, Willis seemed always to be spreading chicken shit on the field, or spraying with weed-killer, whenever they had a summer party out of doors: Elise was sure he only did it because Paul had hassled him. Apparently he wasn't popular in the village. Willis was English, he had married a local girl.

Elise said Paul should ask Willis's son whether Pia had been in contact. He put it off for a few days, but when there was still no news of her, reluctantly one morning he walked over to Blackbrook. It had been a mouldering old place among ancient overgrown apple trees, mossy roof slates thick as pavings, the rooms inside unchanged in half a century. Willis had stripped it back to the stone, put in new windows with PVC frames, replastered ceilings tarred nicotine-brown from cigarette smoke, cemented white sculptured horse-heads on the gateposts, fixed his Sky satellite-dish high on the wall. Its blandness and nakedness made it seem unreal to Paul, like a building in a dream or a film. As he crossed the concreted expanse of the yard, he saw that Willis was running the engine of a tractor, down from the air-conditioned cab, absorbed in listening to it: a sandy, stocky, huge-handed man, features almost obliterated under his freckles.

– There's a snag in the bastard, he said. – It's catching somewhere.

– Is James around?

– What's he supposed to have done?

– He hasn't done anything. I want to ask him a favour.

Willis tipped his head at the interior of the huge corrugated barn. – Hosing down. Don't spoil your shoes. He doesn't do me any favours.

Picking his way past dungy water streaming in the concrete runnels, Paul headed for the sound of the pressure hose; the barn was dark, after the brilliance outside, and the animal stink overwhelming. The boy turned off the hose as he came near, his eyes adjusting to the murk; James was sandy and freckled like his father, but taller, and skinny, hunched over his work, stiff with reluctance.

– How was Pia when you last saw her?

– Why?

– We're worried about her.

He shrugged. – She seemed all right.

– When was this? Have you been to London to see her? Has she been down here?

The boy turned on the hose again, aiming its jet of water into the corners of the pens. – Can't remember when.

– Did you know she'd dropped out of her university course?

– She may have said something about it. I can't remember.

He asked if James knew where they could contact her, but he said he only had her mobile number.

Pia had gone to the Willises at first to play on their PlayStation. She had been bored when she came to stay in the country, she didn't like reading or going for walks: Paul and Elise were pleased that she was making friends, at least. As she got older, Elise thought there must be something going on between her and James, or that Pia had a crush on him, but Pia had denied it flatly, convincingly: she didn't fancy him, they were just friends, they understood one another. It was true that if you came upon them idling around the lanes together, or sprawled watching television, they appeared at ease as if they were siblings: their loose, rangy bodies companionably slack, not strung on sexual tension. Paul couldn't imagine what they talked about. James seemed fairly monosyllabic, lost in thickets of resentment. They caught the train together into Cardiff to go clubbing, or Pia spent evenings at Blackbrook. Willis had converted a barn into a sort of annexe where his sons could live independently, with a games room and a kitchen; in the summer their mother organised this for holiday lets, now that the two older sons had left the farm. Willis had apparently wanted them to stay on, to help develop the business (as well as farming, they made ice-cream and sold Christmas trees, employing several people from the village); there were stories going round about the rows these boys used to have with their father. And the boys had gone.

Elise arranged a dinner party. – Is that all right? She massaged hard muscles in his neck and shoulders. – Are you ready to be sociable yet?

He thought he was ready, but when the party came

he wasn't in the mood for it. They were Elise's friends and not his (she'd said no to Gerald. – I love Gerald, but he's not quite house-trained, d'you know what I mean? Not good at the social give and take). Ruth and her husband came, and another couple they'd got to know while waiting for the school bus. Most of the people they knew in the village were incomers, but Ruth was born here, her brother had inherited the farm she grew up on. She was small and capable, with neat pretty features and curling dark hair tied back; Paul found her constrained and puritan. He and she had argued viciously once about the Welsh language. He was sure Elise complained to Ruth about his absorption in his books and his writing, and about his failure to do his share of domestic duties, even though Elise's work contributed more to the family income than his did.

Elise had warned him he mustn't 'spoil everything' at the party, he was supposed to join in and help the conversation along; but he found it boring, a social music running up and down as accompaniment to the food. All of them around the table, men and women, were somewhere in their early forties; Paul couldn't help seeing on their faces the first signs of their ageing, little lapses of their flesh around the mouth and jaw, puffiness under the eyes, the beginning of the crumpling and crumbling that would turn them into their disintegrated older selves. They discussed costume dramas on television. Someone said that nothing really changes, that wherever you look you find underneath the wigs and dresses the same old patterns playing out, the same human nature. Paul said he thought this was only because the television dramas tried to persuade you of this sameness, that it was a consoling illusion, a sham.

A muscle tightened in Ruth's cheek, bracing against him, as she prodded at her rice with her fork. – What do you mean?

– Human cultures move forward in time as if through a valve that permits no return. The substance of experience is altered over and over with no possibility of return or recovery. History's the history of loss.

– But there are gains, Elise insisted.

– Like human rights, and the treatment of women. The abolition of slavery.

– And contraception.

– Does it follow, Paul said, – that the sum necessarily balances out, gains against losses? Who could decide that we had gained more?

– Or lost more.

– What if extinctions in the natural world reflected the movement of time forwards in our human culture, extinguishing possibilities and qualities one by one, until there were fewer overall, far fewer?

– Shall we all go and top ourselves? said Ruth.

They all seemed to be angry with him, accusing him of nostalgia, of a regressive taste for everything old, of indifference to what had been unjust or caused suffering in the past.

– It's another perennial, Ruth's husband said. – Every generation thinks that what's in the past was necessarily superior. When I was a boy you could leave your front door unlocked, the rock 'n' roll was better, that sort of thing.

Paul couldn't summon the energy to explain that he had only meant the past was precious because it was different, not better. When their guests had gone, Paul and Elise washed up in fatigued silence in the kitchen: they didn't have a machine. He progressed stoically at the sink from glasses through plates to heavy pans that filled the washing-up water with floating rice and turmeric-yellow grease; Elise sorted leftovers, dried and put away dishes, returning the rooms to their daytime selves, shoving the heavy table noisily across the flag-stones. Her clothes had wilted from their carefully prepared bloom: her red stretch dress sagged over her stomach, the skin of her cheeks was oily in the over-head light they had switched on when the guests went. Paul thought he acquitted himself honourably, consid-ering how miserable he had felt all evening, in the flood of bright pointless chatter that no one would even remember the next day. Elise saw social life as a series of complex obligations, to please and be pleased, whereas he didn't see the point of talking, if you didn't say what you meant. The irony was that they had first met at a party, when Elise rescued him from an argument that almost became a fight. Why were women drawn to these resisting frictions in men, which they then set about smoothing away?

Hostile, exhausted, Elise turned her rump to Paul in bed. Usually he fell asleep pressed up against the land-scape of her shape; cast off, he floated, detached, in the cold margin of the bed, not knowing how to comfortably arrange his limbs. Sometimes his wife seemed to him shrunken and caught out in vanity. At other moments she surrounded and surpassed him; he was smaller, his was the deficit, he was the lamed one. Perhaps he was wrong about the dinner parties. Perhaps kindness was all that mattered.

IV

Paul was trying to work in his study: something distracted him, blocking the light at the window. Becky, crouched on her haunches, was tapping on the pane, beckoning him urgently out into the garden. He thought she must want to show him something she'd made: she was good with her hands, like her mother. But she was pacing up and down on the grass, talking on the pink mobile she'd been given for Christmas in a deliberate voice as if she was imitating a grown-up, waving her hands, exaggerating her expressions. Paul hadn't wanted to give her the mobile; she was surely too young for it.

– So how's everything going with you? Becky asked genially into the phone.

Meanwhile she signalled to Paul with her eyes and her free hand, pointing at the mobile, mouthing something. – Cool, she said. – Where are you staying? Is it a nice place? D'you want to talk to Daddy? I could get him easily.

Paul realised this must be Pia.

– They are worried, Becky was explaining to Pia, – but in a nice way.

She beckoned Paul close and then pressed the phone quickly to his ear, as if they might lose her if they didn't keep her trapped inside it. Paul was afraid for a moment that she had escaped. – Pia? Pia? Are you there?

He didn't know what to say. Should he mention seeing her the other day, in the Underground? That might frighten her off, as if he was spying on her, omniscient. When she was younger he had gone for weeks without speaking to her: now the thickness of her silence down the line seemed precious, and he was afraid to put a word wrong.

– Are you there?

– Hello, Dad.

Behind the ordinariness of her voice, whatever place she was in sent back its unfamiliar echo. He put all his skill into coaxing her, not making too much of their contact. She reassured him she was all right, they didn't mention her course, he didn't ask who she was with or what her plans were, nor did he want to tell her over the phone about her Nana. Even while he soothed her he felt some of his old irritation at having to drag communication out of her: she spoke in short reluctant bursts of words, in the slangy accent middle-class children affected. – Funnily enough, he said, – I have to be in London anyway, on Thursday. (This wasn't true, he invented it on the spot.) – Why don't we meet up? We could meet wherever you like. Pia, are you still there?

– Only if you promise not to tell Mum. Or Elise, either.

Pia was an adult, he reasoned, and had a right to her secrets. – All right.

– I'll call you again on Thursday then, she said.

Would she call him? He doubted it as soon as she'd rung off.

Becky asked if he and Pia were meeting and he told her that Pia was fine, but wasn't ready for a meeting yet. Under her freckles Becky flushed pink, perhaps because she guessed he wasn't telling the truth. If he wasn't telling Elise, then he couldn't tell Becky. If she didn't turn up, then he'd tell.

– Was it a good thing I called you outside when I got through to her?

– Very good. He picked her up and kissed her. Her anxieties wrung his heart. – You were like a detective on the telly.

That night he dreamed again about Evelyn: they waited for hours together in a milling, faceless crowd, jostled and queuing for something they never reached, anxious they didn't have the right papers. In the dream it dawned on him eventually that she was queuing to emigrate, that the black hulks, looming alongside the stone platform where they waited, were ships. When he woke he felt lonely, remembering their unconsidered companionable closeness in the dream.

He told Elise he was meeting Stella, which was plausible – she was an old friend who worked for the BBC, he had made several programmes with her. As soon as the train arrived, he phoned Pia. She answered it after the phone had rung for a long time.

– Dad, I don't know if this is a good idea.

She sounded as if he'd woken her up, her voice sticky and slow with sleep. He had been awake for hours; the day to him seemed halfway over already.

– What about this thing you have to go to? she said. – Why don't we meet after that?

– That's later. This evening.

– The evening would have been better for me. I've got things I have to do today.

He didn't believe her. – Where are you? Give me the address, I'll come right now, I won't stay long. I kept my part of the promise, I haven't said a word to your mum, or to Elise.

She was too slow and sleepy to know how to deflect him; he scribbled the address on the margin of his newspaper. It was somewhere off Pentonville Road, and she told him he needed to get off the Tube at King's Cross; after he'd rung off he bought an *A–Z* so that he could work out exactly where he was going. He was surprised that she was in central London, he had expected to have to go somewhere miles out. Eventually he found his way to a block of council flats, bleakly unlovely, rising on a built-up island out of the torrents of traffic that roared unrelentingly all round it. It was hot, the petrol fume rising off the vehicles was as thick in the air as a distorting glass, and it took him a few minutes to find the right system of crossings to use to arrive at the entrance. The block wasn't a tower, only three or four storeys, and around it there was a high wall, which made it look somehow, in its blue and white paint, like a scruffy container ship out at sea.

There was an entry phone: Pia buzzed him in and told him to wait inside the door. A concierge in a little glassed booth, reading the *Daily Mirror,* took no notice of Paul. Fire doors clanged some way off, and he heard Pia's footsteps approaching, resonant in the concrete stairwells. He was unexpectedly emotional, waiting for her. It shook his usual idea of his oldest daughter to find her displaced here, when he had only ever known her insulated by her mother's care: in this place, despite the entry phone and the concierge, she might not be safe. Even while he was concerned, he was also interested by the idea that she must have chosen this, in preference to safety. She swung the last door open. The concierge in his booth said something in a West Indian accent so strongly inflected Paul couldn't understand him; Pia seemingly had no difficulty, she answered quickly, but as if she didn't want to be drawn into conversation. Her tone made Paul wonder if perhaps she wasn't supposed to be staying in this flat, and was avoiding awkward questions.

He was sure as soon as he saw her that it had been Pia on the platform at Paddington a few weeks ago. Her hair was tied in the same low-slung bunches on her shoulders, and this had the effect he remembered from that day, reminding him of girls in gritty Sixties films about the British working classes, with some wornness and marks of trouble on their young faces already, part of their sex appeal. Pia's hair was clean, but her face was pale and not made up; she was wrapped in a shabby black cardigan with its belt dangling loose, which she kept in place, folding her arms over it. She looked years older than when he'd last seen her, when they went out to eat together and he was still thinking of her as a child. Although she might have been trying to cover herself up, he saw in his first glance that she was pregnant. Not hugely pregnant, but enough for it to show up against her angular thinness. He wouldn't have seen it when he saw her on the platform in the Underground because there had been people standing in front of her.

He couldn't imagine how they hadn't thought of this, any of them.

Pia was shyly anxious, managing her father's entrance through a prison-like sequence of heavy metal doors, grim stairwells. Chattering, covering up her nerves, she told him how this council block had been notorious in the Eighties for its drug users and its crime, and how it had been cleaned up in the Nineties, equipped with a security fence and a concierge entrance. Nothing was said yet about the pregnancy, though when Paul kissed her he felt the alien hard lump of it against him. She might even believe he hadn't noticed it. He was embarrassed about how to begin, he was waiting until they had arrived somewhere and were properly alone. They stopped at a red-painted door, off a narrow concrete walkway two floors up. Pia had her keys in her cardigan pocket: just before she opened the door she whispered urgently to him, putting her mouth close to his ear.

– Remember, you promised not to tell anyone about all this.

It wasn't the moment to protest that the promise had been exacted without his understanding the full circumstances. They stepped through a narrow hall space into a small living room, with windows all along one wall. Slatted blinds were drawn down, so that the light was dim, pierced by shafts of white brilliance here and there where the slats were broken or twisted. A big flat-screen television was switched on to twenty-four-hour news, a bed made up on a sofa had been slept in, but not tidied. The whole flat smelled of stale bedding, of cigarettes and strongly of marijuana. A door was ajar into what must be a bedroom, which was also dark: the bathroom and a kitchenette about as big as a cupboard opened off the hall. The bathroom door was off its hinges, balanced against the wall.

– It's a bit of a mess, said Pia, as if she'd noticed for the first time.

She began picking up mugs and plates from the floor.

Paul was thinking that he must rescue her from here, it wasn't a fit place for his daughter's baby to be developing. He was about to say something about this when a man stepped out from the bedroom.

– This is Marek, Pia said. – This is my dad.

Marek held out his hand.

When he guessed that Pia must be living with a boyfriend, Paul's imagination had supplied someone her own age, more like James Willis, or perhaps a fellow student who had dropped out from the university; he had not ever pictured an adult. This man wasn't big, he was medium height with a slight build, but there was nothing boyish or incomplete about him. His slimness seemed packed tight with an energy and authority Paul was not at all prepared for. His hair was dark and curling, cut close to his skull like a tight cap of lambswool: in the dim light he looked at least thirty. He squeezed Paul's fingers in a hard, quick hand and then dropped them; in his other hand he was balancing tobacco along a Rizla paper. Finishing rolling it, he licked the paper in a quick accustomed movement, then offered tobacco and papers to Paul.

– You smoke?

Paul said he hadn't smoked for a long time.

– You don't mind?

The man was lighting up, not waiting for permission: one cigarette more or less anyway wouldn't make much difference in this room. If he was Polish – that was surely a Polish name? – then he might not have been lectured about the effects of smoking on an unborn child. Perhaps from a Polish perspective the whole scare seemed a frivolous fuss. Could this really be Pia's lover? Someone after all had slept on the sofa. Paul might be misreading the whole situation.

– We don't have milk. Pia was still hanging on to the dirty plates she'd collected. – But I could make coffee, if you don't mind having it black.

– Make coffee, Marek said.

He was caressingly, insolently intimate: Pia smiled involuntarily. – It's so hot in this flat! she said. She struggled with her free hand to pull a blind halfway up, then opened the window. – There's supposed to be a roof garden out here. But nobody looks after it.

The city's noise was suddenly inside with them, and a blanching light in which their faces were exposed as if they were peeled. Marek's head was round and neat, and his handsome small features were strained in spite of his smile; his eyes weren't large but very black, framed with thick lashes, dark pits in a pale complexion. Hanging at crazy angles on the wall were Jack Vettriano's couple, dancing on a beach under an umbrella; also a photograph of giraffes in the savannah. There were rips in the fake tan leather of the sofa. The window overlooked a space for parking, and another wing of the housing block beyond it. Between two walkways a sunken area had been filled with earth; weeds had grown tall in it and then died, bleached dry in the heatwave.

– Is this your flat? he asked Marek.

– It's my sister's. She's letting us stay here. When Pia moved out from her mother's, I couldn't take her to the place where I was living, it wasn't nice.

– This is a very strange situation, said Paul. – My daughter appears to be pregnant. Or am I imagining things? What's going on here?

Pia blushed and pulled her cardigan across her stomach awkwardly. – I didn't know if you could tell.

– Make coffee, Marek said. – I'll talk.

– And you've taken out that stud in your lip.

Pia nodded her head towards Marek. – He didn't like it.

– I didn't like it, Paul said. – But you didn't take it out for me.

Marek laughed.

– I'd really like to talk to Pia alone, Paul said. – Why don't you and I go out and find a place for coffee?

He felt the other two were exchanging covert communication in glances.

– It's good here, Marek said. – She wants to stay here.

Paul followed Pia into the tiny kitchen, where pans and dishes were piled up unwashed in the sink, and a rubbish bin was too full to close. – We have mice, she said with her back to him, filling the kettle. – They're really sweet.

– Can't we go out somewhere? We need to talk.

– There's no point, Dad.

– What's happening here, sweetheart? What have you got yourself into?

– I knew you wouldn't understand, she said. – But it's what I want.

– Try me. Try and explain to me.

He couldn't see her face; her shoulders were hunched in tension. He remembered her trudging after him on tired legs across expanses of glacial floor in the museums he used to take her to, submitting unwillingly to the flow of his knowledge, which must have seemed unending.

– OK, he said. – It's OK, if it's what you want.

The coffee she made was instant; she rinsed dirty mugs

under the tap, rubbing the dark rings out of them with her finger. He asked if she'd seen a doctor yet, and she said she had, and that she was going next week with Anna, Marek's sister, to an appointment at the hospital.

– You don't mean for a termination?

She was shocked. – No! It's too late for that. Much too late!

It wasn't clear, she said, exactly how far the pregnancy was advanced; there was confusion apparently about her dates. – They're waiting for the scan. Then they'll know.

She seemed to have handed herself over to this process – its dates and appointments and inevitabilities – in a dream of passivity: he wanted to shake her awake. During all this conversation, Marek could no doubt hear them from the other room, in this flat without any privacy. Paul felt he must tell Pia about her grandmother, but couldn't bring himself to do it in front of a stranger. When they sat talking over the horrible coffee, in the living room amid all the mess of sheets and duvet and overflowing ashtrays, he tried to find out how Marek earned his living, and what kind of prospects he might have for supporting Pia and a child. All the time they talked, the television spewed its news: Iraq, the timing of Blair's resignation, a rail worker killed in an accident on the line, the child snatched in Portugal still missing. It distracted Paul, but the others didn't take any notice. He felt the absurdity of his playing the part of the offended protective father, given his own history with Pia; and it almost seemed as if Marek understood this, reassuring him to help him out, amused at him.

– There'll be enough money, don't worry. There'll be a better place than this, much better. It will all be good.

He said he worked in business, import-export, Polish delicatessen. He was going to make money, with Polish shops opening in every city, every street. Was he a con man, or a fantasist? The condition of the flat hardly suggested a successful entrepreneur: unless he was peddling drugs, small-scale. Paul had spent time in rooms worse than this one, twenty years ago, when he was in that scene. Everything about the place and the situation made him fearful and suspicious on Pia's behalf. And yet, as they talked, he could begin to imagine the power this man had to make her trust him. Smiling, with his cigarette wagging in his mouth, he gestured a lot with his hands, and was somehow amusing without saying anything particularly funny: at the same time he managed to have an air of serious competence, as if there was another message, poignant and melancholy, behind the improbable surface of the things he said.

They had met apparently through Marek's sister. While she was still at the university, Pia had had a part-time job at a café where the sister worked. Paul remembered that Annelies had gone looking for Pia at that café, and that they'd said she had left. She had left, he learned now, because she was being sick all the time, in the early stages of the pregnancy.

– But I've got past that now, I'm feeling fine, I'm really well. I should start looking round for something.

Marek tugged her hair affectionately, as if he was showing something off to Paul, his role as the one who knows best. – I'd rather she just stays at home, look after herself, and make the place nice.

She didn't seem to be doing all that well at making the place nice. But they had only just got out of bed. Perhaps things in the flat got better as the day wore on.

Paul asked Pia to come down to the gate with him when he left. He told her about her grandmother when they were out of sight of her front door, alone on one of the landings in the well of concrete stairs, with its whiff of cheap disinfectant. When she realised what he was saying, her mouth stretched in helpless, ugly crying. He thought how different she was from his other daughters. They seemed to have from their mother a finished, worldly awareness, like a gloss of complexity on their every gesture, on every detail of their appearance. Pia had grown up in the city, but she was raw and artless, with her thick fair hair like straw and big-knuckled hands. Her half-sisters loved her tenderly, perhaps because of this; they took great interest in her entry into grown-up life. Making an effort, she found a tissue in her sleeve and wiped her face.

– I'm all right now.

– I can't leave you in this state. Won't you come out with me, after all? We can buy a decent cup of coffee.

– It was just the shock, that's all. Because I had no idea.

– We could hardly leave it as a message on your phone.

Could she authentically be so grief-stricken, over the death of an old woman she hadn't visited for months?

When she was a child she had wept bitterly over the deaths of her hamsters. Probably she was imagining this baby out of the same reservoir of ready emotion, as if it was a kitten or a doll for her to play with. He couldn't persuade her to come out; they parted at the entrance to the block. At the last minute she clung onto him, pleading with him not to tell her mother. He couldn't begin to imagine how Annelies would react if she knew the full story of her daughter's situation. He quailed at the idea of involving her, or not involving her.

– Don't tell her yet, please, just not yet. You promised you wouldn't.

V

Home from his London visit, Paul found that his routines, which had seemed satisfying enough before he left – the hours working in his study, the long walks, the round of picking up the children from the bus stop after school, the language classes for foreign undergraduates at the university – had hollowed themselves out in one convulsive movement. He was restless, he couldn't sit at his computer. Elise was working on a set of voluptuously dainty Edwardian dining chairs; crowded on the cobbles in her workroom, they seemed to be at their own debauched party, broken up into gossiping groups tilted towards one another, their insides spilling out of rips in the filthy old purple velvet.

– What's the matter with you? She frowned at him, putting down the metal claw she was using to lever out the tacks. There were streaks of sweaty dirt on her face, the air in the workroom was greasy with dust pent up in the chairs for a hundred years. – What happened in London? Didn't they like your idea for the radio programme?

– It's not that.

For the moment he wasn't saying anything about seeing Pia, though he would have liked to hand the problem over and be free of it. When Annelies telephoned, he told her only that Becky had spoken to her, Pia sounded fine. She was living with friends.

– Then why won't she see me, Paul? What did I do that was so terrible?

Paul was going to visit Pia in London again the following week. He would have to tell her that he must speak to her mother, he couldn't hold back any longer.

On the drive into Cardiff to see Gerald, the city's scrappy approaches seemed bleached and exposed in the flat sunlight: corrugated mail-order storage sheds and the back end of new housing estates, a new red-brick budget hotel. Sometimes Paul wished they lived in the city, and thought it was a mistake, their having chosen the countryside. Gerald's flat was at the top of a tall Victorian house beside one of the city parks. All the heat in the house rose up to his attic and beat in through the slates on the roof; his windows were wide open, but it was still stifling. While Gerald brewed tea, Paul stood at the window looking out into the shady spacious top of a copper beech, one in an avenue planted along the side of the park. A tinkers' lorry, on the lookout for scrap metal, cruised past in bottom gear, and a boy sang out 'Any old iron', riding standing up among the rusting fridges and cookers. Paul said it was the last of the old street-cries, resonant and poignant as a muezzin. Although Gerald said the tinkers cheated old ladies out of their money, he couldn't spoil Paul's mood – excited and impatient. He was full of emotions arising out of the painful complications of the past. From his vantage point at the window he half-expected to see a girl he'd known and been involved with, who'd lived round here, and used to walk in this park. He remembered her near-religious attitude to literature; he seemed to see her, striding out below him on the path under the trees – tall and serious, handsome, with slanting, doubting brown eyes. But probably she'd sold her house by now, and moved away.

Gerald sat cross-legged to drink his tea and roll up, using for a flat surface a book he was reading, balanced across his knees. It was about the Neoplatonists of the early Christian era, Plotinus and Porphyry. He explained an idea from the book – how, in its work of imagination, inventing forms, the human mind replicates or continues the work of the world soul, inventing forms in nature. Paul didn't smoke much dope these days – Elise didn't like him doing it, she said it made him boring and made him snore – but this afternoon he needed it. The sleepy heat and the smoking brought back the years between his first and second marriages, when he was teaching in the language school. When Paul had moved to Paris, Gerald had followed him. The patterns of sleep Paul had developed in those days had been 'disastrous', so Elise said; he'd only had part-time hours at the school, often he'd stayed up reading, or talking with the little crowd of his friends, until three or four in the morning.

While Gerald talked, Paul found himself thinking

about Pia's pregnancy, not simply as a difficulty and a disaster. He had a vision of how dumbfounding it was, Pia's originating as a tiny folded form invisible inside her mother, and now inside her unfolded realised self, starting the same thing over; forms folded within forms. How different it was to be male, to feel the unfolding come to an end in your biological self, which could not be divided. The role of the male in this endless sequence was an act of faith, however definite the science. A Frenchman had said to him once that the man's role in making a child was about as much as 'this' – he'd spat on the pavement.

This train of thought may have all been a consequence of the dope.

– Your eyes are rolled up in your head, Elise told him when he arrived home. – That stuff Gerald smokes now is too strong for you, you're not used to it.

James Willis came looking for Paul one afternoon when Elise was out at a sale with Ruth, and the girls were at school. Paul had been getting himself lunch in the kitchen – hunting in the fridge for an end of pâté, desultorily reading the *Guardian*, anything rather than sitting down again at his computer – when the boy was suddenly in the doorway, stooping, worrying about his dirty boots on the mat. In the barn, it had been too dark for Paul to take him in properly, his hunched awkward height, the adolescent hormonal shock still in his face, lips swollen with it, eyes bleary, hands hanging heavy. He was long and pale; when he spoke he addressed his feet.

There was a stud in his lip, Paul saw, like the one Pia had taken out.

James said he'd come with a message from his father, who wanted them to cut back the aspen poplars on the border between their places. Willis's next-door field was planted this year with elephant grass for biofuel. Apparently Willis thought that, because of the trees, the harvester wouldn't be able to turn closely enough at the end of the field.

– If you don't have a chainsaw, Dad said, he'll loan you one.

– You're joking, Paul said. – Your dad's crazy, he's really crazy. Those trees aren't in the way of anything. Have you even looked at them?

The boy shrugged. – I'm just saying what he said.

– Tell him he's crazy. And tell him not to dare to touch those fucking trees. They're on my land.

– He says not.

Willis sending the boy with this message was a cruelty in itself; he must resent his son's attachment, however tenuous, to an enemy household. Paul invited him in, fetched beers out of the fridge. Warily James stood drinking at the table.

– Your father's really wrong, you know, about those trees. Whether they're on his land or mine. There's plenty of room for the harvester to turn.

– It's a big machine.

Paul went on to explain why the biofuel was a bad idea in the first place. He caught a glint in the boy's eye, of derision no doubt, at Paul's citified perspective, the idea that his father would care about the ethics of a crop one way or another. Paul told him he'd seen Pia. James already knew this, he and Pia must have spoken on the phone.

– Do you know about this man: Marek? Paul said, taking a chance. – What do you think about him? Who is he?

James tipped up his bottle, wiped his mouth on his sleeve. – She's told me about him, that's all.

– Do you think she's safe? Should we trust him?

– It's not my business.

– No? Aren't you two friends?

– It's her business.

– And the other thing? D'you know about that too?

He was visibly startled. – I didn't think she was going to tell you yet.

– It didn't need any telling. It was plain as day.

– Oh. I hadn't thought of that.

No wonder Pia had chosen a man in preference to this boy with his burden of suffering youth, blushing, stumbling over his own feet on his way out of the house, pushing his fists deep in his pockets, forgetting even to thank Paul for the beer. She probably imagined that her own youth had been taken off her hands, that she had given herself over to someone who would know how to manage whatever happened. The Willis boys had always been awkward, not fitting in with the other kids in the village. They affected an American twang in their accents and they stuck together, mucking about on the expensive quad bikes their father bought them. The oldest had written off his first car before he left, driving it when drunk into a tree. James at least didn't have his brothers' veneer of showy sophistication.

Paul told Ruth's brother about the Willises and the chainsaw; when he and Gerald walked over one evening for a pint at the pub in the village, Alun was at the bar. He laughed and said Willis was a nutter, but that if the trees were on Willis's land, there wasn't much Paul could do about it, a trim wouldn't do them any harm. He was friendly, but Paul felt Alun always kept him at a deliberate distance, perhaps because of things Ruth told him, perhaps just because of what he would imagine was Paul's type: English, opinionated, arrogant. He wouldn't quite come out on Paul's side against Willis.

Alun was small and broad-chested, handsome; he kept liquorice-coloured sheep on the hills and a small beef herd on the red soil in the better fields; they had a farm shop where his wife sold the fruit from their orchards. Although Paul and Ruth didn't get on, Paul liked her brother's decency and shyness; from the first when they'd moved down here he'd identified him with the landscape and the place, which was probably romantic. Gerald thought he romanticised. Gerald had also grown up on a farm, on the North Yorkshire moors. He had been grateful to leave it behind and didn't have any particular thing about farmers, although it turned out – to Paul's surprise – that he could talk to Alun in an easy way Paul couldn't, mostly about money, money and machinery, how impossible it was for the hill farmers, the endless setbacks that seemed to make up the rhythm of their life. Now there was anxiety about the drought.

Paul really did have to go up to London the following week, to record an interval talk he'd written for Radio 3. In the late afternoon, after he'd finished, he made his way to Pia's; he'd called to remind her he was coming, but she hadn't answered. Pressing the button on the intercom on the forbidding exterior gate, he was relieved to hear the crackle of her voice responding, suspicious and uncertain.

– Pia, it's Dad.

– Shit, Dad. I'm not ready. It's not a good time.

At his exposed back, traffic roared around the island-block. This place really was his idea of hell: the remorseless, ceaseless pressure of vehicles travelling onwards to destinations that in the aggregate were absurd, each under its atomised separate compulsion, brought together in this filthy flow, poisoning the air with fumes and noise.

– But I'm here now. Let me in.

There was a pause; then resignation. – I'll come down.

When she appeared she was in the same black cardigan as last time, over a pink nightshirt and slippers. Her face was pasty and she hadn't brushed her hair, which was pulled out of its bunches and loose on her shoulders; he guessed she had come straight from bed. From under the nightdress her swollen belly poked assertively.

– I forgot you were coming today.

As he followed her up to the flat, something about the

place elated him, even while he was intent on getting Pia out of it. He was bracing himself for encountering Marek again, reading him more deeply, for better or worse: when he realised there was no one home besides Pia, he was almost disappointed. She said they had gone out.

– They?

– Marek and Anna.

The television was switched on, inevitably. The place looked a bit better than last time: at least the spare bedding was folded in a pile on the floor, the blinds pulled halfway up. The smell of dope was pungent, though the windows were open. Perhaps Pia hadn't been in bed, but tidying: in the kitchen there was crockery piled in a fresh bowl of soapy water, and while she waited for the kettle to boil to make tea, she did rinse a few plates and propped them on the draining board. Paul asked about her pregnancy, her appointment at the hospital: into her expression there came the same vagueness as last time. The doctors thought from the scan she was twenty-eight weeks, or something like that. Everything was fine.

– You see. I told you it was too late for a termination.

– And are you planning on keeping this baby? Or putting it up for adoption?

– I don't know. We'll see. I haven't decided what I'm going to do.

She said this as offhandedly as if she was choosing between subjects for her college course.

– Are you eating properly? Aren't there vitamins and so on you're supposed to take?

– Anna's taking care of that.

– People are smoking in this flat. I'm sure you know how bad that is for a developing foetus.

– Oh, Dad.

– What?

– You smoked around me all the time when I was a kid. I used to beg and plead with you to stop.

– Did I? It's not the same thing. Anyway, just because I was an idiot doesn't mean you have to be one too.

Pia dressed in the bedroom while Paul drank his tea. She came out in a new stretch top she said Marek had bought her, grey with huge yellow flowers, pulled tightly across her stomach, showing it off, as was the fashion with pregnancy now. Then, sitting beside him on the sofa, she made up her face in deft accustomed movements, looking in a small hand-mirror, concentrating intently, putting on a surprising amount of stuff: colour on her skin to cover her blemishes, blue lines painted around her eyes, stiff blue on her lashes, colour on her lids, pale lipstick.

– What? she asked anxiously when she'd finished, putting bottles and tubes away in a zip bag. – Have I put on too much?

The mask of beauty painted on her face seemed precarious. When she stood up to brush her hair he was startled, as if there was someone new in the room between them. He imagined her days passing – sleeping late, tidying half-heartedly, dressing and painting her face, waiting for her lover to come home. When he asked if she wasn't missing university work she shuddered, as if he'd reminded her of another life.

– God, no. I was so miserable there.

– It won't be like this, he said, – if you have a baby. Getting up at three o'clock in the afternoon.

– You never trust that I will be good at anything.

He tried to say that this was not what he meant; he just didn't want the baby to spoil her flight and bring her down to earth too soon. – And I have to tell your mother something. She's out of her mind with worry, you can imagine.

– Tell her you've spoken to me and I'm all right. Tell her I'll see her soon.

– Why won't you see her? Just to put her mind at rest.

– It wouldn't, would it? Her mind would be very much not at rest, if she had any idea what was going on. It would be hyperactive. You know her.

There was ignominy for Paul in keeping her secret, as if he was trying to score cheap triumphs over Annelies, fighting with her over their daughter's confidence, where he hadn't earned any rights, given his record. Pia's resistance to her mother took him by surprise.

– She recognises you're an adult, you're free to choose what you want.

Tugging the brush through her hair, Pia looked round from the mirror. – This is what I want. And I'll see her, but not yet.

As soon as Marek and Anna were in the flat, Paul saw that Anna was a force just as her brother was, and that Pia had been drawn to both of them, not just the man. Both moved with quick, contemptuous energy, crowding the place; Paul recognised that they were powerful, even if he wasn't sure he liked them, and couldn't understand yet what their link was to his daughter, or whether it was safe for her. Marek greeted Pia with the same gesture as last time, tugging affectionately at her hair; Pia slid into a daze of submission in his presence. In the flowered top, with her face painted, Paul could see how her languid fairness, freighted with the pregnancy, might be attractive.

Anna's jeans and white T-shirt were moulded tightly to her slight figure: she probably wasn't much older than Pia, but everything about her seemed finished and hardened. Her straight hair, dyed red-brown, was chopped off at her shoulders; her narrow face was handsome, boyish, with fine bruise-coloured skin under her eyes and a dark mole on one cheek. When they were introduced, Paul thought he might have known, from touching her hand alone, that she wasn't British: under the fine-grained skin he seemed to feel lighter bones, a more delicate mechanism for movement. Her nails were painted with black varnish, there were nicotine stains on her fingers. Anna began scolding Pia: had she eaten properly? She was supposed to eat breakfast and lunch too. – What time did you get out of bed? Don't sleep too much: you need exercise.

Pia defended herself half-heartedly, enjoying the fuss made of her.

– It's a meeting of the family, isn't it? Marek brought a bottle of clear spirits from the fridge in the kitchen, and three small glasses. – The new family. It's good that we get together.

– Pretty good family, said Anna, – with no home to go to.

– Anna gets fed up with us, her brother said tolerantly. – Messing up all her nice, tidy space.

– I'm not surprised, Paul said. – It's a small flat.

– Soon, soon, we'll get a bigger one. We'll be out from your hair, Anna, then you will miss us.

Pia said she was going back to work at the café, that would bring in some money. They needed more money than that, teased Marek affectionately, much more. The slivovitz, which Pia didn't drink, was deliciously ice-cold in this room overheated by the low sun striking in through the windows. Paul had come to the flat intending to coax Pia home, at least for a while, to think things over; but he felt himself being drawn farther into her life here, without getting any of the explanations he ought to be asking for. No one seemed to think anything needed explaining. He had no idea whether the possibilities Marek and Anna discussed animatedly were realistic. They said they had been looking for shop premises, although they also seemed to have been approaching shopkeepers to supply them with goods. Marek asked Paul to explain leasehold, which he wasn't able to, not knowing how it worked in any detail. Were these two really going to make money, and look after Pia? Both of them spoke English well, but sometimes they lapsed into Polish, and then Paul found himself looking from one to the other as if he was watching a film without subtitles, which might make sense if only he concentrated hard enough. What would Annelies think of him, seduced like this – or Elise? Marek refilled Paul's glass several times.

Anna said she wanted to develop her own small business, an outlet for friends who made jewellery: 'very original, good quality'. Lifting her hair, she showed Paul silver earrings, little jagged lightning strokes, set with tiny stones, the sort of thing you could buy at any market stall. With a qualm, Paul wondered if they were imagining he had money, calculating he might help them with their projects. For all he knew, Marek could be married, or at least have other women at home in Poland. He even asked himself once whether Anna was really Marek's sister: but there was a trick of likeness between them, not obvious but unmistakable when you'd seen it, in how their dark eyes were set in their skin, so that their awareness seemed gathered behind their faces, looking out.

When he asked, they told him they came from Lodz, but didn't seem interested in talking about their home. Paul had been twice to Poland, long ago, but his idea of it mostly came from the poets he had read. These two wouldn't want him dragging out all those old associations, that old junk, they wouldn't want to know he'd once worn a Solidarność badge to school. They were too young to remember life in the old Poland, behind the Iron Curtain, and he didn't know much about life in the new one. For the moment anyway they were Londoners, absorbed in that, more at home in the metropolis than he was. When he eventually left the flat, remembering his train, he managed to pull Pia half outside the front door, onto the walkway. Probably she thought that he was drunk.

– You have to promise me something, he said in a low voice, urgently. – If they ask you to do anything you don't like, you will call me straight away, won't you?

He saw her eyes widen under their blue-painted lids. – I don't know what you're talking about, she said. – Do you mean drugs?

– Whatever. You don't have to do anything you don't want to.

He wasn't clear himself about precisely what he feared, and was half-ashamed of where such imaginings came from. Was it only because the man Pia had chosen was a foreigner?

She shook off his hand from her arm, to go back inside. – I told you. This is what I want.

VI

Elise's bedtime routine was intimately known to him: the yawns, the cleanser, the glass of water she only rarely touched, the pillow she liked to drag under her cheek, her alarm clock set inexorably for the following morning. One new detail was the glasses she had begun to need to read with. These gave Paul mixed feelings: on the one hand, a chill from the middle age into which she advanced always just a little ahead of him; on the other, a frisson of affection, making him think of a character in one of those mid-period Bergman movies, women struggling to take possession of themselves, their past and sexuality. Was that what Elise was doing? She kept a pile of modern novels by her bed that he rarely looked into; they seemed to him pretty much interchangeable – what people called 'women's fiction'. The trouble with cohabitation seemed to be that you were gripped in some struggle for vindication so convoluted that you couldn't afford to imagine things impartially from the other one's centre.

She would abandon reading with a little sigh, smiling apologetically, but giving out a hum of sensuous submission as she slipped under into sleep, leaving him high and dry, beached in her wake. It was too hot these nights to wrap himself around her from behind; her breasts, if he put his hand on them, seemed scalding; she brushed him away without even waking properly, murmuring a protest. Curled with his back to her at the other edge of the bed, he'd taken to trying to get to sleep by going round and round in his mind the rooms of his childhood home, remembering their obscure corners, which had once seemed banal in their ultra-familiarity and now held the deepest mystery for him. There was no one else to remember them. He inventoried drawers and cupboards: the hairgrips and elastic bands and dust, the crumbling bath cubes, books half full of Green Shield savings stamps. Pins and needles were stuck into shiny paper in a folded card shaped as a flower basket. An old cut-throat razor, with a bone handle, hung around for years after his father had taken to using an electric one. The house itself was gone now, he'd looked for it on Google Earth and, although most of the road still stood, there was a gap where they must have demolished four or five of those mean houses, built shoddily of compressed ash only sixty years ago, as the answer to Birmingham's inner-city slum problem. He had hated the place, but the discovery of its non-existence was a blow, as if he'd been cheated of something.

One night he woke, groaning loudly, out of a nightmare that his mother was dying in hospital, alone, strapped to her sheet in a bed like a metal cot with bars, twitching in violent convulsions, tubes and monitors bristling all over her body. His groaning woke Elise too.

– It won't have been like that, she reassured him, putting her arms around him, cradling him. – They know how to do it, how to ease them out with morphine, making them as comfortable as they can. When Dad was dying the nurses knew just how to prop him up, moisten his lips and hold his hand and speak to him. They know these things.

He didn't believe her, but he was grateful and hungry for her comforting, which turned into love-making, affectionate and familiar. Into that, taking Paul by surprise, came images of the Polish girl: her air of tough disdain, the mole on her cheek, her sloe-dark eyes, young breasts under her tight T-shirt. He imagined the girl carried away in sexual excitement, breaking out in pleading exclamations in her language that he couldn't understand: it was a rough, slightly degrading scene, as if he was punishing her, or proving something. It had not even occurred to him, all the time he was in Anna's real presence, that anything like this was at work in him, saving itself for later. The middle-aged cliché shamed him, his fantasising about one of his own daughter's friends, probably not much older than Pia was herself. He tried to conjure up instead the girl from the past, the one he'd seemed to see from Gerald's window – but she eluded him, her features were blurred.

Paul sat to watch nature programmes with the girls in the little cubbyhole where they kept the television, a

74

room without a window between the hallway and the kitchen; they curled up together on an old broken-backed sofa. If Joni wasn't interested in the programme she stretched herself along the top of the sofa back, biting her comfort blanket and scuffing with her stretched-up foot along the wall, kicking at the edge of a poster for a Lucian Freud exhibition. Becky was driven to distraction by her sister's insouciance; they would fight after she had been patient for long ages, rolling over one another, squealing and hissing and pinching. Separating them, Paul felt their heat, intense and intimate as cubs in a den.

Some of these programmes distressed him, with their casually apocalyptic language. He wanted to protect the girls from hearing that all the beauty of the world was spoiling, its precious places being built over or cut down, its animal life poisoned with pollution. The girls seemed sanguine enough, taking it all in. Perhaps they were hardened through over-exposure; but perhaps a terrible nihilism was being implanted in them, to lie in wait for when they were adult and would understand how to despair. Paul could remember learning in a geography lesson at school about the layered living of the equatorial forest – his imagination had soared at the idea of animals that spent their entire lives in its canopy, never needing to come down to ground level. He had not wanted particularly to travel to the forest and see for himself; the knowledge that it existed was like a reserve in his spirit, a guarantee that spacious beauty existed somewhere.

– I shouldn't worry about it, Elise said. – They seem

to cope all right. Isn't education the best hope for change? This generation ought to grow up passionate environmentalists. The programmes try not to be gloomy, but they have to tell the truth to the children, don't they? You couldn't want to deceive them that everything was all right.

– I'm afraid it makes them helpless. You need such complex contexts, to grapple with the information they're getting.

– Do you? It seems straightforward enough to me. Thank goodness things aren't all left up to the people who understand the complex contexts. If it was up to them, perhaps nothing would ever get done.

Gerald often ate with them in the evenings. Elise didn't mind having him there as long as it wasn't a dinner party. In fact she fussed over him, cooking the things he said he liked, teasing him about how he didn't look after himself properly. Paul had told her about the Scotch eggs and hummus. – Do you ever clean anything? she asked. – Gerald, have you ever cleaned your lavatory? The girls were gloating and giggling, enjoying the game. Gerald said he had bought some toilet cleanser once, and sometimes squirted it in. Wasn't that what he was supposed to do? Paul was sure he was exaggerating, playing along with their joke; he didn't remember the toilet being so very bad. Gerald told them he had a theory, that after a certain point the rooms never got any dirtier: they didn't get cleaner, but they didn't get any worse.

Elise pretended to be appalled. – Won't you let me come round and clean up for you? It will only take a couple of hours. I won't touch any of your precious books, I promise.

It was a joke, but Paul saw with surprise that she half-meant it, too. She didn't care about the cleaning, but she was intrigued by the idea of Gerald's flat, where she'd never been, and she wanted to get a look inside it. Joni wrapped her skinny arms around Gerald's knees, wheedling. – We want to come, we want to come to your smelly flat!

Gerald said he would love to invite her over for tea, he'd get in cake and crumpets specially. – As long as you're not afraid of the spiders.

– Spiders? No . . . Joni was hesitant. – Are they big ones?

– How about bats?

– He hasn't! Becky squealed delightedly, not certain.

– Or cockroaches?

He convinced them that he lived with a menagerie of animals, confessing to Paul and Elise later that the cockroaches were for real. After dinner he helped Elise water the vegetables: he was strong as an ox, could easily carry two full watering cans. Paul thought of him when he was a boy, baling out hay from the back of a tractor trailer in winter, or trimming the overgrowth of their sheep's feet with a paring knife. He had told Paul he used to think up the solutions to maths problems while he worked. To save water, Elise had fixed up a barrel that collected waste from the kitchen sink and the bathroom, to reuse on the garden; after a few trips with the cans, Gerald put in a hose running from the water butt to the vegetable patch. She was delighted with him. They all three sat out with chinking glasses of gin and tonic in the late sunshine, when the chores were done and Becky and Joni were feeding the goats.

– Why don't you have a girlfriend, Gerald? Elise asked.

– It's probably the cockroaches.

– No, seriously. Although I don't suppose the cockroaches help. What happened to Katherine? She was nice.

– She *was* nice. Gerald was smoking surreptitiously, holding the spliff between drags out of sight under his deckchair, so the girls wouldn't spot it.

– And Martine, the one from Heidelberg. She was nice too.

– Went back to Heidelberg.

Elise laughed as if he was impossible, but also as if it gratified her, that he wouldn't be drawn into making much of those girls, giving anything away.

– Why doesn't he stay the night ever? she asked Paul when Gerald had gone to get his train. – It must be awful for him, going back to that dismal flat.

– It isn't dismal. It's how he likes it. He likes to keep his own hours, read as late as he wants, make tea in the middle of the night if he wants to.

– He could do that here, we wouldn't mind.

Gerald had told Paul once that he got panicky in a place where other people were asleep – he had a problem with imagining their breathing or something. This must be part of the story with the girlfriends. If you lived alone for too long, the effort of breaking all your forms of life, to recast them with someone else, might be just too tremendous. Those girls, Katherine and the others, were shaken when they came back from throwing themselves at Gerald with such innocent enthusiasm. There was a cruelty in the blank side he turned to them, when he needed to cut them out.

– It's restful working alongside him, Elise said. – At first it feels funny not saying anything, then you settle into it. I used to think he wouldn't talk to me because I wasn't intellectual.

Paul lied that he needed to go up to London again, to see his agent. He winced at the lie – Elise hadn't absolved him yet, over the lies he'd told at the time he was seeing that girl in Cardiff – but at least it wasn't for his own advantage, only Pia's. Without warning Pia he was coming, he went straight to the flat. All the way there, on the train looking out at the yellowing landscape, and then on the Underground, he was rehearsing how he would persuade his daughter to come home with him. She ought to be looking after herself in her pregnancy, she ought to think responsibly about the future, she ought to be with her family who would love and cherish her best. He might be able to persuade her to pack a bag and leave with him there and then: he would take her home to Annelies, or back with him to Tre Rhiw, whichever she wanted. The idea of restoring her triumphantly made him emotional. His mission sealed him apart from the crowds around him in the Underground, their babble of languages silenced as they swayed together in the heat, strap-hanging, bodies indifferently intimate, faces closed against curiosity.

Arriving at the block, he buzzed the entry phone. Someone seemed to pick up in the flat, but when he spoke into it no one answered, and after a moment it cut off. He hadn't allowed himself to think of this when he was on his way: that there might be no one at home, or no one who wanted to see him. He rang again, and this time no one picked up. Pia's mobile was turned off when he tried it. It was absurd that he hadn't prepared for this eventuality; now he was at a loss. He read the paper for an hour in a dubious café somewhere off Pentonville Road, then tried the mobile and the entry phone again. He made efforts to persuade the concierge to let him in. 'I'm sure they're at home. Perhaps the phone isn't working.' The concierge tried for himself. 'It working. No one in the place.'

Paul spent the day in the British Library, returning to the block in the evening as the sun dropped and the brilliant daylight thickened and dimmed. As he approached he tried to work out which flat was Anna's: one on the second floor with its lights on had its blinds skewed at angles halfway up the windows in a sequence he seemed to recognise, but he wasn't sure it was in the right relationship to where the entrance was, or to the roof garden, whose dead stubble poked above a parapet, a fringe outlined against a sky of deepening royal blue. Again, no one picked up when he tried the entry phone. The traffic roared behind him, a broad river devilish in its night-blare, streams of red and white lights. He crossed to look up from the other side of the road at the lit-up flat. Someone was moving about in there, passing and repassing behind the blinds as if they were tidying up, or getting dressed to go out. If this was the right flat, it could be Pia; but he couldn't attach his feeling to that shadow, in case it was only a stranger's. Or it could be Anna, or her brother. It could have been the shadow of a slight young man.

Paul had forgotten about rescuing Pia; instead he only felt shut out from wherever she was, whatever they were doing. He hadn't been bitten by this anxiety for years, he thought he'd left it behind him with his youth: wanting to be part of something happening, and feeling excluded. He didn't want to go home from here to the quiet of the country. And yet nothing was happening. No one went into the block of flats, or came out of it, while he watched.

Going to Annelies's house seemed preferable to catching the train home; he thought he would tell her finally about Pia. It was about time. Perhaps if she hadn't eaten, he would take her out to one of the Greek places in Green Lanes road. When he arrived, though, she was in the middle of some kind of social occasion. He could smell food as soon as she opened the front door, and hear women's voices and laughter from the room where she had her dining table. He was sorry when he saw what Annelies thought it meant, his turning up unannounced on her doorstep: she braced herself, as if for some dreadful assault.

– It's all right, he reassured her. – Don't worry, everything's fine. If you've got people here I won't come in, I'll ring you tomorrow.

– You have news of Pia?

– Not bad news, nothing to worry about.

– Paul! You think I can wait? You've seen her?

She pulled him into the little front room that was empty, but tidied ready for her guests to move into later, lamps lit, flowers on a table. There were red and white gingham cushions and a striped rug, framed photographs of Pia were on the mantelpiece.

– What? What news?

Paul told her Pia was pregnant, that he had seen this for himself. He said she was living with the man who was the father of the child. For some reason he spoke as if he hadn't met Marek, and didn't mention that he was Polish or say anything about his sister.

– How do you know all this? When did you see her? Today?

– Not today. Last week. But she didn't want me to tell you yet.

– You've known since last week that my daughter is pregnant, and you haven't told me?

– I was afraid that if I broke my promise we'd lose her again, she'd go out of contact.

– OK, Paul. This isn't the end of the world. Our GP is Pia's old friend, he understands everything, we can get her in somewhere straight away, private if it's quicker. Who is this man, anyway? You know where she's living?

82

The crisis, and the idea that Paul had had access to Pia, roused Annelies to defend herself against his way of seeing things, to override it. Her stocky body and stiff wiry curls, her lowered head and shoulders hunched in tension, made him think of a guard dog, loyal to its idea.

– She wants to have the baby. She says it's too late for a termination.

– This is a joke, right?

The voices in the next room had fallen quiet. A couple of women from the party peered round the door, asking if Annelies was all right, as if she might be at some risk from Paul. Annelies said that her daughter was pregnant, and Paul wouldn't tell her where she was. Trying to convince her that their link with Pia was too tenuous to risk breaking it, he imagined that all these women, whoever they were – Annelies's work colleagues or her knitting group or book club – were ganged up against him.

– Who is this man she's with? What does he want with my daughter?

Paul found himself claiming that Pia and Marek loved one another. As soon as they'd come out of his mouth, he couldn't believe he'd said the words. Annelies's contempt was bruising. – You think that makes any difference to anything? What kind of love, if she doesn't want to tell her mother? Just give me her address. Let me go to her. I beg you. Please.

One of the women suggested that if Pia was experimenting with her freedom, it might be best to respect that. Annelies pushed the idea away as if she was brushing off cobwebs. Paul wasn't sure why he stuck it out so determinedly, refusing to tell her where Pia was staying. Perhaps he was afraid of her blundering into a situation more risky than he'd quite let her know. Because of her job, she was expert in the conditions migrant workers sometimes had to live in, and in itself the flat was not too bad. But she would react with passion against the mice and the mess and the dope, and Pia getting up in the middle of the afternoon, and the three of them spinning out improbable plans for the future, improvising recklessly.

He told Elise, the next day, as much as he'd told Annelies.

– You'll have to give her the address, Elise said.

– Then Pia will refuse to see either of us.

– It's her daughter, Paul! Imagine how I'd feel if it was Becky or Joni. I'd never, ever forgive you for holding that back from me.

– But Pia's twenty.

– That's not your reason. You're up to something. I thought you were up to something, all those trips to London. I thought it might be a girl, and then it turns out just to be Pia. Pia, pregnant.

VII

Later that week, Paul woke in the morning to the whine and shriek of a saw, and the burned smell of cut wood floating in at the open window. Pulling on his dressing gown, he ran downstairs and outside to find that Willis had the first of the aspens half down already, in a blare of sawdust startling as blood, petrol fumes from the saw thick in the air. James was with him. Elise in her kimono was already out there; she had abandoned the girls at the breakfast table and now they were hovering in tears at the house door. She was shrieking at Willis, her usual aloofness trampled in her desperation. Paul saw in Willis's expression – filtered through a flirting, quivering fan of the leaves of the murdered and half-fallen tree – that this was exactly what he was cutting down the aspen for: to have the pair of them out in their night-clothes, screaming at him absurdly across a wall on a fine morning, exposed as idly breakfasting while working men sweated. It was as if he were an exorcist and had forced them to appear in their true form at last.

This was an outrage, they ranted. The aspens didn't belong to him, they were on Tre Rhiw land (this was debatable, it wasn't clear from the deeds), it was illegal for him to touch them without their permission, which they would never give. They would sue, they would get an injunction. And anyway, why was he cutting them down in the first place? Willis made his claim that the trees were getting in the way of the farm machinery. – Bullshit, said Paul. – It's pure fucking aggressive vandalism, that's what it is.

James meanwhile leaned on the saw, smiling into the grass and sawdust around his feet, sharing the joke of it all with himself.

– But don't you think these trees are beautiful? asked Elise rashly.

– Trees are just trees, said Willis.

He agreed eventually, reluctantly, to leave the rest of them at least for this one day: probably only because he wasn't really sure either who owned them. When Paul came back from dropping the girls at the bus pick-up, Elise was still in her kimono at the kitchen table, nursing her cold coffee. He was surprised to see she had been crying; she didn't often cry. Soggy tissue was wadded in her palm.

– They belong here and we don't, she said. – No matter how long we live here.

– He doesn't belong here, El. He's English, he comes from outside. You told me yourself, he isn't popular. The other farmers in the village aren't like him: they love this land. And what he's doing is a mistake, even in farming terms: the trees are windbreaks. The aspen suckers help consolidate the soil. He doesn't need to cut them: he's only doing it to get at us.

– But behind it, the reason is real: why he hates us and resents us. He works the land; what are we? We're nothing, we're only playing here. This place where he earns his living is only our pleasure ground. That's what he knows, he knows we feel it. If we live here all our lives, we can't earn that out.

Paul was furious at her fatalism because it was something he was susceptible to himself. – I'm not going to feel guilty, he insisted. – Aren't we working here? Who says that it's his kind of work, mostly poisoning and destroying wildlife habitat, that earns the right to cut down the trees? We taxpayers subsidise farmers like him, to be custodians of the countryside. I'm phoning a solicitor, to get an injunction against him.

– Please don't. Don't make this more horrible than it has to be. I don't want to get in a feud with them. We can plant new trees. We'll put in a new row, on our side of the wall. Ruth says he wants to make enemies of us.

– What's Ruth got to do with this? Did you call her while I was out?

– She belongs to this place, she understands how things work here. We have to respect these country people. Don't forget, it isn't only Willis who's English.

– I resent you bringing Ruth into something that only concerns us.

They rowed as they hadn't done for a long time, their quarrel degenerating almost at once into an ancient idiotic riff over who did most in the house, who was working the hardest, who was having the worst time. While they argued Elise was clearing the breakfast things from the table, scraping Rice Krispies savagely into the compost bin, dashing leftover cold tea into the sink. No one had properly finished eating or drinking that morning. Paul felt excitement mounting, a kind of release. They got onto the dangerous subject of Elise's family. He said he had never been able to work out what her mother used to do all day, apart from choosing clothes and ordering servants about.

– Don't be ridiculous, we didn't have 'servants', not the way you make it sound. Only while we were in Washington.

He claimed there was something unhealthy in how her family hung on to trunks full of papers: diaries and memoirs, souvenirs of dogs and horses, photographs of the houses they had lived in, home movies. Her sisters had hours of taped recordings of their parents reminiscing.

– Who are you keeping it for? Whoever d'you think will be interested?

– I'm shocked, she said. – When I told you about those tapes, I never dreamed you were thinking all this horrible stuff.

– I couldn't care less about the tapes. But you've got to admit, your family carries a lot of heavy baggage.

– No: it's just meanness in you. Something miserable, that wants to shrivel up what other people care about. Does the meanness come from your background, did you get it from your parents? Are you jealous, of all the memories we have?

– I can't believe you've actually used that word: 'background'. What are you, my fucking social worker?

– Don't you *dare* bring politics into this.

Willis would have been gratified to hear them, Paul thought. Probably this was exactly how he imagined the intimate life of people like them, degraded because they had too much time to indulge themselves with thinking.

Elise said she had work to do, and went off to the barn. Paul stood for a while in the cramped tiny bedroom upstairs. The duvet was still heaped on the bed where he'd thrown it off when he heard the saw. Rage at Elise and rage at Willis's assault on the tree were mixed painfully together. The bedroom seemed oppressively feminine, the dressing table with its bottles of perfume and cosmetics, the muslin curtains at the windows, the brass bed frame, the pink-striped duvet cover. How had he arrived at submitting to all this? Downstairs, Elise would be finishing the last of the little dining chairs. She had cut the fabric so that at the centre of each seat there was a single rose, black against a dark pink background. Ruth had found a buyer for the whole set of twelve, and someone wanted pictures of them for a lifestyle magazine, which would be good for business. Sometimes, preparing for one of these magazine photographs, Elise transformed one of the rooms in Tre Rhiw, painting its walls a different colour, purple or pink or green, bringing in furniture from the barn where it was waiting to be sold, whipping up new curtains on her machine. She was paid extra for all this. The hems on the curtains would only be pinned or roughly tacked, as if for a stage set, and she wouldn't bother painting behind corner cupboards or a sofa. This set would become the frame of their real lives for months afterwards, until it was all changed for a new shoot.

Paul threw some clothes in a bag with a couple of books, put his passport out of long habit in his back pocket, his laptop in its carrying case, then left the house the front way, walking to the station on the road rather than using the path through the garden and along the river, so that Elise couldn't see him go from her work-room. The raw gap of the aspen's absence in the sky was a pulse of shock, a murder scene: its felled slender length stretched out along the red earth, new coppery-pale leaves still trembling and sprightly, its death not having reached them yet through the slow sap-channels. Should he have stayed, to phone the solicitors? But Elise was against him doing that anyway. He told himself it was futile to worry about a few trees, when the extreme weather this year was so full of signs of disaster. They were all of them sleepwalking to the edge of a great pit, like spoiled trusting children, believing they would always be safe, be comfortable.

On the train he was devoured inexplicably by the same excitement as on the two occasions he had pursued other women, since he'd been with Elise. Elise only knew about one of these, the last one – the Welsh one, the park girl.

He hadn't done anything of that sort for three years, was not planning on it now, but he couldn't read his book; his heart raced uncomfortably. While the train crawled, scarcely advancing, through the outer London suburbs, he took in the complicated man-made wilderness around the track with intensity, as if it had some message of freedom for him: black-painted walls chalked with white numbers and festooned with swags of wiring, willowherb and buddleia flourishing in the dirt, a padlocked corrugated-iron shed, door ripped off its hinges. The beauty of the massive old stonework and rusted ancient machinery roused a nostalgia sharp as a knife for the old world of industrial work that his parents had belonged to.

There were various friends who wouldn't mind putting him up for a night or two, but he didn't want to see them yet: instead he went straight to the flat where Pia was staying. He told himself this was only a postponement, not a destination. All the way there, he was borne up by the conviction that today his luck was in, he would find them at home, even though when he last spoke to Pia, a few days ago, she had been at work. In the background behind her voice he had heard the noises of a café, the rattle of crockery and chatter. He had rung her to let her know that he'd told Annelies about at least part of the situation she was in. – I know, Pia had said. – She called me. She went fairly ballistic, like I knew she would. She tried to be calm at first, then she lost it. It's all right. It's better she starts getting used to the idea.

It was Marek's sister who picked up the entry phone. When he said he was Paul, she sounded blank.

– Pia's father.

– Oh, Pia's not here.

– Can I come in? I'd like to talk to you.

After a moment's hesitation she buzzed him in, and he found his own way up to the flat. The girl was waiting, holding the door open for him. At first he thought she was not as attractive as he had remembered. She was wearing jeans again, and a sleeveless T-shirt with the logo of an athletics team from some American university. One of her front teeth was cracked and discoloured, she was really very thin; he wondered again about drugs. Inside, she offered him a cigarette, and he enjoyed pulling the smoke down into his lungs. She perched cross-legged, lithe, at one end of the sofa.

– I'm in London for a few days, Paul explained.

– You want to stay here?

It was what he wanted, though he hadn't known that until she offered it. But there was surely no room; in fact the flat seemed more cramped even than the last time he'd been in it, because boxes that must be something to do with Marek's import venture were stacked up everywhere against the walls. The Polish writing gave him no clue as to what was inside. Was Anna imagining that while she slept on the sofa, Paul would stretch out beside her on the floor? He remembered his dream about her.

– It's easy. I stay with my boyfriend.

It didn't matter if she had a boyfriend, it was better. He had never imagined anything else. – I'd like to stay. Only for a couple of days.

– OK, it's fine. You can be close to Pia.

Anna wasn't beautiful exactly, but her movements were sinuous and fierce at once; nothing in her was made coarsely, her wrists and the collar bones visible under her loose shirt fine as porcelain, the beauty spot on her cheek precise as a mark on the mask of one of those nocturnal animals, a lemur or a loris. She explained that she couldn't give him a key to the flat. The keys were given out by the council, only to tenants named in the agreement; it wasn't possible to get them copied. He'd have to call, to make sure someone was there to let him in.

– They watch us coming and going, she said. – We don't know if they will report us to the council, that Marek and Pia are living here. Maybe we'll get turned out: who cares? Soon, we'll be getting a better place.

Anna said Marek was looking for a lock-up to rent, to store the boxes. There had been more problems with the concierge about these. Apparently there were biscuits inside, and Lech beer and jam; Anna said they had got a 'very good deal'. While they were waiting for their business to take off, she was working again at the café, along with Pia; he had only caught her at home because this was her afternoon off. Paul asked whether her boyfriend was Polish; he wasn't, he was Australian, he sold computer software to the retail industry, he did a lot of work in Northern Ireland. – Belfast is a nice place, she said. – Maybe I'm thinking about moving there.

Paul had been like this when he was young: always drawn on by news from elsewhere, always wanting to be beginning again in a new place. But then he had changed his mind, and had wanted to be rooted instead.

He had to use the bathroom. The door hadn't been fixed back on its hinges yet: he tried to pee as noiselessly as possible. Washing his hands, he grimaced at himself in the mirror. When he was a boy he had been pretty, he had had to fight off the interest of certain teachers. Now he was a couple of stone heavier, the flesh of his face had thickened and darkened, his hair had gradually been leached of its colour. Who knew how old he seemed to Anna? And yet it was a fact, it had almost a biological rightness, that men of his age often partnered with girls of her age.

He went out in the afternoon and walked around the streets. He had imagined himself getting away from home to concentrate with a new and cleaner passion on his writing, but now he hardly thought about it, as if he had left it behind in another life. He walked among the crowds and down the side roads until he was tired, bought smuggled cigarettes from a street vendor, then stopped at a bar in Upper Street that had tables on the pavement and read the newspaper over a couple of beers. When he called Elise, she wouldn't pick up. He left a message, saying he was staying with his old friends Stella and John, he would be home in a few days. Stella was his BBC contact. The lie felt bland in his mouth, he shed it effortlessly.

VIII

The days he stayed in the flat slipped into weeks. The first night, getting ready for bed in that tiny living room, it had seemed impossible; he had thought he would have to leave the next morning. He would never be able to sleep here. Pia said it was 'weird' having him stay. He could hear them undressing in the room next door, his daughter and this stranger who might or might not be good for her: they opened drawers, bumped furniture, communicated in intimate low voices that were only just uninterpretable. The plasterboard walls were a perfunctory divide, as if really they all slept promiscuously together, exposed to the sky. It never got dark: light and noise streamed in from the street outside. The traffic ploughed unendingly, only easing off somewhat towards morning. In contrast to this, his bed in Tre Rhiw was a den burrowed deep in the earth.

As he got used to the noise over the nights that followed, he began to imagine it was a tide, and that in the small hours the block slipped its moorings, floating out. Pulling the duvet over his head, he smelled on it the tang of Anna's sweat, her musky perfume. He thought he would never sleep, and then night after night fell into hours of velvety oblivion, waking at three or four in the morning to the trucks outside and the sodium light, not knowing where he was, excited and afraid. Once, the people next door put on loud music suddenly at dawn: probably they'd arrived back from a party they didn't want to be over. Marek came out without hesitation from the bedroom, buttoning his jeans as he went. They heard him pounding with his fist on the neighbours' door, not even bothering to try the bell. Then there was shouting, then silence. There was never any trouble from them again.

On the whole the neighbours in the block weren't bad, Pia said. They were pretty quiet. One tenant upstairs apparently had 'mental problems', as she put it. Mostly he was OK, as long as he was taking his medication, but he had twice left the tap running in his sink with the plug in, and water had poured down into their flat below. If confronted, he got argumentative and violent: they had the number of his social worker to call in an emergency. Marek said it was pointless, people like him being allowed out into the community, to spoil things for everyone else. – If he doesn't want to look after himself, why should we? Paul argued about the cruelty and futility of the old asylum system. He said society had a duty of care towards its weaker members.

– You've seen him? Marek asked. – He's not so weak.
In fact, the schizophrenic was a huge man, with broad

podgy shoulders and waist-length ginger hair, benign-seeming enough when Paul met him a couple of times on the stairs. Apparently he had bought his flat when the right-to-buy scheme was still operative, so the council couldn't move him anywhere. Marek didn't mind Paul arguing with him. He would listen to him attentively, almost fondly; somehow this had to do with his feelings for him as Pia's father, as if their relationship through her pregnancy required him to treat Paul with special consideration, conciliation. He tore open one of the boxes and got out a bottle of vodka flavoured with something he didn't know how to translate; Paul worked out from a picture on the label that they must be rowan berries. Pouring, Marek would patiently explain again how Paul was wrong, how if you were too soft with people they didn't thank you for it, but turned on you in the long run, how if your welfare system was too generous it would only attract a whole underclass of criminals and no-goods, waiting to take advantage.

– I myself will take advantage of it, he said disarmingly, – if you allow me. You must not allow me.

The conventional things Marek said, and his doctrine that could have come straight out of the tabloids, somehow weren't alienating, in the stream of his good nature and boundless energy. He talked about how difficult things would be when the baby was born, but Paul knew he didn't believe this really, his confidence in himself was unfaltering. Whatever Marek said seemed protected behind a habitual humorous irony. His curiosity was restless, he was a repository of information, he picked up quickly whatever he wanted to learn (he had found out all about leasehold, for instance, since he last saw Paul, and was keenly interested in the regeneration work going on at King's Cross).

It was only when Paul had been in the flat for several days that he took in that there were no books in it, none, apart from a tatty dictionary and a couple of recipe books. There were DVDs, most of them Hollywood, along with a few Polish films that looked like thrillers – no Kieslowski or Wadja. He had always had a superstitious fear of being shut up somewhere without books; now that it had happened he hadn't even consciously noticed. Long ago, when he was a student and went home for the summer to work in the brewery, he had built his books almost into a rampart in his bedroom, against the bookless house. Staying over with Pia, he didn't care. He had brought something with him from Tre Rhiw to read on the train, but hadn't opened it. Nor had he unzipped the bag with his laptop in it.

Pia got up early in the mornings to go to the café. Paul buried his face deeper in the sofa cushions while she stepped around in the chaos in the living room, finding the things she needed for work. She was light on her feet in spite of the pregnancy. He was aware of her making breakfast obediently in the kitchenette, because Anna insisted she must eat it. Usually Marek went out not long after Pia. When they were both gone and the door pulled shut behind them, the return of stillness in the flat was a guilty luxury into which Paul sank, chasing the tail end of dreams that seemed exceptionally vivid and important. He got to know the way the light advanced across the floor of the flat, split into laths by the blinds, the day's noise and heat building in the room until he couldn't ignore them. Sometimes when he was dressed he made efforts to tidy the place, not only stowing his bedding in the bedroom, but attacking whatever mess was left in the kitchen from the night before, soaking pans and rinsing plates. It never looked very different when he'd finished. Even with the windows as wide open as they would go, it was always hot, there was always a sweet smell of something rotting, inside the flat or floating in from outdoors.

Several times he visited the café where Pia worked, a place in Islington that specialised in patisserie. The first time he came across it by chance, walking the streets going nowhere in particular; he only recognised where he was when he caught sight through a plate-glass window of Pia in her long white apron, clearing tables. When he had imagined the two girls working together, he had pictured Pia as a clumsy apprentice performing under Anna's tutelage. Surely his daughter, who had been so protected and had never had to work for a living, would not know how to submit to a work discipline? She had failed at university, which should have been easy. But he saw now that she was good at this work in her own right, steady and capable. She carried the heavy tray of crockery between tables without faltering, then returned to take orders, waiting with her pen and little pad, explaining patiently to the customers the array of cakes that rose above the counter, rank upon rank: pink and beige meringues, macaroons, tarts filled with fruit or custard, chocolate truffles sifted with cocoa. The women eyed them with hungry desire, delaying choosing. He could see they were touched by Pia's swollen pregnancy. It wasn't the sort of place Paul would ordinarily have stopped, it was fashionable and expensive, with chunky long tables of oiled wood, cream enamel lamps. The clientele were handsome, well dressed, loud.

While he watched through the window, Pia felt his gaze on her and lifted her head; a smile broke the surface of her absorption in her work, and she beckoned to him to come inside, brought him coffee and tried to persuade him to have a cake. He didn't want cake, but the coffee was good, and he didn't mind sitting there reading the paper, aware of his daughter passing backwards and forwards among the tables behind him, using the tongs to pick out cakes, ringing up bills on the till. When he went in another time, she was making the coffee, using the Gaggia machine, banging out the old grounds and tamping in the new, making shapes in the foam on the cappuccinos. She got used to him, and forgot to be flustered if he was watching. He recognised that he had overlooked, in Pia's childhood, this capacity of hers for steady, graceful work; he had overridden it with his own certainties.

Anna in the café was quite different. Occasionally she came round to talk business with Marek in the evenings, but after the first day, he hadn't seen much of her in the flat. At work she was unsmiling, fierce, effective, a little frown pulled taut between her plucked eyebrows. Her hair was scraped back from her face, and she was disconcertingly lean under the apron tied around her waist: her hard young body seemed in itself a challenge, a form of contempt. Paul saw how the customers were drawn to her as if they wanted to woo her, coax and soften her, and how she played on this, winding the sexual tension tight without giving anything away. Meanwhile she was kind to him as if they were in a conspiracy, undercharging him, bringing him cake to eat that he hadn't asked for and only left on the plate. – Have it, it's good, she said. – Eat. They charge too much. I see the invoices, I know what goes on here. Take it home, eat it tonight.

Anna's default position towards authority was suspicious and derisory, but for some reason – because of Pia – Paul had been excepted. Like her brother she watched scrupulously over him, as if he needed cajoling and swaddling. He asked himself whether there could be anything sinister behind this, but couldn't find it. They knew he didn't have money. The longer he slept on their sofa, the more they must know for certain that he didn't have power. Really, their generosity could only be superstitious and romantic. They must believe in the mystery of the coming child, and how it bound them all together in one improbable shaky family.

– It's nice for you, Anna said to Pia, – to have your father round. It's good.

He did not know what Anna would think of him, the grandfather-to-be, if she knew he was dreaming about her at night. Perhaps she guessed. These dreams occurred at the margins where deliberate fantasy slipped over into sleep, so he wasn't altogether responsible. In one dream he made love to her in a hotel room, horrible like the one at the Travelodge in Birmingham. Anna came from the shower, her hair still sopping; cold water soaked into the sheets and pillows on the bed. She lay with her back to him, he put his mouth to the knobs of her vertebrae, standing out under her skin the colour of pale coffee, cold to the touch and goosefleshed. He ran his hand across her ribs, down her flat stomach, to her gaunt pelvis. In the dream the hot weather had broken and it was raining outside, the windowpanes blurred with running water, the room full with its rushing noise, its gargling in the gutters. The implications of it all were infantile, humiliating. Yet imperceptibly and against all reason, the dreams also began to bind him to the real girl, as if they meant he knew her.

Marek borrowed a van from a friend, a dirty dented white Vauxhall Combo, to take round the boxes of biscuits and beer and try to sell them. Paul had worked driving a van in London more than twenty years ago, before Pia was born: he offered to help, he hadn't anything else to do. Marek didn't like driving. Paul was pleased to fill his days with the kind of work that tired him out without requiring him to probe his inner life. The van handled badly, the steering was shot and the engine hunted in first gear, but he got on top of it and found his way round the old routes, baulked only by changes to the one-way system, or by having to avoid entering the congestion-charge zone. Marek explained to him why the charge was a terrible idea and didn't work. Paul didn't care, didn't bother to argue.

He and Marek were well suited to working together. For long periods of time they didn't talk, then Marek would erupt into a kind of absurd humour, which Paul remembered belonged to this fragmented experience on the road, tangling momentarily in the crazy complexity of local lives and then torn out again. When he closed his eyes at night he sometimes thought he was still driving, carried bodily along, hurtling into the dark. Everyone they met seemed funny. Marek imagined he was a good mimic, although Paul told him all his imitations simply sounded Polish. There were so many Polish shops, and they made sales in Asian and Middle Eastern groceries too. He got used to the special atmosphere of these places, some better, some worse – their stale sour smell, the shelves crowded with faded goods displaced from their natural habitat, pale gherkins floating in cloudy brine, dark rye bread, blue flashes from the insect zappers, the sound of the Polish voices, the metal shutters drawn down over windows and doors when the shops were closed. Some of them kept their windows shuttered even during the day. He picked up a few greetings, yes and no, some names.

Marek brought out Wiejska sausage and bread for their lunch and they ate it sitting in the front of the van with the doors open, washing it down with Coke or paper cups of tea from a café, laced with vodka, not enough to make them drunk, just enough to lift them exhilaratingly a fraction off the ground. They might have been all right if they were stopped. Anyway, Paul never asked Marek if he had any sort of licence to sell his stuff, so if they'd been stopped the drink would probably have been the least of their problems. Marek sometimes made Paul wait ten minutes in a residential street while he dropped in on 'friends'. – It's OK, Marek reassured him. – Only as a favour, little bit of weed. Nothing stupid. Paul seemed to slip back inside that past time when he was heedless and twenty, as though all his substantial life between then and now melted away. Catching sight of his reflection once in a shop window, carrying in a delivery, he was startled to see himself middle-aged.

Marek had found a lock-up to rent in a back lane in Kennington, where he stored the non-perishable goods. In contrast to the filthy noise and traffic, Paul felt when they visited the lock-up almost as if they were somewhere in the country, or in the past, with its red-brick walls, little overgrown back gardens, boarded-up artisan workshops. Pink valerian grew out of the bricks. Once while they were loading up, the van engine idling, Marek asked him about his younger daughters. Paul didn't want to talk about them; what-ever he said seemed compromised because he couldn't adequately explain what was keeping him away from them, here in London. He tried not to picture them too vividly. He told himself he would go home soon, that he hadn't been away any time at all, that they would hardly have noticed.

– You have all girls, Marek said. – Now I've made you a boy.

– Do you know it's a boy?

– I know. I make boys. I have a son already in Poland, ten years old. He's a nice kid. His mother tries to turn him against me, but he doesn't listen. I don't see him very often, it's a shame, but what can you do? I'm here, I send money.

– Is Pia aware of this?

– She's OK, she's cool with it. This woman in Poland hates me. We're never even married, she was married at the time to someone else. It's all a big mistake. Except the kid: he's fine.

He took out a photograph from his wallet. A skinny boy in shorts was on some climbing apparatus, grinning over his shoulder at the camera. He was very fair, but with his father's black eyes and small skull, neat and round as a nut.

At the end of Paul's first day's work, Marek insisted on paying him, tucking folded notes into his shirt pocket. Paul saw that, as a point of honour, he must accept, although he tried to say that the work was in return for their letting him sleep on their sofa. As it happened, he really didn't need money at that moment. When he'd visited the cash point, expecting to be overdrawn, he'd found he was several thousand pounds in credit; this could only mean that the money left over from his mother's savings had gone through probate and been paid into his account. He had planned that he would give a couple of thousand of this to Pia at some point, to help with the baby, but he hadn't said anything about it yet. He did his best to spend what Marek gave him on drink and food for the flat. Adding up the hours, he calculated that this delivery work probably paid him better than writing.

Paul called on Stella and John in Tufnell Park. At the door Stella had to wrestle with the dog, a tall overbred animal, all silky locks and nerves, which leapt on visitors in ecstatic welcome.

– She's shameless, Stella apologised, tugging its collar.
– She's anybody's. Come on in.

The dog's nails skittered on the tiles in the big hall, which was elegantly untidy, doubled in a huge mirror in a crumbling gilt frame. A mounted stag's head was a paperweight on top of a pile of issues of the *TLS*. Paul thought that Stella's kiss on his cheek was tinged with reproach: no doubt she'd been talking to Elise and had concluded he was up to his old games. He recoiled for some reason from reassuring her that he wasn't. Stella was diminutive and forthright, with dangling earrings and a pixie haircut: she had done Classics at university. She and John were his friends and not Elise's; Elise said Stella reminded her of the head girl at school.

Paul passed the evening in his usual chair in Stella's study, drinking John's twenty-five-year-old Talisker; John was out with clients, he was a partner in a law firm. The dog subsided into hopeful repose on its rug, making efforts to hold its eyes open, folds twitching on its shallow forehead.

– Elise is in a state, Stella accused him. – She's no idea where you are. You told her you were staying here: I felt awful when she rang and I didn't know what she was talking about. What's going on, Paul? Are you behaving like a shit again?

– It's not what you think, he said vaguely.

– I don't know what I think.

– I'm looking after Pia.

– She told me Pia's pregnant. Is that where you are? The poor kid. Have you any idea what a disaster a baby would be, at Pia's age? She'd be crawling up the walls with frustration.

Paul said that it was too late to do anything about the pregnancy.

– So who is this guy? Do you trust him?

There were original Eric Ravilious prints on the walls of the study, a Barbara Hepworth maquette on a table, on the bookshelves first editions of Hughes and Larkin. The room was intensely familiar to Paul, like a second skin; yet the smell of the van was also on his clothes – garlic sausage and petrol and hot rubber – and the traffic still seemed to be in his blood, surging round him in its abrupt stop-start rhythm. He got into an argument with Stella about education, Pia's education in particular. He was surprised, hearing his own pent-up belligerence spilling over.

– It's all a sham, the liberal fiction of enlightenment. Education's a caste system, a narrow gate set up to process children. In order to pass through, they have to be broken, then put back together. Middle-class parents invest it with fetish value because they were tested and broken themselves, they pass on the hidden damage.

– What rubbish you're talking, Stella said. – The trouble is, for Pia everything's at stake here; it's real, it's not just you upsetting people at parties.

Eventually, even while they went on arguing, Paul relaxed, felt at home again, forgot about the raw new phase of his life at the flat. He thought affectionately about Stella, sitting opposite him straight-backed, earrings shaking in emphasis, the dog's head lying in abjection in her lap. In long-ago Greenham days, she had been one of those who broke through the perimeter fence to spray the silos, and was repeatedly arrested. She was honourable and conscientious. At the end of the evening she persuaded him to call Tre Rhiw. Tactfully she left him alone with the phone and went to make coffee. He expected to get through to the answering machine. It shook him when he actually heard Elise's voice, tentative at the other end of the line, even tremulous.

– Hello?

– Elise, it's me.

His voice seemed to fall into the empty quiet of the

house at night. She had not been watching television when he rang – he would have heard it in the background. He was surprised she was awake so late.

– Where are you?

– I'm at Stella's.

– No, you're not. I know you're not, I rang her.

– I really am here tonight. I'm ringing on Stella's phone: do 1471 afterwards if you want.

He explained that he was staying with Pia, that his mobile was out of battery, he had forgotten to bring the charger with him. He knew Elise must be listening for something else, for more than this. She ought to be fortifying herself against him, to punish him; and yet her voice in his ear was disconcertingly intimate, as if his call had caught her unprepared, before she could conceal herself.

– You could at least have spoken to the girls.

– I know. I'm sorry. I'll ring them.

He waited for her to ask when he was coming home.

– Actually something's up here, Paul. I think Gerald's ill.

– What kind of ill?

She said she was worried he might be having some kind of breakdown. – Maybe it's nothing, he just seems strange to me, he's behaving strangely. I thought perhaps you ought to come back, that's all.

– What do you mean by strange? Don't you always think he's strange?

There was silence, he thought she must be searching

for the right words to describe what was worrying her.
– How do you know this? Have you spoken to him?

– Listen, it doesn't matter. Take no notice of me, I'm probably imagining things.

He forgot to ask whether Willis had been back for the rest of the trees.

IX

One morning Paul drove Marek to Heathrow for a meeting with one of his exporters, who had a few hours in London between flights. He was also apparently an old school friend: short and plump, with a shaved head and cherub mouth. Marek was always in jeans, but this man wore a business suit and a thin leather tie, carried a briefcase. With one arm round Paul's shoulders and one round his friend's, Marek introduced them.

– Not only my driver, also father of my girlfriend Pia, who is very lovely, dear to my heart.

Paul was pressed into the heat of this stranger, smelled on him the different spice of Warsaw, where he had woken and breakfasted that morning. They shook hands, the man's eyes glittering and clever.

– Marek, you're become a family man?

– I like family! Marek insisted. – The right family, I like it.

Paul joked. – I'm sticking with him, to keep an eye on him.

– And how is Anna?

– You know Anna. Always on my case, we have to build the business up. She's a slave driver.

– It's good for you! Without Anna you're too happy, you'll be lazy.

Marek and his friend bought pints of lager at eleven in the morning, in a simulacrum of an old-world pub, panelled in stained wood, carved out of the vast vacancy of the airport. Paul left them to their planning and walked around; he had no role to play in their business, and knew anyway they would soon lapse into Polish. He loathed airports. He had not been in one for a couple of years – they had not had the money recently to travel abroad. Out of some superstition he'd inflicted on himself, he'd never eaten in an airport or an aeroplane, as if they were an underworld and he feared that if he tasted their fruit he'd leave something of himself behind. Today he let himself be washed along in the slow flow of people in transit, carried past the repeating loop of shops. Even the real things these shops sold – whisky, a book about the origins of the First World War – seemed degraded by the place into shadows of themselves. He bought himself a paper, but didn't sit down to read it. Instead he found himself staring up at the departure boards.

It occurred to him that he could go anywhere, right now. There were all those thousands sitting in his account, enough to buy himself a ticket; and his passport was – he checked – still in the back pocket of these trousers. On the way to Heathrow, he had had no thought other than returning with Marek into London after the meeting. But Marek could drive himself. Sooner or later, in the next week or so, Paul had meant to go back to Elise and the girls at Tre Rhiw: that was his real life. But what if he didn't go back? What if his life continued somewhere else, and was real differently? The lettered shutters spelling out the place names on the board flickered over with their soft susurration: Dubrovnik, Rome, Odessa, Cairo, Damascus. His idea wasn't cerebral; the assault of his desire for it, dropping through him like a current, unhinged him momentarily. He had enough money, even if he gave half to Elise, for a ticket anywhere, and a room when he got there. A room while he sorted himself out. Enough money to get by for a while because he knew how to live frugally.

For ten or twenty minutes, while he dwelled inside this possibility, it was so real that he felt afterwards the unfinished gesture in his muscles, his clenched jaw; he had meant to walk over to the information desk, ask about last-minute tickets, find out where he could go, get out his card from his wallet, pay. He would have to take the van keys back to Marek. It was a door that stood open, through which he could walk lightly, carrying nothing. This was the sort of thing he used to do; something unfinished in him, which had been set aside and forgotten, stepped up to the adventure with fast-beating heart. He imagined himself walking out from a room somewhere else, in a few hours, into a different light: to buy clothes, toothbrush, razor, which he would not know the names for. He would find a bar to eat in, or buy food on the street. The place might be dirty and poor, it might have stone ramparts where the population strolled to take the air in the evenings, it might overlook the sea, it might not. Paul felt himself at a pivot in his life, swinging dangerously loose: if he moved, he would go over to the information desk and everything would follow on from there. He had only to keep still. If he went, he couldn't be forgiven, or forgive himself – freedom would carve out an empty space in him for ever. A message drifted through his cells, from his bones, that he must keep still. Eventually Marek came to find him.

Pia's ankles swelled and the doctor told her she had to rest, take time off from work. She wasn't sleeping well at night. Marek was solicitous, sat with her big white feet in his lap, massaging them. When Paul vacated the sofa in the mornings she settled herself there and switched on the television. Sometimes she didn't even wait for him to clear away the bedding, didn't bother to pull up the blinds. Listlessly uncomfortable, she kept shifting position. She made her face up by the artificial light.

– Won't you let me read to you? Paul asked one day not long after the Heathrow trip, when Marek hadn't needed him, he was doing business somewhere else in the city. At a loose end, Paul had even thought of going to the library and starting some work. He couldn't bear the idea of Pia filling her head with the kind of drivel they put on television in the daytime. If he bought *Great*

Expectations or *Emma*, perhaps he could abridge as he read, if he saw she was getting bored.

– Read to me? Dad, have you forgotten I'm twenty years old?

She was adamant, as if she suspected him of trying to smuggle in under cover some scheme for getting her back into education. All she would agree to was his borrowing DVDs from a local rental place, which they watched together in the afternoons. Her taste was not what he'd expected, not sentimental. She liked clever thrillers, *Michael Clayton*, *No Country for Old Men*. They began on the first series of *The Wire* together; she was much quicker than he was to pick up what was happening.

– Aren't you missing your friends? he asked her. – What about your old girlfriends from school? Or from the university.

– I did see some of the girls from school at first, when I moved in here. Once I knew I was pregnant, I couldn't go out drinking with them, and that's all they ever want to do. I only miss James.

– James Willis? Really? Isn't he a bit of a clown?

– James and me are soulmates. We think the same things at the same time. One of us says what the other was just about to. That's why we never could go out together.

– He's always tongue-tied if I try to talk to him.

– That's because you're you, Dad. You're not the easiest person to talk to.

He told her about Willis senior coming to cut down the poplars at Tre Rhiw.

– Was James involved in this? He's never mentioned anything about it.

– He was the one wielding the fucking saw.

She laughed, and he began to remember all the detail of that morning, which from this perspective in the flat seemed highly comical. When he told her about his quarrel with Elise, she took Elise's side, she said it wasn't worth making an enemy of Mr Willis for the sake of the trees. It was clear she couldn't really remember which trees he was talking about, and she said they could always plant some more. Paul had wondered if she might take the opportunity of backing him against Elise. She hadn't always got on with her stepmother. Elise could be blunt sometimes, and when Pia was younger, Elise had found her obstinate and unresponsive. Sometimes when she first came to stay with them, before Becky was born, she was patently sick with misery, away from her home; but however Elise coaxed her, she had insisted with a little false smile that she was fine, sitting on the edge of her bed, swinging her feet. There had been something heart-wringing, exasperating to Elise, in how she had unpacked her rucksack so neatly and arranged her trainers in pairs against the wall.

The shape of Pia's pregnancy as it grew was fearsome, a bloated dome; her belly button turned outwards, she stretched the cloth of her T-shirt across it to show it off to Paul. He wouldn't lay his hand on her belly when she offered, if the baby was kicking; but sometimes unavoidably, at close quarters in the crowded flat, they knocked up against one another, he and his grandchild-to-be. Pia's mood seemed to Paul to be changing as the pregnancy advanced. Her girlishness fell away, she was less capricious, more brooding. Once she said passionately that she wished her Nana could have seen the baby, and he realised then that he'd stopped dreaming about his mother since he came to the flat. She began to make a little collection of baby clothes. When he remembered her balancing her tray and patiently picking out cakes in the café, he wondered if she might after all be gifted for motherhood when it came. Perhaps the women who found it easiest were those who didn't fight against relinquishing their own will.

He tried to make the flat pleasant for his daughter to spend time in, buying flowers and bringing home fresh food, plenty of fruit. Marek commiserated over her being stuck on the sofa all day, but it was difficult to imagine him doing this sort of domesticated shopping. Instead he arrived back with pieces of equipment he had got at bargain prices: a complicated pushchair on three wheels, a baby alarm, something improbably called a baby gym. There wasn't room to unpack these from their boxes.

He called Tre Rhiw from a pay phone in Upper Street. While he waited for Elise to pick up he felt trepidation, half-expecting to be transplanted back inside their last conversation, with its intimate unguardedness, late at night. In the blaze of afternoon, however, her voice was quite different, brusque. She conveyed that any talk was snatched out of a day impossibly busy, between the pressure of orders in the workshop and looking after the children.

– You've managed to find time to call, she said. – That's good of you.

He couldn't argue with her outrage, didn't try to defend himself. But it seemed laid on in thick strokes, like a mask over some other excitement. He fixated on the idea that she had been conspiring with Ruth against him; or with her sister Mirrie, who had been at Tre Rhiw for the weekend.

Over the phone the girls sounded years younger. Becky was shy and he could hardly squeeze information out of her. He could picture her blushing behind her freckles, murmuring into the mouthpiece, holding herself still in concentration.

– What are you doing in London, Daddy?

He told her he was staying with her older sister. Becky seemed to know about the baby, giggling diffidently when she mentioned it; he explained this was why he was keeping an eye on Pia, to make sure everything was all right. Joni was perfunctory, as if she'd half-forgotten him already. She couldn't wait to hand the phone to her mother.

– Did Willis come back? he asked Elise.

– He came back. She gave a hard, short laugh. – He offered to sell me back the trees cut into logs.

– The man's unbelievable.

– Yes, well. I've had other things to worry about.

He asked after Gerald, whether she'd had any contact with him. Elise didn't appear to be anxious any longer that he was having a breakdown. – He's been spending a lot of time out here, she said. – I think it's good for him. He and Mirrie got on well together.

This didn't seem likely to Paul, but he didn't comment.

Anna called in after work to tell them Annelies had come looking for Pia at the café. Luckily, she said, no one had mentioned Pia's connection with her, or given away that Pia was living in her flat. They would only give her Pia's mobile number, which Annelies already had.

– I'll call her, Pia said. – I'll go and see her. I really ought to.

– You don't have to. It's your choice. Don't let her blackmail you.

Paul encouraged Pia to get in touch. Anna seemed lit up with hostility to the idea of Pia's mother, as if Pia was a refugee from some oppression. Beside Anna, Pia seemed steady as a rock, calming. No doubt Annelies's performance in the café – she hadn't been happy with their non-cooperation, apparently – had given some flavour of how she might judge her daughter's new friends, their rackety household, their prospects.

Paul hadn't yet met Anna's Australian boyfriend. He was away for some time in Belfast, and then even when he was back, Anna didn't mention him often. If she did, it was with a smothered impatience; was he too malleable, Paul wondered, or not malleable enough? Anna began spending more time at the flat again, and Paul knew he ought to go, to make room for her in her own place, although she never hinted at this and he believed she might not want it. In some crazy way they had accepted him as part of their improvised family. Marek teased him affectionately, calling him an intellectual, caricaturing him as an otherworldly idealist. In the evenings, or even in the afternoons if Anna wasn't at work, Paul was aware that she and Marek were sometimes fuelling themselves, apart from all the dope they smoked, probably with pills or coke: they went off into the kitchen or the bedroom, claiming to be talking business, and came back wired and jumpy. They kept this stuff away from Pia with exaggerated protectiveness: and from Paul too, out of a kind of courtesy, touching and faintly insulting, as if they thought he was too innocent, or just too old.

One evening Marek took Pia out for a meal, because she had said she was going mad, stuck all day in the same place. While they were out, Anna talked to Paul about their troubles at home in Poland. The windows in the flat were all open, cool air was blowing in at last after a day when the heat had never moved. The orange sky outside was barred with shadows: clouds gathered on the horizon in the evenings, but didn't come to anything. They sat without switching on the lights, Anna cross-legged on the sofa beside him, hair falling into her eyes, dabbing with the end of her cigarette in the brimming ashtray. She spoke in her usual abrupt sentences, fatalistic. Their father was ill, he had been diagnosed a year ago with bone cancer. She wondered if the diagnosis was accurate: it was well known that Polish hospitals made mistakes.

– Will they give him the best care? I doubt it. I don't trust them.

He listened sympathetically, asking tactful questions. She said her father was a strong man, physically small but very strong, who had never had one day of illness in his life. He had been a supervisor in a factory making household cleansers, but now he had been off work for months. 'Who knows what chemicals they used there, or if they gave him the right protection?'

Their mother was alive, but their parents were separated. Paul began to understand while she was talking that she and Marek hadn't seen their father since he'd been ill, or even spoken to him: and not for some considerable time before that, either. He didn't ask why. What Marek paid him for a day in wages would have bought them a cheap flight home. Anna sat with her shoulders hunched almost to her ears: defiant, estranged. He was overwhelmed by his attraction to her, as if she was a miserable beautiful animal, huddled in captivity.

She bent forwards to stub out her cigarette and in the orange light he could see the small mounds of her bare breasts inside her loose vest, surprisingly soft and plump against her skinny torso. He put out his hand and felt the hem on the neck of her shirt between his fingers, then touched her hot skin, reaching down inside the dark under the cloth, cupping his hand around one breast, feeling its nipple in his palm. Its soft flesh seemed quite separate from the rest of her: the softness seemed to send an unexpected, hopeful message. For a few seconds Anna didn't pull away from him. But when he leaned forward to kiss her, she darted her head down and bit him on the inside of his forearm, not hard enough to break the skin, but enough to make him yelp and jump back. She shook her finger at him, laughing and frowning.

– Naughty, naughty.

He remembered how his boy's desire had stirred for the robber maid in Hans Andersen's *Snow Queen*, who tickled the throat of her pet reindeer with her knife. The bruise Anna made on his arm stayed in his skin for weeks.

He dreamed he was in Willis's yard. In the dream something in its blanched, clean-swept order was uncanny, its light like the thick honey stillness before a storm. Willis's horses were dipping their heads to dash away flies above their half-doors, and he could hear their hooves shifting on the cobblestones out of sight. There seemed to be some kind of whitewashed arcade around the yard, like a cloister (this was only in the dream, not at the real Blackbrook). Paul was aware at the edge of his attention of a figure moving in and out of its intense shadows: working stiffly, bending her long back. A metal bucket clanged against stone flags, a mop was sopped in water. He couldn't see his mother's face, but he knew for sure it was her; he recognised an old nylon dress she used to wear for housework: white zigzags on navy, slubbed and limp-pleated. Even in the dream he thought how this dress had lain neglected at the bottom of his memory, and was excited by rediscovering it. Who knew what other discoveries were waiting for him, if only he could push farther inside the yard?

That was all, nothing else happened. He only remembered the dream at all because he was woken in the middle of it by some kind of disturbance in the flat. He sat up abruptly, sweating, throwing off the duvet, thinking he'd been roused by sounds of violence. It might be the schizophrenic upstairs: had he started trouble? There was banging from somewhere. Before Paul had collected himself completely out of the dream, he shouted out for his daughter, to see she was all right. Then there was silence, only not empty, more like a wakeful aftermath. He identified too late the noise of lovemaking that had broken through his sleep: banging probably because their bed was cheap and pushed right against the wall, perhaps noises forced out from between the lovers' clenched jaws, however Pia may have tried to keep them from her father's ears. No wonder this thrilled in the air as violence. Paul had been embarrassed to wonder, the first nights he slept in the flat, whether his presence behind these flimsy walls might be inhibiting for his daughter and Marek; he had reassured himself vaguely, when he never heard them, that they might not be making love anyway, in her advanced state of pregnancy, or that the walls were soundproof after all.

The bedroom door opened, Pia came out in her nightshirt, closing the door behind her. He thought she was very angry.

– Dad? You shouted.

– I'm sorry. I think I woke up out of a dream. A nightmare.

He was sitting up on the sofa with the duvet pulled across his lap. In the light from the street lamps her shirt was fairly transparent, so that he saw her distended shape – long legs, mounded stomach, breasts growing heavy – almost as if she stood there naked, intimidating. The pregnancy appeared to him for the first time as the blatant outward sign of his daughter's secret sexual life.

– How long are you going to be staying, Dad? Because there isn't really room here. Isn't there anywhere else that you could go? This really isn't working out.

He took out two thousand pounds at the bank, which they gave to him in a brown envelope. When he went to say goodbye to Anna at the café, he pressed the envelope into her hand.

– Please take it, he said. – I got some money un-expectedly. You'll have a lot of extra expenses over the next few months, with your father's illness and everything.

The place was busy, humming. At several tables people were waiting to have their orders taken.

– Oh. Thank you.

Anna looked quickly at the envelope, she didn't open it to see inside, only put it away in the money bag the waitresses wore around their waists, glancing to see if the other staff were watching. She must have felt the thickness of the wad of notes, though. He didn't know how to read her expression, whether she was offended by the present, or grateful, or even slyly triumphant.

– It was very good of you to put me up at the flat. In my hour of need.

– It's no problem.

She was remote, as if his gift had turned him back into a stranger, a customer. He had imagined kissing her before he left, just a grown-up peck on the cheek. But there was no way he could carry it off in front of all these people.

X

The aspens' absence beside Tre Rhiw, as Paul came up through the garden, disfigured every-thing. Planes of sky and slanting field were exposed in a new relationship with the house, which was thrust nakedly forward. On the near side of the garden wall was a line of new, very young trees, each with its stake and its beige protective casing – this planting undertaken without him was another shock. Around them the earth was still raw, but above the little casings leaves of brilliant yellow-green fluttered out like flags, flaunting their growth. Elise must be watering them every night, in this dry heat. The doors to the workshop were open at both ends and Paul walked through it, half-expecting to find her.

The house door stood open too. He heard the televi-sion as he crossed the yard, where the sunlight struck with a new ferocity because it wasn't filtered through the trees; for a moment he was blind, coming into the smoth-ering dimness of the hallway. Peering into the cubbyhole where the television pictures weakly danced, he took in a lungful of its familiar stale morning air: musty cushions, little girls' farting, souring milk spilled from their cereal bowls.

– Hello! It's Daddy! Becky said in cheerful surprise, making no move.

– Where is he?

Joni had to crane to see him around the bulk of Gerald, who was slumped on the sofa between the girls. The girls were snuggled against him, and Gerald had his arms round both of them. Before Paul's eyes learned to adjust, he seemed more like a blockage of the light than a positive presence. Then he made out where the black hair was pushed behind Gerald's ears; the ears stood out as pale, delicate for a man of his build. He was looking up at Paul.

– Oh, it's you! said Elise, arriving out of the kitchen, wiping her hands on her striped butcher's apron. She was wearing her hair in some new way, pulled loosely into a tail at the nape of her neck; she must have allowed it to grow longer since he left. He hadn't thought he'd been away long enough for anyone's hair to grow.

– You could have phoned, she said. – To warn us you were coming.

– But here I am. Who helped you put in the trees?

– Gerald.

Gerald seemed to have gone back to watching the television. The presenters of these children's programmes were manic, they contorted their faces with dismay or were orgasmic with enthusiasm.

127

– I'll put coffee on, Elise said. – Would you both like coffee?

– Please, said Gerald, not looking up again.

Paul followed her into the kitchen. In the light he saw that his wife's hair was growing out, an inch from her parting: not grey exactly, but a faded neutral, weaker than the strong honey colour of the rest. He couldn't sit down yet, he was too restless, moving about the room, picking things up and putting them down – the pepper grinder, blackboard for shopping lists, plastic bottle of washing-up liquid, vanilla pod in a jar of sugar – as if they might have altered while he was away.

– For goodness sake, said Elise, lifting the hotplate cover, putting on the kettle to boil. – Sit down, Paul.

The kitchen smelled of baking, little cakes were cooling on a wire rack. He tried to catch her around the waist from behind. Something had changed in how she moved and held herself. He thought she was wearing an unfamiliar perfume.

– Not yet, she said, pushing him away. – Let me make this coffee. Why don't you put up the umbrella, and we'll have it in the yard? The weather's so lovely.

– I noticed how, with the trees gone, the yard's in full sun.

– We have to not be thinking of those trees all the time. It's pointless getting worked up about them.

– Tell me about the day when Willis came back.

– Not now.

She explained that she had paid for the new aspens

out of Evelyn's money; she had thought it was a good thing to spend it on, something that would endure and would be a reminder to them of Evelyn, for at least as long as they lived at Tre Rhiw. Her tone was as if she was justifying herself, rather belligerently.

So far the new trees were doing fine, they had all survived.

– Gerald dug and I gave the orders. We got them all planted in a day.

– Good team.

– It was good for him. Paul, he was in a bad way.

She dropped her voice, stirring the coffee in the pot, imagining Gerald must still be in the cubbyhole with the children. At that very moment Paul watched through the kitchen window as Gerald stepped out, blinking, into the yard. He stumbled, surprised by the bright light, unearthed from where he had been hibernating. Hands pushed in his pockets, head down, he started with his usual shambling walk down through the garden in the direction of the path along the river to the station. Paul didn't point out his departure to Elise.

– When he was first here he couldn't read a book, or even a newspaper. I had to phone his department at the university, to say he was sick. Some days he didn't get up, except to use the lavatory. He lay there with his eyes closed, or watched television. He started to smell, even the girls noticed it. In the end I had to run a bath for him, I made him get in it, then while he was in I put his clothes in the washing machine. I bought him a toothbrush and clean underclothes. Ruth said I ought to get a doctor. I was frightened of him doing some harm to himself.

– El, you should have told me how bad it was. I'd have come home.

– I did try to tell you, when you phoned from Stella's.

– Not the full story, not like this.

– I asked him if I should get a doctor, and he said it would help if he had his antidepressants, so I drove into Cardiff to pick them up from his flat. You never told me what that place was like. It's a horror.

At the thought of the flat, the full coffee pot seemed to quake for a moment in her hand.

– And did they help?

– Did what help?

– The antidepressants.

– Oh, yes, I think they did. Anyway, he's much better than he was. Tell him the coffee's ready, would you?

– He's gone. I watched him leave five minutes ago. I guess he didn't really want coffee.

– Who's gone? Gerald? Where?

– He walked down the garden, I presume in the direction of the station.

Elise ran out into the yard, then halfway down the garden, and stood shading her eyes with her hand, looking for Gerald; but he was out of sight. She rushed back into the kitchen, pulling off her apron, as if she was going to go after him. – My God, you have no idea! What were you thinking of, to let him go? You have no idea how serious things have been here.

– He seemed all right to me. He's a free man: if he wants to catch a train home, that's his business. You said he was better.

– But does he have money for the train? Does he have his keys?

– If he doesn't, then I suppose he'll have to come back.

Elise came at him with her fists upraised. – Everything's been so uncertain. And then you come blundering back into it, with no comprehension.

She hit blows on Paul's shoulders and chest that were only slightly painful, distracting because he had to hold his face away from them while he tried to catch hold of her wrists. Then she smacked him hard across his cheek, which hurt more, so that he pushed her and she fell against the draining board. Crockery smashed into the sink.

Becky and Joni, roused from their television slump, watched from the door.

– Where's Gerald? Becky asked, as if appealing for the one sane person in all this mess.

– He's gone, Elise said, sounding blank, bereft.

She picked up a tea towel to wipe tears from her face, then reached out for one of the rock cakes cooling on the wire rack. – I shouldn't eat these. The calories will only go straight to my thighs.

Paul poured the coffee and made the girls milkshakes. They all four sat subdued around the table, eating cake.

Gerald didn't come back.

In the afternoon Elise played Leonard Cohen in her

workroom, while she worked on dismantling and repairing a broken old lacquer box, inlaid with mother-of-pearl, that Ruth had bought in a country sale. Paul went through his post, which Elise had piled on the desk in his study, and his emails.

Something had happened between Gerald and Elise while he was away. Elise wouldn't talk about it.

– If you mean sex, she said, emphasising the word contemptuously, – then you're barking up the wrong tree. I know how your mind works. But he isn't like you.

Paul tried to be reasonable. – All right then, it wasn't sex. I'm glad it wasn't.

– How dare you? How dare you take yourself off and disappear to London without any warning or explanation, and then come back and think you can call me to account, that you've got any right to know about my private life?

– I haven't got any right. I'm not asking you because of right.

When he said he loved her, she only sobbed furiously, carrying the plastic tub into the yard to hang out the washing. Paul guessed she had thrown herself at Gerald, and he had rebuffed her. Or that she had been planning on throwing herself, just about the time when he arrived home, spoiling everything. He found himself imagining in detail her going in to Cardiff to fetch Gerald's antidepressants, parking the car beside the grassy city recreation ground, looking for the number on the tall gloomy old house, using Gerald's keys to let herself into his flat: a busy competent woman, on a charitable errand. She would have been shocked by the mess; she must have saved up examples to exclaim over to Ruth afterwards: mouldy pitta breads in the fridge, the crack in the wall, the stained toilet. Perhaps she even washed some dishes. In his mind's eye, she wasn't in a hurry. He saw her closing the door behind her when she first arrived, leaning for a long time with her back against it, taking in everything. Before she even started looking for the pills, he imagined she sat down in one of Gerald's broken old armchairs, holding her bag on her lap, closing her eyes, laying her cheek against the greasy ancient chintz, just breathing in the empty space, the stale hot air. In his pictures she had her hair fastened in the new way.

– Gerald's different, Elise said. – He lives more truthfully.

Paul was miserably perturbed and jealous, he tried to argue with her that truthful wasn't enough. It was one of the fixtures of their life together, that Elise found Gerald comical, and disapproved of his indifference to material things. But now she was suffering with a breathless excitement, she jumped whenever the phone rang, and sometimes Paul knew she had been crying. Paul slept in the cubbyhole. There was bedding already folded away on the sofa, which must have been Gerald's. In the middle of the night he woke up stifling, and had to go walking around outside in the grass, wearing only his boxers and a T-shirt, afraid of ticks on his bare legs.

The stars shone brilliantly, the goats detached themselves, pale forms, from the surrounding dark, they came trotting over to the fence, eager with curiosity to watch whatever he was up to. An owl hunted in the fields nearby. He missed London.

Elise asked him about Pia's flat, but as if she couldn't make herself properly interested in his life there.

– How's Pia then? What's this boyfriend of hers like?

He described Marek cautiously, making him out to be somewhat more sensible and businesslike than he really was, never mentioning the existence of Anna. He waited for Elise, who managed their bank accounts, to notice the missing money, but she didn't say anything, so either she didn't register it or didn't care. Perhaps she assumed he'd given it to Pia. When he spoke to Pia on the phone she said everything was fine. The swelling in her ankles had gone down, they were pleased with her at the hospital. She had been to visit Annelies, it hadn't gone too badly.

Paul took over watering the new trees. The drought was supposed to end soon, according to the weather forecast. James Willis delivered the logs cut from the old trees, and Paul paid for them, stacking them in the outhouse, even though when he looked it up he found that poplar wood wasn't supposed to burn well. One evening they all went out with Ruth to watch for otters: apparently there was a family of them living further up the river. Ruth's husband had seen them playing in the moonlight. Elise shivered in her sleeveless dress, because they'd left home in the late sunshine and she'd forgotten to bring a cardigan. Ruth warned the girls that the otters were shy, they probably wouldn't put in an appearance. She showed them a dusty depression on the bank that might be where the otters slept by day, and their spraints nearby, blackish messes of fish scales and fragments of bone, probably eel bones. They watched from behind a screen of hazel stems on the opposite bank; the moon rose out of sight, its glow seeping into the sky from behind the hill, then sailed overhead.

Paul was touched by the girls' obedience and patience; he felt the discipline in their little bodies huddled against him. Elise wrapped one of the blankets she'd brought to sit on around her shoulders – they waited for more than an hour, but didn't see anything. Becky pleaded for them to stay longer. She was sure she had spotted something in the water, 'a little ripple, like a nose poking up', but Elise complained she was going numb with cold. She tried to keep her voice perky and joking, but Paul could hear the effort in it. On the way back Becky sulked; Joni whined and was tired, and Paul carried her. It was the first time she'd let him pick her up since he'd been home. She laid her head on his shoulder, her fine baby hair tickled his cheek. That morning at breakfast she hadn't allowed him to cut off the top of her egg; pouting, she had said she wanted Gerald, 'Instead of *you.*'

Paul began writing something new: not a memoir exactly, but a recollection of his earliest interest in nature.

He tried not to think too hard about it, but felt hopeful that it might come to something. At junior school he had won as a school prize a book on exploring the countryside, which had set out all the different animal footprints diagrammatically, as neatly labelled black ink blots: badger, fox, roe deer, red deer, and so on. He had dedicated himself to learning them, along with the animal droppings, the leaf shapes and the different nuts and berries, as if nature was a kind of code, like learning Latin; if he only worked hard enough at breaking the code, he believed he could break through to the mythic world of beauty he intuited behind it. He borrowed more nature books from the central library in Birmingham, catching the bus into town to change them on Saturday mornings. Afterwards he used to meet his father, who knocked off on Saturdays at midday, outside the corrugated-metal gates of the screw factory where he worked. If Paul got there early, then he started in on the pages of the first book, leaning with his back against the gates in the cobbled street whose walls were the windowless back ends of factories. It hadn't occurred to him to look for nature anywhere in the world around him. The books were safe in their nylon string bag between his feet. In those days, even at weekends, he would have been wearing ankle socks and his school lace-ups, his skinny knees would have been bare below his shorts.

– Go and make sure he's all right, Elise said, meaning Gerald.

It was first thing in the morning, she was in the bathroom still in her nightdress, cleaning her teeth, spitting into the sink, watching Paul in the mirror.

– You go.

He had come upstairs from his sofa in the cubbyhole, needing to pee; he wasn't sure whether, the way things were between them, he should go ahead while she was in the room.

Her eyes fixed him. Wordless, she scrubbed vigorously behind her back molars.

– He'll be fine. We'd have heard if he wasn't.

She spat again. – All right then. I'll go, she said.

– Of course he might not be there. In the summer he spends a lot of time at his parents'.

She ran the tap in a fierce spurt.

Later that morning he heard her drive off in the car. He walked around the place, having it all to himself for the first time since he'd been back. He tried the drawers in the lacquered box Elise was fixing, used the hose to water the trees, and then the vegetables and the borders and tubs, though it was the wrong time of day for this. Inside, invading the suspended stillness of the house, he looked for more to do, but Elise had washed the breakfast dishes, so he tidied up vaguely, straightened the duvets on the girls' beds. It was already hot in the rooms upstairs, where the sun beat through the roof. His study was cool. He sat reading through a book on ecology and elegy that he'd been sent for reviewing. After a couple of hours he heard the car come back. Elise walked quickly through the house to her workroom, heels scraping on the flagstones in the yard. She must have put on her dressy shoes to go out. He followed her.

– How was Gerald?

She was wearing eye-shadow and lipstick, and a new silky shirt, printed with lilac-coloured flowers, which he hadn't seen before. It was more or less an hour's drive into Cardiff: she couldn't have spent any time with Gerald, even if she saw him.

Squinting at the sewing machine, trying to thread the needle without her glasses, sucking the thread and coaxing it to a point, she claimed she didn't know what he was talking about, that she'd been out with Ruth to look at a dresser for sale on one of the farms. He didn't believe her. Perhaps she'd gone looking for Gerald and he'd been out. Or perhaps she'd found him, and he'd closed himself against her.

– OK, I just thought you said you were worried about him.

– He's your friend, Paul. You're the one who should be worrying.

They ate leftovers for lunch together, under the umbrella in the yard; Elise said they ought to invite people round for a barbecue the next day, before the weather broke.

– If you like.

He heard her telephoning round.

– I left a message on Gerald's phone, she said. – But why don't you try him? Try and persuade him to come. It would be good for him.

Paul tried dutifully. Gerald's phone was switched off; he left another message.

Elise spent the next day preparing food: marinated chicken and fish and vegetables for the barbecue, little deep-fried Middle Eastern patties, a cheesecake topped with nut brittle, home-made prune ice-cream. Paul thought she was doing too much for an impromptu occasion, but she turned on him angrily when he tried to say so, her face hot from the frying. She sent him to Abergavenny in the morning with a shopping list, mainly for drinks; he drove all the way into Cardiff instead, and called in on Gerald, half-expecting he wouldn't answer the door because it was still too early. If Gerald was surprised to see him – possibly Paul stood just where his wife had stood the day before and not been invited in – then he only hesitated for one moment, puzzling, swaying slightly on his feet (small, like his ears), before he turned without a word, as was usual, and preceded Paul through the dank old air of the three flights of stairs to his lair under the roof.

Inside the flat, black plastic bags of waste paper and kitchen rubbish lay open on the floor, the hose of a vacuum cleaner plugged in at the wall snaked on the carpet; the windows were thrown up high and the plum-dark leaves of the copper beech outside were bruised and brooding in the wind that was supposed to herald different weather. Neither of them commented on the cleaning in progress; Paul felt uncomfortably as if he'd stumbled into his friend's privacy. Gerald made tea, meticulous in his measuring and stirring. He said he was trying to give up smoking, and was baking his dope instead into chocolate brownies made from a packet mix; bringing some in a cake tin from the kitchen, he offered them to Paul, who wasn't tempted. The brownies looked dry. Gerald munched through two with an air of despatching a necessary routine. He asked after the little girls, and then showed Paul a book he was reading, about the variations among different cultures in the language used to categorise emotion.

– The Ilongot in the Philippines have a word to describe a reaction to the violation of a community norm.

– Don't we have words for that in English?

– Can you think of any?

Paul could only think of words that weren't emotions, like 'respectable' and 'scapegoat'.

– And *toska*, in Russian, Gerald said, – means 'how one feels when one wants some things to happen and knows they cannot happen'.

– Very Russian.

– That's the point.

Paul invited him to the party that evening, suggesting they could drive back together now; Gerald said he was busy in the afternoon. – I'll let you know. I might come over later.

– Elise worries about you. She thinks you're in a bad way.

– I was in a bad way. I'm feeling better. Elise persuaded me to wash, which was a place to start, for which I'm grateful. And she drove over here when I was at your place, to get my pills for me.

Paul pretended he hadn't known this. – She came in here?

– She dropped something actually. Will you take it for her?

Gerald hunted through the heaps on his desk until he found a printed silk scarf Paul recognised. It smelled of Elise.

– Did the pills work?

– They did what they do. Under the nuanced cultural variation, the blunt chemical truncheons. It's not a fine science.

Elise complained that he'd been gone for hours; Paul didn't explain where he'd been. It was his job to get the fire going in the big barbecue that Elise had built out of stones from one of the ruined outhouses, the grill made by the local blacksmith. Becky and Joni arrived home with the first contingent of guests, children and parents from the school. The gang of children was soon running wild, looping around the house and garden, a few tiny ones staggering after them, down to the river where Becky womanfully scooped up the babies to safety and Joni swung from the branch of a tree to show it was hers, kicking out her legs over the water. Then they ran back again. Their parents shouted warnings and prohibitions.

Elise had made a summer punch, with mint and borage and strawberries floating in it, served in a glass jug frosted from the freezer. She had showered and washed her hair, and looked composed and demure in the new flowered shirt. He heard her tell the otter story as if it was funny, that he and the girls had wanted to stay on, staring at nothing in the dark, while she was frozen stiff. At first he could tell she was careful not to drink too much, because she had to manage heating the patties up in the oven and getting them onto serving plates, while keeping watch over the barbecue; once everyone had had something to eat, she allowed herself to be more reckless. One or two of the smallest children had fallen asleep by this time and been put into the beds upstairs; the rest were playing hide-and-seek all round the house and garden and in the fields. Light was withdrawing behind mauve bars of cloud on the horizon; a fume of shadow spread under the old apple trees in the meadow, the children's skulking or speeding forms indistinct in it, their noises amplified: a thud of footsteps if they were going for home, or the sudden yelp and relinquishment of defeat. The older children were organising this game, one of Ruth's boys and a girl. Joni didn't grasp the rules, or refused to play by them; she kept on running and squealing even after she'd been touched.

– I needed this, Elise said, swallowing mouthfuls of the punch thirstily, relaxing, dropping against the back of her cane chair. – I've been looking forward to this drink all day. Isn't this perfect? What a perfect evening!

Perfect food too, everyone agreed.

Paul was talking to Carwen, a friend who was the

education officer for the nearby conservation area, about what he'd been reading that afternoon, in the book on elegy, about the asymmetry in complex systems – how painstakingly long it took to construct them, and how almost instantaneously they could be destroyed: as true of social and cultural systems as it was of living organisms.

– It's tragedy, built in to the very structure of things.

– You could choose to look at it like that, Carwen said. – But if I'm allowed to be a brutal scientist, destruction is also cleansing, it liberates the way for new systems.

– Isn't that how tyrants have justified their wars? asked Ruth.

– We can't afford to see it in that time scale, Paul said.

– Don't you hate that word tragedy? said someone else. – Everything's a fucking tragedy nowadays. They use 'tragedy' when they just mean an accident, or anything sad.

– Don't spoil things, Paul, Elise said. – Don't be all doom and gloom.

But in fact he was enjoying himself. He was buoyed up by his hopes for his new book. And he felt affectionate towards these people, even some of them he didn't know very well, even Ruth. Ruth looked pretty, she was wearing some kind of long patterned smock over jeans and it made her seem less buttoned-up, more girlish. She had been nice to him since their vigil waiting for the otters – as if she withdrew somewhat from her solidarity with Elise, and felt sorry for him.

He took a call on his mobile, hurrying farther down

the garden, where the signal was better. Elise tensed in her seat when she heard it ring, and he knew she was distracted from her own conversation, trying to work out who it was: afterwards he beckoned her to come over, so they could talk. Unsteady on her high heels when she stood up, she slipped out of the shoes and came in her bare feet across the grass. Bats were sketching their flight across the grey air. In the dusk her face was blurred, he could only clearly see her pale clothes, the dark of her cleavage where the top button of her shirt was undone.

– Who was it? Was it Gerald? Is he coming?

Her speech wasn't slurred, but aggressive; some layer of concealment had been stripped from between them. Where their feet bruised it, the grass sent up its yearning green smell, tugging at his emotions. He seemed to guess how Elise felt, eaten up as if something essential was passing and she was prevented from reaching it, so that all she had to give, all her bloom, was going to waste.

– It's Pia, he explained. – I have to go. Something's up, I don't know what, I don't know exactly where she is, but she's left the flat, she needs me to drive and pick her up.

– Oh, shit, Paul. Shit! You can't drive anyway. You're drunk.

– I'm not. I've only had a couple of glasses.

– Why can't she go to Annelies?

– She's already somewhere on her way here. She was hitching, she's at a service station but she doesn't know which one, she's going to phone me back.

– Can't she get a bus or something?

– She's pregnant, El. And I don't even know what's happened, to make her leave. I'm afraid for her.

– All right. OK.

– I'll come and make my excuses to everyone.

XI

Before he started the car, he checked his phone for messages from Pia. He saw that he had missed a text from Gerald, saying he was on his way to the party. He didn't see any need to pass this on. Gerald would be there in person soon enough.

Paul was sure he was all right to drive, although he had probably had more than the couple of glasses he'd owned up to. He liked night-driving. The empty roads weren't banal as they were in the day – drawing the cover of darkness around them, they were transformed as if he was speeding through a different landscape, charged with mystique. He was full of apprehension for Pia. He had no idea what the matter was. She had refused to go into detail over the phone, she had been tearful, terse, desperate. Had she found out something about Marek, which she couldn't live with? Perhaps he had been arrested, or they were going to deport him; perhaps it was something private, worse, some worm of deviancy or cruelty that he, Paul, had lived alongside and not detected. Perhaps Marek had only waited until Paul was out of the way to reveal himself. When he tried to imagine the man he had liked, he came up against the locked door of Marek's unknown life. Already the time in that London flat was receding as if it had never belonged to him. When he thought about it from his perspective at Tre Rhiw, he was shocked at the casual drug-taking, the unfocused future, the lack of any genuine preparations for the baby's arrival.

These anxieties circled round and round in his mind, but he also experienced a certain exhilaration: here he was, flying through the night towards his daughter when she needed him. This rescue seemed a simplifying and cleansing thing; a pure demand that he could meet and live up to. On the motorway he found himself, even at this late hour, backed up behind slowed traffic at some point after he'd crossed the bridge into England, funnelled into one lane. At least the traffic never stopped moving, and it didn't take him too long to reach and pass the cause of the delay: there had been an accident, long enough ago for an ambulance to have arrived and for the police to be in charge. Two small cars were slewed across the road, facing the wrong direction altogether; the barrier along the central reservation was buckled, debris and broken glass strewn everywhere. Superstitiously, and out of respect, Paul didn't look to see if anyone was badly hurt; he was aware that among the fluorescent jackets of the rescue services a few dazed young people stood around, woken up out of their lives into this disaster. He accelerated into the emptiness of the motorway ahead. When his phone buzzed, he pulled over onto the hard shoulder, more scrupulous after seeing the accident than he might have been. Pia texted that she was at Strensham services, and Paul answered that he'd be with her in less than an hour.

At that time of night the service area was ghostly: the staff outnumbered the customers, they looked around in the foyer from where they were grouped together, talking, when he walked in. One man was pushing a bucket on a wheeled trolley, washing the floor. Paul saw Pia in the café at once, bundled up in a windcheater with her back to him, her hair in two bunches, rucksack propped against the table beside her. The sight of her alone there, so intensely familiar, pierced him, and he hurried forward to claim her. When she turned around he saw that she had put the stud back in her lip. She was very pale. She hadn't made up her face, and her sulky expression reminded him of her childhood.

– God, I couldn't have waited here another moment, she said. – They're all staring at me.

– I expect they're only concerned about you. A pregnant young woman waiting here alone, late at night. You're a bit of a mystery. And what were you thinking of, hitch-hiking? You should have called me, right away.

– I had a lift with a guy in a lorry, but he was turning off here. It's better if you're pregnant, they don't try anything.

– I didn't realise you'd hitch-hiked before.

She shrugged. – Well, I never told Mum when I did it, obviously.

When he bent down to put his arms round her, she leaned her head submissively against his jacket.

– What's happened with Marek? Why have you left?

– Nothing happened.

– But you're all right? He hasn't hurt you?

She pushed her empty cup angrily across the table, and he didn't ask anything more about it for the moment.

– Do you want another coffee, or anything to eat, before we set out?

Pia only wanted to get going. In the car she rifled through the CDs in the glove box and announced he hadn't got anything decent to play; she put on the radio, which he had tuned to classical music, then turned it off again. Restless and uncomfortable with the seat belt round her, she arched her back and shifted in the seat; he remembered Elise doing this when she was pregnant. He felt triumphant, driving home with Pia sitting beside him – as if it completed whatever mission he had begun weeks and months ago, when he first went to look for her. He was bringing his daughter home, he would look after her.

– Don't get the wrong idea, Pia said, shifting again, as if the accusation erupted out of her physical irritation. – Nothing happened.

– Something must have happened.

– I changed my mind. That's all.

– Something must have happened to make you change your mind.

She turned her face away from him to stare out of the window. This stretch of motorway was lit, the tall stems of the lamps flicking past and the hanging veils of light giving the space an empty grandeur, cathedral-like. Then they came out on the bluff above the flat estuary valley, and saw ahead the two lit bridges coiling over the water into Wales. Paul was careful not to speak, in case he deflected whatever was coming. If she had found out something shameful, she wouldn't want him to have guessed at it.

– It was me, she said. – It was my fault.

As if he had asserted something different, she insisted that Marek was a good man, he and Anna were kind, generous people. And Marek really loved her. She was sure that he wanted to have a family with her, he meant it.

– I don't know why I did what I did.

– What did you do?

It was so stupid, Pia said. She had pretended that the baby was Marek's.

That wasn't really as bad as it sounded. When they first got together she hadn't had any idea she was pregnant. She had liked Marek, he used to come into the café to see Anna; she liked his way of making a fuss of her, it seemed romantic. He was different from the English boys she was at university with, grown-up compared to them. And he was the first one to realise why she was being sick; he asked her about her periods and everything. As soon as she understood, she knew Marek wasn't the father, because she'd been feeling these things for a few weeks before anything had happened with him. But he had taken it for granted that the baby was his, naturally enough. And she hadn't put him right. At first she'd thought if she was going to get rid of it anyway, there wasn't any point in putting him right. But then she hadn't got rid of it. The dates they'd given her at the hospital had confirmed what she already knew; she had lied to Marek and Anna about these.

A momentary spatter of rain made Paul switch the windscreen wipers on.

– So, who is the father?

– Who d'you think? James, of course.

– Oh. Paul considered this. – Does James know that he is?

She shook her head. No.

He drove without saying anything for a while. They passed the site of the accident he had seen on his way over: there was still single-file traffic past it, but the emergency services had all gone and men were manoeuvring the smashed cars onto a breakdown truck.

– You're mad at me, Pia said. – I knew you'd be mad at me.

– I'm not mad at you.

But he did feel obscurely hurt, and disappointed. He had been ready to feel outraged by Marek and Anna, and now instead he felt uncomfortable and guilty, as if he was implicated in Pia's deception of them. She had seemed steady – a steady, fair English girl – and she had not been. He had imagined her given over in good faith

151

to her adventure; now he couldn't help picturing their surprise, or disgust, or distress, when they read the note she said she'd left behind. Pia said they wouldn't know how to find her – they didn't have her mother's address, they only knew Paul lived somewhere in Wales. She would change her mobile. She had never told them anything about James. And anyway, they wouldn't want to find her.

Her voice was small and bleak.

– I want to feel free. I just want to be my own person again.

On the approach road to the village, she asked him to drive her to Blackbrook and drop her off there. It had not occurred to Paul that she wouldn't be coming with him to Tre Rhiw, at least for this one night. At the idea of arriving home without her he lost his temper, stopping the car, pulling it into the grass verge so that shoots of bramble grazed along the window on his side.

– You're being unreasonable, he said. – It's two o'clock in the morning. We can't wake them up at this time. There's nothing that can't wait until tomorrow.

– We can ring the bell on the extension. Only James will hear. I've tried his phone but he's got it turned off.

– I think you ought to listen to me, after I've driven you this far.

Pia undid her seat belt and opened the car door, clambering out heavily. A blast of night air disrupted the warmth inside the car; the drift of fine rain passing over, damping the baked earth, had roused a rank vegetable stink. Paul knew where they were: beyond the dense invisible hedgerow of hazel and blackthorn, the green shoots were standing a foot high in Willis's fields.

– I know my way from here, Pia said. – It's easy.

– Don't be ridiculous. It's pitch dark.

– I have to talk to James.

– Talk to him in the morning.

She set out walking ahead of the car along the road, visible in his headlights, encumbered, obstinate, her back set in resistance to him, then stumbling over something, a pothole or a stone. Cruising after her, he wound his window down.

– What about your rucksack?

– I'll get James to come for it tomorrow.

– OK, I give in. Pia, get in the car. I'll take you.

She was breathing heavily when she climbed back in. He thought she was crying; she wound the window down on her side, and pressed her face out into the night. Where the drive forked at Blackbrook, Paul took the lower track, leading towards the converted outbuildings where James had his room. As he drew up outside, a security light clicked on and a dog barked up above them, at the main house. Paul thought how he hated Willis's conversion, featureless and glaring with its new ceramic roof tiles and plastic windows, the old barn's soul exposed and dissipated.

– This is a really bad idea, he said.

– Don't worry.

– You know Willis is a nutcase. And he hates me.

– Everything isn't always about you, Dad.

They got out together and Pia pressed the doorbell. They waited while she pressed it twice more, hearing it ring inside. Crouching at the level of the letter box, knees apart, she called through in a voice that she tried to make subdued and penetrating at once.

– James! James!

Someone inside thudded down an uncarpeted wooden staircase. Pia only just scrambled up in time before the door swung inwards; Paul saw how, expecting James, she sagged forward in relief. But it was Mrs Willis instead who stood behind the door: stout, stubby, grey-black hair cut short so that it stood up on her head like a brush. She didn't look her best, roused from sleep presumably, glaring and defensive, in an incongruously feminine pink nightdress.

– What's up?

– I'm really sorry, Susan, Pia said. – I didn't think you'd be sleeping over here. I didn't want to wake you. I wanted James.

– Did you now!

The woman's intelligence came awake behind her eyes and darted between Paul and Pia's face blotched with tears, her swollen shape. Behind Susan Willis the hallway and staircase had the neutrality of a holiday let, with no comforting accretion of belongings or mess.

Paul was helpless to stop himself sounding English and effete. – I tried to persuade Pia that it was an unreasonable hour. But she was adamant.

Adamant wasn't a word he even used.

154

– Is he here? Pia persisted, desperate.

At that moment James appeared on the stairs in boxers and saggy T-shirt, bare legs fuzzy with blond hair, face bloated and blinking from sleep, missing a couple of steps in his fuddled state and only just saving himself from falling headlong by grabbing the handrail. Susan Willis was still staring at Pia, calculating, bemused – but not preparing to be outraged or devastated, Paul thought. He'd only seen her in passing before; he'd spoken to her once or twice when he was sent to buy ice-cream and she was serving in their shop. He hadn't recognised then this reserve of irony in her. Perhaps she was sleeping in the annexe to be apart from her husband.

– She says she wants to talk to James, Paul said. – But we could come back in the morning, if you'd rather she didn't stay.

– She can stay if she likes, said Susan warily. – If it's what James wants.

– What? James said. – What's she doing here?

– She wants to talk to you. It looks like you might have something to talk about.

– It's nothing to do with me, said James.

– No, it is, Pia said.

– This is what she told me, Paul said, – in the car on the way down here.

– I pretended it wasn't to do with you. I almost came to tell you the truth once. I bought the ticket at Paddington and then I didn't get on the train. I got on and got off again, at the last minute.

– I don't believe you, James said.

He was rubbing his fists in his eyes, shocked out of his deep adolescent sleep, doubting and resistant. Pia looked shocked too, as if the revelation wasn't going the way she had pictured it in advance.

– It's a girl, she said shyly. – Apparently it's a girl.

When Paul was born, his mother had been expecting a girl, they had had a girl's name ready. There was some old wives' tale: you dangled a ring on a thread over the unborn child, watching to see if it spun clockwise or anticlockwise. So much for old wives' tales. Evelyn hadn't been disappointed, she'd been relieved. She'd said to him once when he was still living at home that she hadn't wanted a daughter, to be born into drudgery. A son could get away into a different life. Perhaps she had felt otherwise about it later, when Paul in his different life had left her behind – didn't visit often enough, didn't know how to turn over on the phone with her the interminable, essential detail of her everyday. A daughter might have been a better bet.

Paul sat for a while in his car after Pia had been swallowed up inside the Willis's house. Evelyn, when she was alive, would have hated the idea of Pia pregnant and unmarried; she wouldn't have understood why they were all taking it so calmly, as if it wasn't momentous. The world turned and the old forms, which had seemed substantial as life itself, were left behind and forgotten. There wasn't any place he could go now to remember his mother. Perhaps her name was written in a book in the crematorium – or did they only do that in churches?

156

– name after name in neat black calligraphy, with an embroidered bookmark on the opened page, furred with dead moths and dust. He preferred to think about her in the dark. She had been visiting him again, since he came home – but with less ferocity than at first. In her dead self, in his dreams, she could even seem forgiving, the knots of her anxious fearfulness loosened. Paul was so tired, he almost fell asleep there in the car. He didn't want to drive the last quarter of a mile.

Searching everywhere inside the house, he wasn't sure what to expect. Was Gerald here somewhere, with Elise? Party mess was piled up in the kitchen, dirty plates, sleazy regiments of bottles, leftover food not put away in the fridge. Upstairs, the spare mattresses were dragged out onto the girls' bedroom floor, extra children were curled heaps under duvets or in sleeping bags. All of them were asleep amid signs of wild play cut short, the toy box upended, dressing-up clothes trampled on the floor where they'd been thrown off. He touched the door to the bedroom across the landing, which stood open as always: swinging back soundlessly, it revealed only the landing light trapped in the mirror, the expanse of white counterpane on their bed undisturbed, Elise's make-up bag on the dressing table disgorging pencils, tweezers, pots of colour. The open window rattled on its catch; the flurry of rain had stirred up smells of earth and growth in the garden. Moths batted inside the luminous paper globe on the landing behind him.

Elise was extravagantly absent.

Were all these children safe, alone in the house without her?

From the window he thought he saw pale shapes moving in the meadow. He went downstairs again, deliberately clattering, running the tap noisily in the kitchen, calling out of the back door for her. Coming from the lit indoors, when he stepped out into the yard and then across into the garden it felt as if he pressed against a skin of darkness and then broke through it, having to step cautiously and lift his knees, wading in a thicker medium, not sure where he was putting his feet down.

– El? Where are you?

She seemed to break through something, too, when she was suddenly ahead of him, the night thinning out around her form. She must have pulled a jumper over her shirt when it turned chilly, but he knew from her height in relation to his shoulder that she was still barefoot. He intuited across the space between them her intensely familiar sceptical scrutiny, invisible in the night.

– Paul? Is it you? What have you done with Pia?

– I've left her at Blackbrook. She wanted to be with James.

– That's good, because there are children on all the mattresses. What was it all about? Is she all right?

Paul told her more or less what had happened, Pia's deception and escape, waking Susan Willis in the middle of the night. – I can't believe we're mixed up with the appalling Willises now. Actually genetically mixed up with them. It's a nightmare.

Elise said she'd thought there was something funny

with Pia's dates. She had looked too big in the pictures she sent Becky.

– Was it a good party, after I'd gone?

– It was a drunken party. We drank too much.

– Fun drunk or hazardous drunk?

– Anyway I'm sober now. I've been sober for hours. I went out to walk under the apple trees by myself. It's amazing what you can see and hear in the dark. Your eyes get used to it. It was lovely there.

– Did Gerald turn up?

She answered airily, lightly. – He did turn up. But you know what he's like. He doesn't say anything in company. He just sits there – exasperating really. You're wondering all the time whether he's judging everything, or just oblivious to it.

– He doesn't like parties much.

– Someone brought the speakers outside and we danced, but Gerald wouldn't join in. Then I looked round and he'd gone. I suppose he caught the last train. But I'd told him he could stay. I mean, this was almost his home for weeks, when he was ill. We were very close, when he was here and I was looking after him. One night I had to hold onto him for hours, Paul, he had such an attack of horrors. Nothing happened, you understand, except that I held him.

Paul took this in.

– Never mind, he said. – You know what he's like. That's what he does, he comes and goes. He lives in his own world.

Garden flares stuck in the plant pots had burned out

159

hours ago, the yard was dark. They peered in through the window at the lit-up kitchen: the piles of dirty washing up, the greasy leftovers, the chairs displaced, bunches of dried herbs and corn dollies and postcards pinned to the beams and thick with dust, school notices bristling on the fridge door.

– Whoever lives in this house, Elise said, – I'm glad it's not us. It's a filthy mess.

– Me too. I'm glad about it.

– I'd hate to have to go in there and get started on that washing up.

Her voice was careless; massaging her shoulders, though, Paul felt her disappointment and humiliation, resistant as a knotted rope. Her jumper slithered under his working fingers, against the silky shirt. Through his hand, he seemed to be in touch with the surge of her inner life, which mostly wasn't disclosed to him: deeper and more chaotic than it ever showed itself in the words they exchanged. He felt as if he hardly knew her, this wife and mother of his children. When they first met he had been drawn to Elise because she seemed complete and fearless, with all the bright presumption of the class she came from. Now, it was as though she was stepping out of that identity – leaving it behind like a husk – into something new and more precarious. He was stricken and desiring, imagining her walking about alone, before he came home, under the trees in the meadow where the children had played in the twilight. What had she been thinking, all that time?

– Let's not go inside just yet, he said. – Let's walk.

– It's some crazy hour of the night, you know. We'll be shattered tomorrow. Those kids'll be up at the crack of dawn.

– I know. But it's nice out here.

At first they were both blind again, when they turned to face into the garden, because they'd looked too long into the kitchen light. Paul promised to get up first with the children in the morning.

– All right then, Elise said. – I don't mind, if you promise.

Only Children

I

Cora on the eve of her wedding day, twelve years ago.

Before dawn she had woken in her parents' house, her childhood bed, to the sound of rain pattering and rushing, intimate around her, on the roof, in the gutters. Net curtains, blowing out into the rain through the open window, were soaked at the hem. She got out of bed and knelt on the window seat, where some of her old dolls and teddy bears were still arranged, out of habit – she wasn't infantile, but her childhood really wasn't far behind. The house was in a terrace over-looking a narrow strip of park: she leaned out of the window, breathing in freshness from the saturated earth, the drenched, labouring trees. She didn't care about the rain spoiling things, she didn't care anything about the outer shell of the wedding, which so devoured her mother: flowers and guest list and caterers. Cora hadn't been brought up as religious, and she'd never belonged to any church, but her religious instincts were strong;

she was concentrated in the mystery of what she was undertaking. Also, she imagined herself in a continuum with the serious, passionate women whose weddings she'd read about in novels: Kitty in *Anna Karenina*, Anna Brangwen in *The Rainbow*. She was twenty-three. The rain seemed blessed to her, sitting alone in her washed-pale pyjamas at the window, thoughts reaching out into the night. She had a vision of herself as a figure outside her own self-knowledge, emblematic, almost sacrificial.

It had cleared up anyway later in the morning, the sun had blazed on the grass in the park pearled with little drops as she walked on her father's arm, white dress dragging in the dirt of the Cardiff city pavement, from the front door of their house to the little church on the corner. They normally only came to this church when it was used for concerts; Cora had performed on the clarinet in here, on occasions organised by her music teacher. Her mother had been agonised, wanting to pick up the dress out of the wet dirt, afraid to countermand her headstrong daughter. Cora had loved the weight of the skirts kicking against her limbs; she had loved the passers-by, dog-walkers in the park, stopping to watch; she had laughed at her mother.

She thought of these scenes now with derision. They made her sick.

Now she couldn't even live with Robert. She was living in her parents' house again, sleeping in her old room, although she had changed everything.

* * *

Robert waited for her to come home from her work at the library. He didn't have a key to this house, so he waited in the park. The weather was hot for spring; taking off his pullover, he knotted it round his waist, feeling he must be even more conspicuous than usual (he was six foot four, fifteen years older than Cora, big and loosely put together, clumsy), among the few dog-walkers and mothers with pushchairs and small children. He hadn't brought a bag, only a slim briefcase, supposing he would be going back again by train to London later. He hadn't spoken to Cora for weeks. She wouldn't answer his calls, and he only knew about the job at the library because his sister had told him.

Cora wasn't expecting him. The kind of work Robert did – he was fairly senior in the Home Office – made him think calmly about the interview he needed to have with her, certain things it was time to ask her straight, arrangements they ought to put on an established footing. He was used to grasping bleak necessity firmly. He was only agitated, anticipating the first moments that she saw him, in case she hated it that he was lying in wait for her. What would he see in her face, before she put up the guard he had got used to: disgust? An instinct for flight? Cora was tall – not as tall as he was, but as a couple they had occupied an exaggerated space – with long legs and a narrow high waist, shapely hips. He remembered that she didn't run badly, as a girl apparently she had even got to a certain level in county championships as a sprinter – but her trainers had said her technique was too eccentric to go farther, with her big feet flying out at an angle, hands raised at the wrists. She hadn't minded, she had been bored already with the hours of training; she had preferred poetry.

In the end Robert need not have worried: he was expecting her from the wrong direction. Cora must have had minutes to observe him and adjust her expression behind her sunglasses before she decided to come up behind him and touch him on the arm.

– Hello. What are you doing here?

That flat brightness was in place, deflecting him as if it was a light in his eyes. In his confusion he hardly recognised her; she was wearing clothes he didn't seem to remember, a skirt and a short-sleeved white linen blouse. She looked good, but surprisingly much older than he ever imagined her. He saw how completely she filled out this latest performance, as if she had lived like this for ever – single, resourceful, bravely dedicated to her modest job, perhaps with sources of secret suffering. Her hand looked naked without its wedding and engagement rings. She still wore her hair long: thick, clean light-brown hair, chopped off crisply below her shoulders. His arm ached in hyper-awareness where she had touched him.

– Sorry. I hate springing myself on you like this, without warning. But as you didn't want to talk on the phone, it seemed the only . . .

– All right. Never mind. D'you want to come in? It's lucky I noticed you standing over here. How long would you have waited if I hadn't seen you? I'm hot, I need to get a cold drink.

On the doorstep, fishing in her straw basket for the key, for a moment she couldn't find it. She had lost innumerable keys over their years together; she'd be humiliated if she'd lost this one now. He was as relieved as she was when she dug it out from among the rest of the female apparatus in there: purse, apple, sunscreen, mobile, make-up bag, book, tissues.

The house inside was blessedly cool, shadowy because before she left at midday (her job at the library was only part-time) Cora had pulled down the blinds at the windows. Without asking, she made Robert a gin and tonic – what he always drank. She poured herself tonic, put ice and lemon in it, then, after hesitating, splashed gin in it too. They stood in the kitchen.

– So . . .

– I haven't come to pester you, he said. – It's just a few practical arrangements, about the flat and so on. Of course, half of it's yours.

– I don't want half the flat.

– All that's settled with the lawyers. But I ought to have your name taken off the mortgage, in case anything happened to me and you were liable. And we ought to take your name off the bank account too, I suppose. If you think that's best.

He suffered, seeing her name beside his on the cheque book and bank statements.

– I've brought instructions you need to sign.

On the kitchen table, he began unzipping the briefcase.

– I don't want anything.

She turned and went pacing with her long stride around the ground floor of the house, carrying her drink. He followed her. Self-conscious about her height, she always wore flat shoes; today they were brown brogues, decorated on the toe with a flower cut out of the same-coloured leather.

– I can't talk about this now, Robert.

– You've done things up very nicely here.

– Oh God!

It was an undistinguished late-Victorian terrace at the thin end of a long park, smaller inside than it looked from the front; her parents had bought it shortly after they were married, in the late Sixties. Robert had trouble making out his in-laws' old house now, underneath what Cora had done to it since she inherited: knocking the two reception rooms into one, extending the kitchen into a new conservatory, sanding the floors, painting everything white, getting rid of most of the old furniture. She had had the building work done while she was still living with him in London; they had talked at first as if she would sell the house when it was finished. He spotted some of her father's framed geological maps still on the walls, kept presumably for their aesthetic appeal. This question troubled him: whether it was still the same place as it had been when Alan and Rhian lived here, or whether a house was a succession of places, blooming one after another inside the same frame of stones and brick and timber.

Cora was experiencing Robert's presence in here as a shock to her whole system, her breathing felt smothered and irregular, her voice seemed to her shriller and more childish, sounding inside her head. When he wasn't present, her idea of him dwindled to something small and convenient as a toy; she forgot how he crowded her perceptions. Her rooms – which were her new life – seemed smaller with Robert in them; and he wasn't properly interested in the nuances of her taste, the lovely mugs she'd chosen for instance, one by one, with such delight in each, for the kitchen. Habitually Robert ducked when he came through doors, even if he didn't need to, and he smelled, not a bad smell – sweat and wool and soap and something else, oaky with a high note of lemon – but intrusively masculine and over-powering. He had on an awful shirt: she knew he would have bought it in a cellophane packet, on his way home from work, from one of those shops for tourists. His hair – like very dark old tobacco, threaded with grey – hung in lank locks over his collar; he needed a haircut. She couldn't look properly into his complicated ravaged face, strong beard-growth speckled over shaven jowly folds, because its familiarity filled her with shame. It was unbearable to imagine now her earliest intimacies and confessions with Robert.

Without asking, he put on the news on the television in her bare white sitting room, stood watching it while swallowing his gin, swishing the ice cubes round in his glass, grunting ironically at something political, which of course he would know all about from the inside. Was she supposed to stand around waiting in her own house, while he caught up on the latest scandal? She snapped up the blinds at the front windows, and bold squares of light sprung onto the bare boards. Nothing could shake his hierarchy of importance, where work was a fixed outer form, inside which personal things must find their place. Once, she had gloried in cutting herself to the right shape to fit it.

– I'm surprised you managed to make the time to come down, she said.

Innocently, he said he thought they could manage without him for an afternoon.

Just an afternoon.

– I don't want anything, she said, to attract his attention. – If you leave me anything and then you die, I'll just give it to Frankie.

– That will be your choice, of course, he said reasonably. – Anyway, I'm not planning on dying any time soon. But I wish you'd let me give you some money now, until you're settled. You'd have a right to it, in any court of law. You put your share into the flat. He turned the television off. – Nice set.

– You want to control me by paying for me.

Funnily enough, he clearly remembered her saying the same thing to her mother when they were arguing years ago over the wedding. It had been nonsense then; afterwards she and Rhian had cried and made up, as they always did. Was there any truth in it now? Very likely he did wish he could control her, but he had surely given up, out of realism, any belief in the possibility. Bruised as he was, he believed he truly didn't want her, in her brave new venture of living here, to fall flat on her face

172

or want for anything. And he had no use for the money himself. But in case she was right he didn't press her, he only asked her to sign the papers relating to their joint bank account.

– They've started the inquiry into the detention-centre fire, he said. – I'm giving evidence next week.

This was momentous, but neither gave away their reactions to it.

– Frankie told me. Oh, that reminds me: she's coming to stay this weekend, bringing the children.

Frankie was Robert's sister, Cora's close friend, Cora's age. It was through Frankie that they had met in the first place. Cora and Frankie had done English together at Leeds; Frankie's much older brother had taken time out of his already busy life to come to her graduation.

– I know. She told me. She's looking forward to it. Will you mind the invasion?

Cora flinched as if he'd caught her out: these rooms weren't well designed for children, with white walls, rugs on the polished floors to skid on, treasures displayed on low shelves.

– I'm not lonely, you know, she said angrily, writing with the usual flourish her boldly legible signature.

In the library Cora sometimes felt as if she had fallen to the bottom of a deep well. It wasn't an unpleasant feeling. She hadn't known that there could be a job like this, pressing so weightlessly on the inner self, allowing so much space for daydreaming. At first she had thought it might be her duty to encourage the borrowers, talking to them about the books they were choosing, but she quickly learned that they looked at her with shocked faces if she tried, as if their reading was a private place she'd intruded into. The whole point of her role was to be neutral, she realised, not engaged or committed. The hand-to-hand exchange at the issue desk – taking the books, opening them, date-stamping them, handing them back – was a soothing ritual of community. Even when she was helping the asylum seekers who came in to research information on the Internet in support of their appeals, she never discussed the content of what they were looking for; they only strove together through the process of finding it. This exemption from the effort of relationship seemed to her to be a relief to them both. In London, for eighteen months, she had visited a failed asylum seeker awaiting deportation (the problem was not at this end, but with the Zimbabwean authorities, where the crumbling bureaucracy made obtaining the necessary paperwork impossible). The memory still produced guilt and confusion: she had not liked him, she had let him down.

If she was on a morning shift, her first task of the day was to do the health-and-safety checks, making sure the place had been cleaned, the shelves were securely bolted in place, and no one could trip over the carpets; she was also supposed to go outside into the little garden between the library building and the street, checking for needles left by drug users. (She had never yet found any; perhaps they had them at the libraries closer in to the city centre.) The library was at a junction on a busy road carrying traffic in and out of the city from the valleys. It was a Carnegie endowment from the early twentieth century, built like an odd-shaped church with two naves at right angles and high windows of greenish glass, mournfully aloof from the squat, bustling shopping street of fast-food joints, quirky cafés, cheap mini-markets, hairdressers. Inscribed in stone above the entrance were the words 'Free To The Public', which moved Cora and made her nostalgic for the idealism of another era, although many more things were in fact free now. The staffroom looked over the Victorian city cemetery, a conservation area for wildlife. Sometimes she ate her lunch in there.

Cora told her fellow library workers she was divorced, which wasn't true, yet. Annette, the librarian in charge – long, dramatically ugly face, red hair, resilient jutting bosom – was divorced with grown-up children. At first Cora had been wary of her slicing ironies and touchy proneness to take offence. It was always Annette, scathing and jollying in an outbreak of noise, who tackled the occasional unruly drunk wandering in. Cora found herself imitating some of Annette's patterns, although Annette must be twenty years older. She began making her own brown bread for sandwiches, and joined the choir that Annette sang with, which met one evening a week and would try anything from Pachelbel's Canon to a Beatles medley. One weekend they had sung for charity in a shopping centre in town.

Inside the library the noise from the roads was muffled, like the light through the wavering greenish glass of the windows. If it was raining outside, or if the sky grew dark, then the intimate atmosphere intensified around the clacking of the computer keyboards, the bleeping of the scanner. Strip-lights were suspended from the ceiling by chains. After stamping and putting out the newspapers in English and Urdu and Arabic, Cora would print off the 'holds' list of books requested by other libraries all over the county, then begin to work through it, locating these books on the shelves, scanning them and fastening labels to them with elastic bands, ready for collection; she would be interrupted every so often by borrowers wanting something at the issue desk. The librarians conferred together in murmured voices.

In her teaching job at a further-education college in London, Cora had been active and forceful; she had worn herself out preparing classes and marking, standing up for her students, fighting threats from bureaucracy. Yet she'd always felt that this work, which in anyone's eyes could have amounted to a real career, was provisional, while she waited to do something real with her life. In her job in the library, which paid less than half as much and hardly began to use her capacities, she could imagine herself growing old. But she tried not to let her imagination run away with her. She knew how you could deceive yourself, falling into one of those pockets of stasis, where you could not see change building up behind its dam.

The weather stayed fine for Frankie's visit. Making up extra beds in the spare room on Saturday morning, Cora heard their car draw up outside and the familial tide spilling out, Frankie's chivvying and encouragement, whimpers from the baby. Cora dawdled downstairs through the house's last held breath of emptiness and quiet, waiting on the bottom stair until one of them actually rang the bell – 'Let *me* do it' – pushing open the letter box in a scuffle of excitement, peering through – 'Is she in?' – then poking in small hands and turning them to and fro in the hall's dimness, as if it was water. When she did open the door, they were suddenly shy on the doorstep, both of them stripped down to their shorts in the heat, skinny torsos pale: Johnny the eldest, her godson, red-headed, shuffling behind his dark-haired sister, shoving her forward as if she was an exhibit.

– Cora, look! he said.

Lulu held up her arm to show off pink plastic bracelets, making them fall one way, then the other.

– Hello, you two.

Hugging and exclaiming over them, it was as if she pushed herself with an effort out of her adult solitude; this had not happened when she saw the children all the time in London and must be another aspect of her new life. Frankie struggled in last, laden with bags, the baby on her hip. She had given up trying to keep her shape, after this last birth, and wore whatever loose clothes she pulled first out of the high-piled ironing basket – sometimes her husband Drum's shirts – over tracksuit bottoms. Cora was self-consciously aware of the summer dress she'd chosen, after trying on other things in front of the mirror.

– Shit, it's hot! Frankie said. – The motorway was a nightmare. I've been dreaming of your nice bathroom. Hold him, will you, while I use it?

Magnus had been woken up out of his sleep. Red-cheeked, strands of auburn hair darkened with sweat and pasted to his head, smelling of regurgitated milk, he squirmed in Cora's arms, opening his mouth to bawl. She walked into the kitchen and then on into the garden to distract him, kissing the top of his head and talking encouraging nonsense. The linen dress had been the wrong choice; it would soon be crumpled and look like a rag. The other two were getting drinks from the tap, standing on a chair, spraying water everywhere because they had turned it on too hard. The baby was transfixed by the sight of next door's cat on the wall; then he screwed his head round to stare with serious scrutiny at Cora's face, taking her in. She seemed to see for a moment that he looked like Robert: surrounded by her husband's family, she was ambushed.

In their time at university together, it had been Cora and not Frankie who was sure she wanted children. Frankie was clever, she had got a First, she had been set on a career as an academic; this was a surprise to people when they first met her, because her looks were sporty and unsubtle: round, pink, handsome face, messy chestnut curls, calves that in those days didn't have any spare fat on them, but were as substantial as young tree trunks. She had dyed her hair black, painted kohl round her eyes, taken drugs, but all her efforts couldn't erad-icate the glow of sanity and good health. When Cora fell in love with Robert, she thought she might lose her friendship with Frankie: it had been one of the elements of her old life that she had been calmly ready to trample underfoot in order to have him. But the friendship had only grown gnarled and tangled, woven around all the complications and surprise developments in their lives since. There were so many sensitive spots to beware of that they hardly bothered to try.

After lunch, Frankie fed the baby, the light gleaming on the skin of her breast where the tension tugged and puckered it. Cora wiped surreptitiously with a cloth around the sticky chair backs and edges of the table where the children had been sitting.

– Are you supposed to drink coffee? she asked.

– Hell, I don't care, Frankie said. – I do everything. I shouldn't eat this, for a start; look at the size of me.

As well as brown bread, Cora had made courgette cake, which was still warm. Johnny and Lulu carried slices into the garden on their palms. Johnny nibbled at his like a bird, dipping his head to it; Lulu tried to coax the cat to eat hers. Frankie sighed, relaxing, admiring the cake and her cake plate and her coffee mug, white china with a pattern of blue leaves.

– You've got everything so nice here. Don't think I've changed my opinion about the awful mistake you're making, leaving Bobs. But I'm jealous too. Everything here's deliciously calm and organised. London's vile.

– It isn't exactly that I've left him. We both agreed to try living apart for a while.

– Rubbish, he's desperate. You left him. Just because

he's an inhibited stick doesn't mean he isn't in torment.

– He keeps trying to give me money, Frankie. He turned up the other evening, waiting in the park to catch me on my way home, with a briefcase full of forms and papers. He wants to make over half the flat to me. That's how he thinks about relationships. It's horrible. As if the whole thing in the first place had been like arranging a contract or a piece of legislation. It didn't occur to him to ask me how I was feeling.

– It shows how he's suffering, that's just what he would do. Don't pretend you don't know him.

– I told him I wouldn't touch anything. I don't want any of it.

Frankie groaned. – You think you're so high-minded, but you're both just as bad as each other.

Open-mouthed, the baby fell asleep, away from her nipple, milk trickling at the corner of his mouth; she lowered him cautiously into his car seat. – By the way, I've got a new life-plan too, she said. – You're going to hate it. But you have to tolerate it, if I'm tolerating yours. At least mine's virtuous. I'm going to train for the ministry.

– Which Ministry?

Cora was thinking politics.

– *The* ministry. You know, the jolly old C of E. To be a vicar. Can't you just see me in a dog collar?

– You aren't serious. You don't even believe in God. You used to be a Marxist. You used to hate the establishment.

– The Church can be fusty, agreed. But behind the façade there's all this anarchic stuff about truth and social justice. We need that.

Reasonably, Frankie explained that if she'd been born in Baghdad she'd be a Muslim, or a Baha'i or a Jew, but the revelation most naturally to hand was the one she was born into, however imperfect and incomplete, because it was woven into her history and culture.

– So I love Protestantism. I sort of love it, romantically. The whole strenuous wrestling-for-grace thing, inside the individual soul. That does it for me.

– But you don't believe in the impossible bits, like Jesus dying and rising again?

Frankie's face sometimes took on a certain expression of tactful patience if she thought Cora was showing her ignorance, or failing to understand a difficult idea. – Well, I do, though I'm not sure it's helpful thinking about believing or not believing it, in that kind of either/or way. I don't suppose I believe in the Resurrection literally. For me it's a way of expressing the mystery of renewal, as a narrative.

Cora felt her own face stiffening in hostility, false sympathy. Apparently Frankie had been going to church off and on since Lulu was born. She had spoken to her parish priest, and then to a Vocations Adviser; they had told her she could do her training part-time, so she thought of beginning when Magnus started nursery. If Cora tried to imagine what Frankie meant by grace, a kind of ash seemed to settle inside her, sinking down through her chest like a blight. She didn't feel any longer that she had a soul, and she thought then that she hardly knew her friend, they were only connected out of habit. Love is a kind of comfortable pretence, she thought,

181

muffling everyone's separation from one another, which is absolute. Probably she had more in common with embittered Annette at the library than with Frankie.

– What does Drum think about it?

Drum, Frankie's husband, worked for the campaigns-and-policy division in a major charity.

– Well, of course he's a militant atheist. But I think he thinks it'll keep me happy. Or at least he thinks it'll keep me off his back.

Cora offered to put suncream on the children playing in the small back garden. She had eradicated from inside the house every trace of her parents and their long lives here, almost zealously, as if she couldn't bear to be reminded of it; and yet she had never dreamed of touching the garden, apart from where the new extension encroached into it. Otherwise it was still laid out just as her mother had it: low walls overgrown with roses; a crazy-paving path meandering in the grass; a dwarf pear tree, which was blossoming now. Only Cora didn't have Rhian's gift for gardening. Nothing grew quite as well as it used to: diseases rioted among the plants, slugs ate them, the roses were arthritic and blighted with black spot, the lawn was full of dandelions, she forgot to water things in pots. Sometimes she knew they needed watering, and obstinately put off doing it. Every time she stepped into the garden, even while it soothed her, she also suffered from her failure.

Later in the afternoon Cora and Frankie and the children processed across the road and along beside the iron railings to the park gate, bearing – as well as the baby – blankets and cushions, shrimping nets, picnic supper, plastic cricket ball and tennis ball, a bottle of rosé and glasses. Both women knew they must look like an idyll from the kind of old-fashioned children's book they used to read. Other sections of the long park that ran through this eastern part of Cardiff for more than a mile were given over to cultivated beds, bowling greens, a rose garden; at its far end there was a lake with a clock tower built as a little lighthouse commemorating Scott's expedition to the Pole, because the *Endeavour* had set out from Cardiff docks. Opposite Cora's house the park's ambitions were less strenuous: winding paths, grass worn thin under the spreading trees, dusty shrubbery. Older children were already in possession. Johnny eyed them warily: bikes dropped on their sides in the grass, a football game in progress, goals marked with T-shirts stripped off in the heat, girls paddling calf-deep in the brook. Cora had played in this park all through her childhood, felt as if it was yesterday the ooze of the stony brook between her toes, her mother's dread of broken glass and lockjaw.

They had forgotten the corkscrew and she went back for it; the others watched her summer dress flickering past the far side of the railings, her unhurried long stride with head held high. She waved to them, but Frankie, throwing the ball at Johnny's bat – he could hit it if she threw from about a yard away – was annoyed and alarmed at how unreachable Cora was these days. Always she had had a surface poise like a thick extra skin, which

Frankie had admired and envied; she supposed you had to be beautiful to acquire it, as Cora was. It had something to do with being so much looked at, deflecting an excess of attention, to protect yourself. But in the past she had been passionately available to her friends, beyond the act of herself; in fact she had used to seem to Frankie uncomplicated, in the best sense – admirably not opaque. Now, her spontaneity was extinguished. You knew about disillusion, but you didn't really believe in it as a tangible force, or anyway not in its coming on so soon – after all, they were only in their mid-thirties. In Cora's expression, it was as if a shutter had dropped with a crash, one of those dismal metal ones that shopkeepers install in areas of high crime. Frankie felt disappointed in her brother and Cora; she thought they should have had more resilient imagination than to have let their relationship collapse. They shouldn't have given up so easily on being happy, even if it was about not having children, which it might be, though Cora denied it.

Frankie crouched businesslike over the rosé when Cora brought back the corkscrew; both friends felt the strain at the idea of the weekend stretching out ahead of them to be filled. It was the first time Frankie had come to stay since Cora had moved to Cardiff ten months before; both had looked forward to it and now they were both thirsty for the first kick of alcohol, as if they might otherwise run out of things to talk about, which had never used to happen.

– Before you say anything, I know I'm not supposed to drink this, either, while I'm breastfeeding.

– He's such a feeble baby, you can see it's taken its toll.

Huge Magnus, on his back on a shaded corner of blanket, slept with clenched stout fists, reminding Cora of a pink plastic doll she'd had whose eyelids closed when you tipped it. They talked about the library, and although Frankie pretended to be sympathetic to what Cora described, the peaceful routines and absorption in administrative tasks, Cora was as defensive as if her friend had voiced the conventional pieties: that she was wasting herself, in a job where she wasn't using her brains or her education. Cora wished she was alone; one of the girls in the choir had offered her a spare ticket for something at the theatre – it didn't matter what. Yet the sunshine and the children's noise and the playful scrap of breeze, riffling the pink candles in the horse chestnut, made out of the park an image of blissful leisure.

– Bobs thinks, Frankie said, drinking down fast, – that you can't forgive him for the fire at the immigration removal place. But I said you couldn't be that irrational. How could you think it was his fault? He has to take responsibility, in the chain of command, that's how things work in government. But it's not personal. It's not morally his fault, in a way anyone could blame him for. You couldn't think that.

– I thought you were the one going into the Church. Your idea of conscience seems pretty flexible.

– So you do blame him.

– Of course not, Cora said. – I know he's an impeccably good man. Good in a way I'll never be. But those centres are unspeakable, it's a horror that they even exist. I can't talk about it, it's too awful.

– What do you mean, good in a way you'll never be?

– Nothing. She added – I can't imagine Robert saying that, about me blaming him for the fire. Whatever he thought, he wouldn't actually say it.

– Perhaps not in so many words.

– You shouldn't make the words up, Frank. They're important.

– You're right, I'm sorry.

– It's OK.

– Only I did know what he was thinking. He is my big brother.

– You never could know, not for absolutely sure.

They shifted positions on the blanket, each dissatisfied with the other, Frankie unpacking hard-boiled eggs and yoghurts from a cool-bag, Cora stretching out on her back and pulling up the skirt of her dress in a semblance of sunbathing. Lulu wandered out from the shrubbery to sit astride her, showing her an earthworm in a seaside bucket.

– Look at my snake.

– Don't bounce on your Auntie Cora.

– She's not my auntie.

– I don't mind, Cora said. – She isn't bouncing very hard.

But Frankie lifted Lulu by the armpits and swung her away, protesting, skinny legs bicycling wildly. Only the memory of the contact with her heated little life remained across Cora's pelvis and flat stomach for a few moments, vivid and distracting as when, the other week, Cora had had to pick up a starling that flew by mistake into the house and dazed itself, flashing round the ceilings and against the windows – its racing metabolism had seemed to leave its trace in her hands for hours afterwards.

There had been no loss of life during the fire at the immigration removal centre, but a detainee in his fifties, an Iranian, had died of a heart attack a day later, which was why the ombudsman had been asked to conduct a private inquiry. Recent inspections had reported a somewhat improved regime at the centre since the scandals of the early days, and the local fire chief had been paying regular visits. The usual decision had been made against installing sprinklers – too prone to being activated in the event of detainee protest – but Robert didn't think this would constitute a significant criticism, the ground having been gone over so thoroughly in previous inquiries. It wasn't clear that sprinklers would anyway have made a significant difference to the spread of the fire. Building design defects – a failure to plan for the need to isolate sections of the centre in an emergency – were much more likely to crop up, but blame for those could hardly be laid at his door, as the centre had been operative for two years before he came into his present role. The problem came back to the perpetual tension between allowing the detainees to associate – they weren't supposed to be under prison discipline – and the difficulty of managing large-scale protest, or controlling them safely in any emergency.

It shouldn't be too bad for us, Robert had reassured Frankie. He'll say, of course, in the report that these aren't very nice places. How could anyone imagine they might be nice? We can only be required to try to make them function as humanely as possible in the circumstances. It could have been so much worse. Staff followed procedures pretty well, the disturbances that started the whole thing were quelled rapidly, the individual who set the fires had a history of instability and had only been brought in the night before, there was a model evacuation, even the damage to the buildings had been limited. The couple of detainees who did abscond were picked up within hours.

This fire had happened a year ago, when Cora was still living with Robert in London, in Regent's Park; he hadn't told her right away that it had implications for him, not because he was hiding anything from her, but because she seemed at that point to have stopped taking an interest in his work. (She had stopped watching the news, as well, and reading the papers.) He thought she must still be grieving for her mother, but this didn't reassure him, he felt himself helpless to put up any argument against the blind force of her feelings, where he couldn't follow her. Also, he noticed that she had started avoiding undressing in front of him in the bedroom, turning her back so that he couldn't see her nakedness when she stripped off her top or stepped out of her knickers, hurrying on her pyjama top before she'd even taken off her skirt. He turned his eyes away from her, he went into the bathroom and took his time cleaning his teeth, he became scrupulous to protect her privacy, took her inhibition inside himself. It began to be their routine that he stayed up late, working on papers, long after Cora had finished whatever marking and preparation she had to do. Almost always she would be asleep, or pretending to be asleep, by the time he turned in.

Eventually Cora had learned from Frankie about the fire. When Robert arrived home in the flat from work one evening, Cora was already in bed. She said she was ill, she couldn't stop her legs trembling; she must have a fever or something.

He was still in his suit jacket and loosened tie, skin sticky and gritty from his Tube journey. – Why don't you take a break from teaching? he said. – You're putting yourself under too much strain.

– Is that what you think it is? she said bitterly from where she was huddled, clasping her knees in her pyjamas with her back to him, staring at the window. The late sunshine showed as shifting yellow rectangles on the thin muslin curtains.

– I don't know. What is it?

– I told you, I'm ill.

He put a hand on her shoulder and it was true that she was burning hot, scorching him through the thin cotton.

– I saw Frankie, she said. – I went round there after my last class.

Frankie was pregnant at the time with Magnus, having some medical problems.

– How is she?

– She told me about the fire at the removal centre, and the inquiry.

He knew at once it had been a mistake to keep this from her. Nothing would convince her now that he hadn't been hiding it.

– You don't have to worry about that. I'm confident it's going to be all right. Some effective work's been done in those places since the early days.

He tried to reassure her that no one had been hurt, that the man who died had a pre-existing heart condition, which was in his records. The curtains at that moment were blowing into the room, lifted on a breeze from outside. Cora uncurled herself onto her back, gazing at him.

– Robert, you frighten me sometimes. What does it feel like, to say those things?

Under her scrutiny he felt himself transparent, hollowed out.

– Sorry: am I talking civil servant? It's an occupational hazard.

– I don't blame you for anything, she said. – Only you use this calm and steady language about things that aren't steady.

– No, of course they're not.

– Things that are horrors really. Filthy and bloody.

– I suppose it's force of habit.

– Someone has to do it, I know that, she said heavily. – I know that, in comparison, I don't do anything.

When for a while Cora had visited Thomas, the Zimbabwean detainee, he had been at a removal centre in an old building outside Brighton, converted from a private school, with a spreading cedar – left over from the past – still in the garden, where the detainees were not allowed. Even as a visitor, she had been body-searched and made to leave her fingerprints. The shaming details of the place – Thomas had told her that when they brought him in they used fabric leg-restraints, so he couldn't run – still recurred, not in her dreams, but when she was defenceless, alone with herself, skewered by her guilt (she had been his only contact in the outside world, and after eighteen months she had stopped visiting). Robert's fire, however, had been at one of the new purpose-built centres: brick buildings on brown-field sites, as blandly featureless from the outside as mail-order depots or units on an industrial estate. The brutality of Victorian prisons had a negative moral weight, pressing heavily on the earth; this modern apparatus for punishment stood lightly and provisionally in the landscape, like so many husks, or ugly litter. The appearance of the buildings, Cora thought, was part of the pretence that what was processed inside them was nothing so awful or contaminating as flesh and blood. The buildings made possible the dry husks of language in the reports that Robert read, and wrote.

Frankie was going to drive back to London on Monday morning when Cora went off to work. Saturday night was rather a flop. The two women had promised themselves hours of talk once the children were asleep, but by the time Cora came downstairs from reading Johnny his story, Frankie, who had put things in the dishwasher, was yawning and ready for bed.

– God, I'm so pathetic. It was the wine in the sunshine. It's the bloody baby. Literally, I'm dozing on my feet: look!

She presented her moon-face for inspection – broad nose, big cheeks, thick dark brows – pegging her eyelids up with her fingertips; her girlish looks were gaining gravitas, personality stamping on them strongly as a mask. Cora began to believe in her as a vicar. As soon as Frankie had taken herself upstairs, Cora felt excessively wide awake; resentment dispersed like a fog lifting, and affectionately she tidied away her visitors' mess, thinking she would have made a more organised mother than Frankie. Pouring herself another glass of rosé, she stalked round the ground floor of the house in her bare feet, thirsty for contact and explanation now there was no one to explain to. Her lovely rooms, unappreciated, wasted their charm on the warm evening air; the windows were open, and footsteps passing in the street sounded unexpectedly close. The dishwasher churned in the kitchen. The usual quiet of the house was thickened by the sleeping children in it, their restlessness and rustling and little cries: inexperienced, she stopped at each new noise, listening anxiously.

As it grew dark, she lit the candles meant to enchant Frankie, then met herself accidentally in the mirror above the fireplace in the front room, ghost in her own house, with a shocked hostile look, unlike the carefully prepared scrutiny she usually allowed herself. In the mornings, or before she went out, she put on her make-up and arranged her clothes satisfactorily, as if she existed as a mannequin outside herself, whose beauty must be served. Catching herself unawares now, she seemed to see something that she had squandered, and had to answer for, and couldn't. Her face wasn't broad and dreamy, suited to quiet work at the library, as she liked to feel it from inside: the weight had fallen off her jaw and cheek bones, she looked questing and thwarted. The mirror was old, foxed, an antique, divided in portions like a triptych, in a thin cracked gilt frame. In the empty grate beneath, a fan of folded gold paper was arranged with some pinecones sprayed gold.

She did not want to see herself, or think about herself. The appetite for communication, which Frankie had roused and then frustrated by going to bed, broke in dangerously on the steady rhythm that her days had fallen into. Tamping down her restlessness, Cora put on the television, with the sound turned low. She remembered watching a different television in the childhood room that had occupied this same space, where she had once known how to possess herself confidently. That sitting room had been poky and papered in her mother's cautious stab at 1970s taste – stylised pink flowers on a mud-green background. Now that it was gone, Cora regretted that she had not kept even one scrap of this paper, which must have been one of the first things she opened her eyes on; although when she was a teenager, she had complained to her mother that it made her feel like a frog in a pond. But she had begun work on the house in a kind of frenzy, wanting to alter everything after her parents' deaths, which she had not foreseen, and which had struck her terribly. She had always thought they would come into their own in old age, they would have a talent for it. Dad's fatal heart attack, however, had come only two months after he took early retirement from teaching mining engineering at the University of Wales Institute; a year later, Mum was diagnosed with acute myeloid leukaemia. Cora had taken six months off work to nurse her.

Magnus cried several times in the night (poor Frankie, who was trying to get him to sleep through), and on Sunday morning Johnny and Lulu woke up early. Cora dozing in her own bed heard them, excited and tentative, testing the freedom of the downstairs emptied of adults, conferring in miniature voices, Johnny chiding and bossy: 'You mustn't touch, Lulu!' She gambled that they wouldn't break anything, and wondered idly what it would mean to have a sibling to explore with. They would be stepping with bare feet where the sun, on another fine day, crept its long, low, early light along the blond floorboards, warming them: Cora liked doing that too. If this long spell of lovely weather was unnatural, she could hardly make herself care. They would be entranced as well by the next-door cat, meowing through the glass from where it waited every morning on the sill outside, though she determinedly wasn't feeding it.

Luxuriantly she turned over under the cotton sheet

that was all she needed these warm nights, closing her eyes, floating at the edge of the dream she had woken from, of a long pillared hall like a temple, sloping down out of sight. Sometimes sleeping alone, after twelve years of marriage, was a huge relief; it was blissful to stretch her limbs across an empty space, weightless and free. In her memory, sometimes, Robert beside her in the bed had been a brooding and oppressive mass in those last months, weighing down the mattress on his side until she had to cling to her edge so as not to roll into him. She had lain tensed in the cramped margin, his sexual need gnawing at her ('sexual need' had been her mother's ashamed phrase for it), though she obstinately ignored it, and he never tried to touch her if she didn't want him to. At other times in her new life, however, Cora was so scalded by her solitary nights, sodden with dreams and longing, that she crawled downstairs to sleep sitting up in one of the armchairs. Then, her empty bed seemed ignominious, as if she was an old woman already, having lost everything.

After breakfast Frankie took the children to the little church along the road where Cora was married, while Magnus slept and Cora listened out for him. She made a picnic, thoughtfully putting in wet wipes and kitchen paper, bibs and nappies and changing kit. 'You're a genius,' Frankie exclaimed, and Cora saw how she almost went on to say that Cora was gifted for motherhood, and would have taken to it naturally, but stopped herself in time. Returned from her immersion in spirit, or whatever it was, Frankie looked washed with some new shine that made her impermeable to Cora. She had actually put on eye make-up and lipstick, combed out her mop of hair. Church had made the children momentarily big-eyed and solemn. Lulu was sucking her fingers wrapped in the skirt of her dress; the three of them composed a picture of wholeness and grace. Some great-uncle or other of Robert and Frankie's had been a bishop; Frankie's Drum belonged to that world too, his family had a big house and land in Scotland somewhere. These patterns were remembered in the blood, Cora thought sceptically. It didn't even spoil the picture of wholeness when Johnny flung a door open in Lulu's face and there were howls, Frankie shouted that he was an 'absolute bloody idiot'. Long ago, when they first met in Leeds, Cora had felt the difference of class background as an uneasy terrain dividing her from Frankie, in crossing which Frankie must somehow make the first move, propitiatory. Cora had been brought up a socialist. Her father's father had been an electrician in a coal mine and had volunteered for the International Brigades in the Spanish Civil War. She had used to burn with a sense of the wrongs done to her forefathers in history.

The friends got on more easily on this second day of their weekend together, because they'd stopped expecting too much. They drove up to the folk museum at St Fagans; almost carelessly, they let slip the old strenuous habits of their intimacy, and were nice to one another instead, even polite. Their lagging progress round the Welsh farmhouses and cottages done up in the styles of different periods, with smoking hearths or fumy gas-lamps, gave adequate shape to an aimless day; they bought flour from the water mill, rode in the horse-drawn cart. There were goats for Lulu to love and dread, and their picnic was blessedly wasp-free. Cora took them backwards down the row of tiny terraced houses from Merthyr Tydfil, furnished as a historical sequence: starting in the 1970s, they retreated to the early nineteenth century, because that was the only way she could bear to do it when she was a romantic girl, passionate against modern degradation, besotted with a purer past. Now, the past choked her, its tiny stuffiness, antimacassars and flat irons, rag rugs and faded photographs of dignified assemblies of Baptists, all men. Frankie peeked, when an attendant wasn't looking, into a massive old Bible in Welsh, which Cora couldn't read although her mother's family had been Welsh-speakers. Discreetly, neither of them mentioned religion when they stepped into the Unitarian chapel, with its democratic pulpit in the midst of the congregation, its clear light from windows of plain glass.

The longed-for idea of children was always remote from the reality of hours that Cora actually spent with Johnny and Lulu and Magnus. Caught up for the day in their clamour and tangled joys and crises, her skin printed with the hot impress of little bodies, it hardly occurred to her to feel the old cruel twist of her own lack. She couldn't want somebody else's children. She would be relieved – however much she liked them – when somebody else's were put to bed at the end of the day; she couldn't yearn after these completed persons, who belonged to themselves. Frankie's children only made her envious when they were absent, reduced to an idea; and in any case, the lack that had used to be savage pain was flattening into a duller wincing, in the more general ruin of her life. The great thing was to carry it off, so that no one pitied you. Cora knew that she was naturally good at this. Walking round with Lulu on her hip, explaining things to Johnny without overburdening him, she was aware she made a picture of a clever aunt, or a favourite school teacher. An uncompromised adulthood could make a clearer air for children, sometimes, than foggy mothering. Once, when Frankie had taken Johnny in search of toilets and Lulu tripped, Lulu was not inconsolable, accepting Cora's comforting as second best. That would have to do. Other families, passing their little group burdened with pushchair and bags, would not be able to tell immediately which one was the mother.

Frankie found herself explaining, while the children were on the slide in the playground and Magnus slept, how our modern sensibility, deprived by scientific rationalism of a mythic dimension, was floundering in darkness. – We've subjected religious beliefs to the wrong kind of scrutiny, as if they needed to be true in a scientific sense. So we're desolated by our cleverness, in an empty universe. We need the symbols and stories that embody the idea of another dimension, beyond the one we actually inhabit.

– But just because we need them, that doesn't make them true. Maybe there isn't any other dimension.

– No: the fact that we need them is what makes them true. We bring that dimension into existence, our imagination in creative collaboration with the life-forces outside us and the mysteries of physics, which otherwise have no outlet into being known. Those forces are incomplete without our faith as we're incomplete without their existence beyond us.

Cora wasn't interested, she was drawing with the toe of her sandal in the bark chippings of the playground.

– Have you left Bobs for somebody else? Frankie suddenly asked. – Is there anyone else?

Cora turned on her a look dishevelled, tragic. – Can't you see there isn't anyone else?

– You could have him bundled out of sight somewhere.

– Well, I haven't. There isn't anyone.

– OK. Don't be mad with me for asking. I didn't really think there was. I thought that if there was, I'd see the signs, and be able to tell.

– I'm not mad with you.

– Only I'm still so perplexed at what went wrong between you and Bobs. Because in spite of all the differences between you and what everyone said, I always believed you were one of those truly balanced couples, really good together.

– What did everyone say?

– Oh, you know, the usual: the gap in ages. The difference in sensibility: he was too sober for you, that sort of thing.

Cora saw a balanced couple, as in some idealising old

painting: the wife's hand, with her one glove off, held – almost as if they didn't notice it – in the husband's; he stood behind where she sat, they smiled out of the frame, not at each other.

– Was it because he refused to go for IVF or something?

– He didn't.

– Oh, really? I didn't know . . .

– It was nothing to do with that. Frank, I don't want to talk about it. Even with you, I can't, not yet. You were just wrong, about us being balanced together. That was just your wishful thinking, like the religious-dimensions thing. You weren't wrong about Robert, but you were wrong about me.

Frankie put her arm around her friend, having to make a little effort at forgiveness and empathy, because Cora had always thought she was free to slash around destructively in her friend's sacred places ('wishful thinking' she had called her faith), whereas Frankie knew she had to be more circumspect in Cora's. Frankie thought this had to do with Cora's having been the only child of devoted parents, used to them tiptoeing round her inner life, as if it was a perpetual wonder. Frankie and Robert's parents (there were two more siblings between them), who had been often absent anyway, and had sent their children to boarding school, were killed in an accident in a private plane in Tunisia when Frankie was sixteen. Her father had been advising the government there. It had made an added complexity to Cora's marrying Robert that, in the years after their parents' death, her older brother had played the role for Frankie of something like a father. There had been an inward upheaval for her when she first began to guess what Cora wanted, as if at the broaching of a taboo: who knew what dangers would follow? She did not know whether Cora had ever registered the struggle it had been for Frankie to adjust to seeing the new shape of things – love, between her brother and her friend – cleanly, without prejudice. Now, she had to adjust all over again.

She thought she could remember having something like the same argument about religion with Cora when they were twenty-ish, except that they had adopted opposite positions to the ones they took now. Cora had been mysterious, Frankie had been the debunking rationalist. In those days, too, Cora had worn the same look of suffering sensibility, maddening and touching; only then, behind her look, she had been buoyant, expectant, full of appetite. Now, she submitted to Frankie's hug, stiffly. Then someone shunted into Lulu on the slide and Frankie had to get up to go and rescue her.

After the disruption of Frankie's visit, it was a relief to Cora to feel the atmosphere of the library close again over her head: its greenish light, high peeling pink walls and subdued hush, altered by little blares of different sound, reminders from outside, when anyone pushed open the outer door. At other moments, she wanted Frankie to come back, so that she could manage things better, be more kind to her friend; definitely, she hadn't been kind about her plan to go into the Church. She lifted her eyes sometimes in the midst of whatever she was busy with, to where there were encouraging panes of stained glass – blue and yellow squares with red diamonds – above the issue desk, in a strip around the base of a glass dome, where dead wasps collected in dingy heaps. No doubt the architect had had in mind a library as it might have existed in a Burne-Jones painting: dreaming members of the public opening their minds in a jewelled light to Tennyson and Keats, rather than to Large Print Family Sagas and True Crime.

Cora had been afraid that seeing Frankie might spoil her time at the library; she had a horror of discovering that this new respite she had found, at the bottom of the deep place she had fallen into, was only another thin skin of self-deception. But as soon as she was making her usual round of checks on Monday morning, poking into the escallonia and Rose of Sharon bushes in the small wedge of garden for non-existent needles, she fell back into weightlessness, buoyed up by the unhurried current of routines outside herself. She had left Frankie behind at the house, packing the children's clothes and toys chaotically into huge plastic Ikea bags. On Sunday evening they had put the children to bed and watched a detective series on television; Frankie was asleep, startling occasionally at her own soft snores, long before the murderer was exposed. In the morning, making their farewells, they had embraced exaggeratedly but almost perfunctorily, covering up something that hadn't happened between them. 'It's been lovely.' 'It was lovely having you.' They had smiled too much, eager to be rid of one another, feeling the strain in the present of their old closeness.

Because of the public coming and going, the library could never have the airless inwardness of an office workplace; there was always something desultory about their hours passing, not because they didn't all work reasonably hard, but because in the end all their work was in the service of the mystery of reading, which was absorbed and private. Cora imagined herself in an outpost of culture, far removed from the hub, like a country doctor in a Chekhov story, ordering books from Moscow. One of their regulars, a petite sprightly woman with dyed black hair and a mask of thick make-up, brought in a painting done in an art class, wrapped in a black bin-liner, to show them: a clown juggling with stars against a purple background. Cora helped an Iraqi man search online for a news article on an American bombing raid on Fallujah, and when he had printed it off, he said emotionally that 'This was what I came to your country for', although she wasn't sure whether he was grateful for the free access to accurate information, or incensed at British involvement in the massacre of his countrymen. She developed a benign fantasy about an elderly man who wore a silk scarf and had a suffering, distinguished face like Samuel Beckett's; he borrowed European art films on DVD – Visconti and Chabrol and Fassbinder – and Cora imagined that he recognised a fellow spirit in her, although they never exchanged anything more than the change for his payments of £2.50.

After school, as well as a rush of mothers with younger

children, a group of teenage girls in blue uniform shirts and trousers and headscarves came in from the local comprehensive, ostensibly to do their homework together, putting their mobiles out on the table in front of them and texting frequently, conferring and confiding in strained whispers that never grew raucous, although Brian occasionally hushed them. Brian was meticulous and waspish, he did the cryptic crosswords and read French and German novels in the original; he was Senior Library Assistant and added up the cash at the end of the day. Brian and Annette, the full-timers, had been in libraries for years, and displaced a lot of their frustrations into the arcane politics of the library service; they were haunted by the threatened introduction of RFID machines, which would check out books automatically. The other library assistants were more like Cora, they had fallen into the job for one reason or another, and might not stay: a boy who was involved in amateur dramatics, a woman who'd given up her teaching job while her children were small, a shy girl with a shaved head and piercings, who took out all her nose- and lip-rings whenever she came to work, though no one had ever asked her to. Cora had realised at some point – she always realised it too late – that she had roused the resentment of the other assistants because she was too friendly with Annette, or because of things in her manner that she couldn't help; they thought she was bossy, or high-handed. Annette said not to worry what anyone thought, she never worried.

– People have to put up with me, she said. – They have to like me or lump me.

Cora took her lunch into the cemetery next door, strolling between the scuffed trunks of the pines that lined the avenues, stopping to read the inscriptions on the gravestones: Protestants, Catholics, Welsh, Poles, Irish, Italians. Sometimes she had to make way for the white van of the cemetery workers, but she had the place pretty much to herself; there were hardly any new burials here and not many people visited the old ones. 'Of your charity, pray for the repose of the soul of Mary Hanrahan.' A sub-lieutenant *'mort pour la France'*. An amusement caterer, whatever that was, with a monument as ornate as a fairground organ, including Jesus and a lost sheep; dock pilots; a tobacconist. She calculated how old they were when they died; how many children were lost; how long the wife outlasted her husband. Herbert William Alexander lived only thirteen days. Twin brothers both drowned, one aged seven, one aged twenty. William Tillet died in 1896 aged seventy-six, 'for over forty years with Messrs George Elliot and Co. of the Wire Rope Works, West Bute Dock, Cardiff'. Magpies and floppy crows, whose feathers fitted like old mackintoshes, picked around in the turf. Notices explained that for conservation purposes an area of the cemetery was left to grow like an old-fashioned hay meadow, and was only cut once in autumn, encouraging a variety of wildflower species and of wildlife. Green woodpeckers fed on the warty mounds of ants' nests. The grey squirrels, whose skittishness was startling in the heavy quiet, were so fearless she got close enough to see their quick panting: one pounded intently with both front paws, digging to bury a pine cone, chucking up dead leaves and earth behind him in a frenzy.

On a bench, with her face lifted to the sunshine, Cora felt like a convalescent put outside to build up her strength from day to day; only she didn't like to ask herself what she was building it for. There was a circularity in her recovery: if she was happy she was bound to look to the future – but she could only be happy in the present. Saving herself from having to think, she took her book into the cemetery to read while she ate her sandwiches. She wasn't reading anything strenuous these days: women's novels, commercial novels, some of which, she and Annette agreed, were remarkably well written, better than much so-called literary fiction, more true to life. She hardly ever thought now about what she had learned when she did her English degree. Her imagination was crammed with women's stories, most of which began with a collapse like hers, some loss of faith or love, losses more catastrophic than anything she had endured. She devoured them, one after another, turning the pages with hasty hands, impatient for the resolution. As soon as she'd finished one, she would start in upon the next.

When she wasn't reading novels, she was working slowly through a book setting out the fundamentals of geology, which Brian had recommended when she told him about her father's maps. She planned to enrol in a geology evening class in the autumn. At first she had only hung the maps on her walls because they comforted her obscurely; they were so familiar she hardly looked at them. In the old days she and Mum had used to tease Dad for preferring diagrams of rocks to paintings and literature. Recently, Cora had begun to take an interest in what the different colours meant, even though it was the sort of exact scientific subject that was alien to her, and she found it difficult. She had taken the meaning of the maps for granted when her dad was alive, but it became strange, after his death, to think of the layers hidden beneath her feet, beneath the city pavement and the park – mudstone and sandstone, overlaid with glacial sediment. Dad had been tolerant and patient, charming, good with his hands. He had been in Militant Tendency – Trotskyites inside the Labour Party – when he was young, but left because he didn't like the way they talked about ordinary people. He had approved of Robert, even in the time when her mother was set against the marriage, before she came round. Between Cora and her father, relations had always been painfully tender, each trying to shield the other from whatever they discovered that was ugly or disheartening. When he died she had felt a kind of shame, as if his decent and cheerful life had been maliciously blotted out.

Cora changed her mind, and decided that Robert was right in his desire to put their relationship – or the end of it – on a more formal footing. Perhaps here too she was influenced by Annette, as with the brown bread: a divorce was a clean, businesslike thing, better than this current mess between them, impossible to explain when people asked. Anyway, mightn't Robert be better off if they were properly divorced? She ought to cut him free of her, so that he could find someone else. Perhaps he would get back in touch with his old girlfriend, whom Cora had displaced. She rang him at work to arrange a meeting – somehow she didn't like to speak to him on the telephone that would ring in the Regent's Park flat where they had had their lives together. Before she rang she thought carefully about what to say and in what tone of voice, so as not to raise his hopes in the wrong way; and then after all that she only got through to his PA.

– Elizabeth? It's Cora.

In the old days, Elizabeth had thought she was scatty; Cora would have been ringing because she had locked herself out, or because she'd forgotten to buy something for supper and was asking Robert to get it on his way home. Robert had met all her requests or difficulties with the same calm seriousness with which he would have attended to a message from the Home Secretary's office, but Elizabeth had felt their affront to the importance of a senior civil servant, although she had had to be polite. Now, she must enjoy being flatly, casually indifferent. The world had got on without Cora.

– I'm sorry, he's in a meeting.

– Would you ask him to call me?

There was a moment's hesitation, which was almost personal. Elizabeth wouldn't use her name. – On which number should he call?

Robert wouldn't have given her any detail of the

collapse in his home life, except what was functionally necessary.

– Tell him I'm in Cardiff. Well, he knows that.

– I'll let him know. He's very busy this afternoon.

Putting down the receiver, Cora was flooded for an unexpected instant – before she quashed the weakness – with nostalgia for the old-fashioned wife-identity she had forfeited. She had hardly cared for it while she had it, had scarcely used the word 'wife' about herself, or thought of Robert as her husband. In the first years of her marriage, the conventional category had seemed somewhere below what she aspired to be to him; more lately, it had seemed above her range. She made up her mind not to wait around for Robert's call. It was her day off from the library, she had plans to go into town to buy fish at the market. Determinedly, she was feeding herself properly, cooking from her recipe books with fresh ingredients, although sometimes, sitting to eat alone at the place set with her heavy silver knives and forks (a wedding present to her grandmother, on her mother's side), on the soft old wood of the dining table in the conservatory, with the doors open to the evening light in the garden, she could hardly finish what was on her plate and had to scrape into the bin what she had so scrupulously prepared. She daren't stand on the scales to see what weight she'd lost.

Robert called her back almost right away; they arranged to meet for lunch in London the following week. She suggested the National Portrait Gallery restaurant, because although they had both liked it, they had not gone there much together. He discussed her days off at the library as respectfully as if they existed in the same category as the time he contrived to squeeze between his appointments in the diary Elizabeth kept for him; he was so cavalier with his importance that Cora was anxious he must not get the wrong idea about why she wanted to see him.

– You were right, she said abruptly. – We ought to sort things out more sensibly.

– Sort them out?

– For your sake. It isn't fair.

There was a short pause, while he puzzled over what lay behind her words. – When you say, 'sort things out' . . . ?

– I mean, financial and practical things.

– It's all right, I thought you must mean those.

When he'd rung off, she stood with the receiver pressed to her chest, pulling at the coiling wire of the phone, doubting whether she had done the right thing. Was there any truth in the possibility that she was manipulating him, or playing with his feelings? Could anybody think that of her plan for lunch – or that she was meddling with him, planning trips to London, because she was bored? Horrified, she almost rang Robert back to cancel, but realised that would only seem worse, she would only be digging herself in deeper and deeper. She burned with how far she didn't trust herself.

By the time the day came for her London journey, these qualms had lapsed; on the train she thought only about how best to arrange things with Robert. She didn't know anything about divorce law, except that these days it wasn't necessary to prove that anyone had committed adultery, or been violent or mentally cruel. It would have been sensible to research it on the Internet before their meeting, but she hadn't had a connection set up yet at home, and couldn't have looked up anything so private at the library. Anyway, she recoiled from typing the word casually into a search engine, as if it was only a topic like any other. She found herself picturing Robert calmly as an old friend. Divorce seemed an exaggerated and crude instrument for prising them apart when they were already so remote.

She had allowed herself an hour or so to look around the gallery before lunch. After the assault of heat and crowds in the Tube and on the street, her consciousness sank into the cool interior like dropping gratefully underwater, then bloomed towards the otherness of the portraits. Concentrating on the twentieth century, she shivered in her sleeveless dress, pulled on her cardigan, drank stories in unguardedly; when it was time to meet Robert, she was borne up in the lift by an elegiac vision of lives piled high, one after another, full of colour and incident, involuntarily expressive of their era. She arrived at the restaurant a few minutes early, and ordered a prosecco while she waited. The particular present – cacophonous acoustic, well-dressed people (no doubt she'd forgotten already how not to look provincial), celebrated view of the mauve-grey roofscape – lost its power for a moment, dislodged by the weight of the long past.

Robert saw Cora before she saw him: exceptionally

attuned to her, he even saw her mood of grave gener-
alised regret, and didn't want to spoil it. He had no idea
about clothes, but did see that she looked less like London
than she had when she lived with him: it must be the blue
cardigan with its small buttons, which suited her, but
made him think of a school teacher (he didn't have any
up-to-date idea of what librarians looked like). Reflectively
she was eating the cherry from the top of her drink.
Attractive women usually made him feel tall and too
bulky; although Cora was slim, she had always seemed
to be made to his scale. She had a narrow waist, but her
hips were shapely, as wasn't fashionable now. Making his
way towards her between the tables, he ignored at least
two parties of people he recognised; when Cora caught
sight of him she half-stood up, knocking over her glass,
which fortunately was almost empty. By standing she
meant to convey, Robert understood, that she was his
host and had convened their meeting: he must not try on
any air of entertaining her. He tried to think how he could
defer to this respectfully, without letting her pay.

– I shouldn't have had that prosecco, she said,
blushing. – It's gone straight to my head.

– D'you want another one?

He hoped that didn't sound as if he wanted to make
her drunk.

– No, thank you. Thank you for coming. I suppose
you're very busy.

Hanging his jacket over the back of his chair, loos-
ening his tie, he admitted that the reorganisation was a
bit of a nightmare.

– What reorganisation?

Robert looked sharply at her: could she really have missed it? Inside the Westminster village, it was easy to forget with what little interest the public outside followed the earthquakes that consumed them. He explained that part of the Home Office was being separated off as a Justice Ministry.

– Oh, yes, of course, Cora said vaguely.

The procedural aftershock, he said, had disturbed even the farthest reaches: he was helping to make sense of the creation of the new Borders and Immigration Agency.

– Is that a good thing?

He was never exasperated with her, but he wouldn't set out his serious interest in the issue for her benefit, either, if she wasn't really interested. – Well, I've been spending rather more time than is pleasurable in Croydon.

– Croydon?

– Where the Agency is based. I'm still at Marsham Street, but I've wanted to see what they're doing on the ground. I suppose Croydon's the ground, or part of it. Though sometimes there one seems to be in some kind of middle air – it doesn't remind one much of earth. What shall we eat?

Neither of them, looking at their menus, could read them at first. The effort of their conversation, that appeared so easily offhand, actually dazzled them, blanking out everything else. In the moment of catching sight of Robert and knocking over her glass, Cora had thought that he was impossible, 'just impossible'; but she didn't try yet to disentangle what the thought meant. He wasn't handsome, she had never thought that, though she had liked his looks, and other women liked them. His nose was good, straight; his eyes were in deep hollows under brows that, without her supervision, were growing bushy. His shoulders and hands and feet were generous and his movements rather shambling. He hadn't looked much younger in his late thirties, when she first met him. Some men altered exaggeratedly in form from the child they had been, more than women ever had to; and yet sometimes in Robert's guarded look you saw what he was as a boy – shut up in those horrible schools his parents had paid a fortune for – more plainly than in a more boyish man. Over the years this glimpse of his childlikeness had come to pain her more than the more obvious thing people thought: that she had chosen a father figure.

When they'd managed to pick something from the menu and order it, Cora told him she'd been looking round the gallery. – As I came into the restaurant I had the weirdest sensation, as though our present had turned into the past already, and we were all over with too. Doesn't it seem strange to you sometimes, how we only live in this one moment of the present? Like a light moving along a thread which stretches out behind us and ahead. I mean, why is it *this* moment, and no other?

Her metaphysics always went somewhere under Robert's radar, which was tuned to practical effects. – We're not over with, though, he said.

Did he mean their relationship? She was alarmed:

he had never protested at her going to live apart from him, accepting her decree fatalistically. But she realised he only meant that they weren't dead. They were stuck with themselves, with their ongoing lives. To distract him, she brought out her suggestion about his old girlfriend.

– Robert, you ought to get in touch with Bar.

He didn't know straight away who she was talking about.

– With Bar? What an extraordinary idea. Why would she want to see me? Why would I want to see her, for that matter? Bar's probably married with five kids, on a farm somewhere.

She saw he didn't even notice what he said about the five kids.

– I don't really want to discuss this now, but perhaps everything would have been better if you'd stuck with her in the first place. There are people smiling over at you. Do you know everyone?

– I hardly know anyone, he said, not turning round to see. – How extraordinary of you to bring up Bar, all of a sudden.

– What do you think about this weather? Cora said brightly, as their food arrived. – Is it global warming?

Outside the window, which ran the whole length of the restaurant, the delicately nuanced monochrome of the top of the capital – lost in its secret quiet above the seething busyness below – was bathed in a transforming sunlight. There wasn't a cloud in the sky; glass and metal surfaces on the rooftops flashed like signals.

Robert lifted his eyes from the plate set in front of him, only to look at her.

– Probably only a normal climatic variation, even if within a changing spectrum.

They both ate all three courses of the set lunch. It all seemed delicious to Cora – in Robert's familiar orbit she recovered her old appetite. She had calves' liver with creamed cauliflower and crispy bacon. Robert's portions vanished as easily as if they were snacks, and he drank a couple of glasses of Bordeaux – he wasn't a wine buff, he was bored by too much fuss, but he liked fruity reds. He had to eat, to fuel his big frame and his indefatigable stamina, and he could drink a lot without it having much effect on him, although he usually didn't drink at lunchtime.

It was strangely ordinary, eating together.

– I suppose we ought to get a divorce, Cora said, towards the end of her salmon with hollandaise. Robert had been reaching with his knife and fork for an extra potato. He put the knife and fork back on his plate and for a moment rested his hands, clenched in fists, on the edge of the table, staring down into his food. Cora was appalled by the idea he was going to cry, and by her own tactlessness – although, when would have been the right moment? It would have been absurd to wait to discuss it with their coffee, like *petits fours*.

But of course he would never cry, probably not on any occasion – Cora had never seen him do so – and certainly not because of a woman, in a restaurant full of acquaintances. That was nonsense, it wasn't how he was made. He was just taking in with the appropriate seriousness what she had said. What kind of man would have gone on to take the potato?

– I don't know much about it, she went on quickly, covering up her confusion, explaining how she hadn't yet fixed up the Internet at home. – Isn't there something about irretrievable breakdown? We could go for that.

– Is it irretrievable?

She knew she flushed, and in her embarrassment was suddenly furious with him. – My God, yes, Robert. Have you no idea? Doesn't it *feel* irretrievable to you?

– Then you're right, we ought to go ahead with a divorce. There's no reason not to.

– It would leave you free.

He made one more necessary effort. – Frankie tells me there isn't anyone else.

The idiotic formula sounded incongruous, coming from him; she wanted to cover up his shame.

– You don't need to worry about that, truly. Not on my side. All I want is my solitude. You probably think that's nonsense. But I would like you to find someone and be happy. That's why we should divorce.

After a moment's thought, Robert helped himself to the potato after all, and cut it up carefully into pieces on his plate. Cutting up all his food before he started eating was one of the irritating habits Cora blamed on the form of education he'd been forced into.

– If it's what you want, he said eventually.

They agreed that both of them would contact their solicitors. Cora would go to the same firm in Cardiff who had dealt with her parents' mortgage, and then their wills, and then the transfer of the property into her name. Finishing her salmon, she had to dab her eyes once surreptitiously with her napkin, but she mainly felt relief at getting the painful discussion over with. Afterwards, however, it was difficult to start conversation up again. Casting around in her mind, she rashly asked Robert about his session at the inquiry; he replied that it hadn't gone too badly. The day-to-day running of the centres was contracted out, and the primary remit of his team was contract letting and agreeing procedural guidelines; as far as that went, the questioning had been sympathetic. They had nothing to cover up; in fact, some of the work they were doing had been commended. He paused to take a mouthful of his wine; Cora guessed he was calculating how much more to say to her, weighing the chance of provoking one of their disputes against his desire, always, to give her the whole picture if she asked, which was his kind of truth-telling. Despite their relatively easy ride, however – he went on – he wasn't sanguine about the outcome. She mustn't repeat this, of course. But there was something in the air that made him think the press wouldn't let it go. The Iranian who died turned out to have been someone, and the story was starting to make waves.

– What d'you mean, someone? Everyone's someone, you know.

– I do know. All I meant was the kind of someone

the press can attach a label to, if he comes to a sticky end.

The Iranian was a journalist, he'd been living in London for years, not bothering to renew his visa; some of his short stories had even been published in translation by a small press over here, in the Eighties. He'd been touted around the usual literary festivals and readings for a while. He should never have been refused asylum, it had clearly been an error, by their own criteria – the adjudicators could be idiots, that was often half the problem. It would have worked against him that he hadn't done anything about the visa until he was picked up. The man had been depressed, he'd had a drink problem for years, everyone had forgotten who he was, probably he hadn't even looked presentable when he came up in front of the tribunal. It seemed he'd managed to alienate his lawyer and ended up representing himself – he'd made a bit of a mess of it, ranting and not making a lot of sense.

– And then he died.

– He had a dodgy heart. It could have happened at any moment, anywhere.

– But it happened there. He had to die in one of those places.

– It was a bad way to go. There are worse ones.

Cora was determined not to row with him; she didn't point out that a journalist and writer might have met one of those worse ones precisely in Iran, where Robert had been trying to send him. Sometimes she was tired of herself, pushing against his reasoning, chipping away at it, as if he was in her path like an immovable rock. It had been the same before he moved to immigration, when he was in prisons. She baulked at the detail of what he oversaw; he said that someone had to oversee it, so long as the government had an immigration policy, or wanted to lock people up. He said he'd rather do it himself than someone else, who would do it worse. Delivered with his authority, that sounded like an unassailable defence of what he did; but so were her qualms unassailable, they came from deep inside her nature, she couldn't learn to suppress them, or want to, although she had tried when they were first together and she was very young.

– What were the things the inquiry commended? she asked.

Robert explained that his team was working on a new scheme, whereby within a few days of application each asylum seeker would be allocated a 'case owner', who would manage their case through every stage, from the initial interview through to integration into the UK. Or deportation, if necessary.

– Was this your idea?

– My recommendation, in a Review.

– It sounds like a good one. For them to have a continuous point of human contact.

He couldn't let her plaster him with good intentions. – It should be more efficient. Speed things up, help move the backlog.

The waitress brought the pudding menu.

*　　*　　*

After her mother died, three years before, Cora had been in a bad way.

Through the last months of her mother's illness, she had made a good nurse, resourceful and resilient. Robert had been moved to find that the wilful girl he married, with her strong gift for pleasure, had this patience in her. When, after a spell in hospital, Rhian had come home to die, Cora had risen to the occasion as if it were a test, like other tests she'd always passed with flying colours. She hid her own desperation from her mother; she worked as if she was part of the team of doctor and cancer nurses who came to the house, and they had praised her steady, unsqueamish caring. – Whatever happens, I will be with you, she had said to her mother calmly, and her calm had seemed to help. Rhian had been querulous in life, but was rather stoical at the conclusion of it. Near the end, Cora had seemed to know how to make the dying woman more comfortable on her pillows, lifting her so gently and exactly.

Carelessly, Robert had presumed – without thinking about it – that this new strength would be part of Cora permanently. However, as the months passed after Rhian's death, she was hardly recognisable as that capable nurse, wise instinctively about entrances and exits. Her old energy seemed irrecoverably broken. She wouldn't talk to him about her parents; wrung with pity for her, he wondered uncharacteristically if counselling would help, but she insisted she didn't want to talk to anyone. Drooping from her usual straight height, she complained of period pains, nursed a hot-water bottle to her stomach, went to bed early, watched television in the day. If they made love, it forced tears out of her eyes, which she tried to hide from him. He imagined her collapse as though she had drawn too deeply upon subterranean reservoirs of her nature that, once tapped, couldn't be replenished by any ordinary process of rest and recuperation. Her spirit seemed darkened and poisoned, and Robert suffered because he felt himself inadequate to clearing it.

Rhian had died in February; after Easter, Cora insisted on going back to teaching. At least it meant she had to get dressed in the mornings, and she had to prepare for her classes and mix with her colleagues and students. But he was afraid it was too soon. One evening when he came in late from work, he found her sitting on the side of their bed in her coat with her knees together and a grey face, as if she had dropped there when she came in and hadn't moved since. Her heavy case, crammed full of books and marking, was at her feet.

– How long have you been sitting here?

– I don't know. What time is it?

Unwisely, kneeling to take off her shoes and help her out of her coat, he reopened a suggestion he had made before, and which she had fiercely rebuffed. Why didn't she give up teaching at the FE college? A friend of his had contacts at a private school, the conditions there would be so much easier, she could take on part-time hours to begin with, the kids were eager to learn.

Cora shrugged her arm out of her coat sleeve, pushing him away.

– Why can't you get it into your head that I wouldn't

work for a place like that, if it was the only school left on earth? I actually happen to prefer the kids I teach. They don't have much of a chance in life, I don't pretend I can do much to alter that. But at least I'm more useful, teaching them basic literacy skills, than cramming pampered brats for Oxbridge. And I don't have discipline problems. I'm an experienced teacher. Where do you get your ideas of what goes on in a place like ours: from the *Daily Mail*?

– But look at you. You're desperate with fatigue. You owe it to yourself to take it easy. Just for a few months, till you're feeling better.

– I suppose you're blaming my principles now, for me not getting pregnant?

He was slow to rearrange his insights in the light of this new element; he must have shaken his head, he thought afterwards, like the bewildered ox he was.

– Getting pregnant? Is that what you want?

– Oh, Robert: how could you not know?

– But aren't you having those injections?

She said she had stopped having the injections two years ago: he was astonished, but didn't question that she hadn't discussed this with him at the time, or ever told him. She said that she had 'wanted it to be a surprise'. He accepted that in this area of experience women had a natural primacy, and must make up the rules according to their own mysterious intimations.

In two years, nothing had happened. This last week, she had been hopeful, but when she got home tonight, her period had come.

– I suppose that Rhian knew about it?

Not only Rhian, it turned out, but Alan too. Part of Cora's grief was that they had been cut off without ever knowing their grandchildren.

Without having gone through the long build-up, with its slow cycles of anticipation and disappointment, Robert was plunged suddenly into the extreme end of the angst of childlessness. But he put himself entirely at Cora's disposal. He would do whatever was necessary, if it would make her happy. Anyway, without thinking about it much, he had also always wanted to have children, at some indefinite future point. That seemed the right inevitable shape of their family, if they were a family: between the two of them, the vaguely sketched-in graduated sequence of their children, two or three – never babies when he imagined them, but sturdy children in shorts and sunhats, with fishing rods, and their own plans. His picture was made in the mould of himself and his own siblings, and from the phase of childhood he had enjoyed most (when he was at prep school, and had spent summer holidays with his parents and siblings – apart from Frankie, not born yet – in a house at the top of steeply wooded cliffs in Devon). He had believed too, without acknowledging it to himself, that children would seal the bond of his marriage with Cora, which otherwise, even after all this time, he thought of as provisional and precarious. She might, if there weren't children, remove herself one day as arbitrarily as she had thrown herself at him in the first place.

* * *

So, three years ago, they had found themselves in the waiting room of a clinic in a handsome Georgian house in Wimpole Street, on the brink of their first appointment with the fertility doctor. Robert had made discreet enquiries of the right people, and found this was the place that got the best results. It was a close, wet June day, rain blowing in a warm mist in the streets, the pavements greasy with it. Cora, who had hardly noticed for months what clothes she put on in the morning, had dressed with feverish care for this appointment, as if she needed to seduce the doctor, not consult him. Now she was suffering because her Betty Jackson satin print blouse, with a bow at the neck, was stained with damp, and anyway was surely wildly inappropriate, making it appear that she wasn't serious about the whole process. She couldn't look at the other couples waiting with them. Afterwards, she wondered if she had hallucinated the fact that the walls of this room were covered, every square foot, with photographs of babies, of smiling mothers and couples with babies. It seemed too manic to be probable; and wouldn't it be an insensitive message, anyway, to blare at those who might, after all efforts, still fail to conceive?

Robert beside her was a dark mass, in suit and tie because he'd come from work to meet her here. Chairs in any public place always seemed too small for him, and it was surprising to see him reduced to a client or a patient in a queue like everyone else, as if all his body language by this time involuntarily exuded authority and control. He didn't give any sign, however, of minding waiting, or of wanting to be anywhere different. She wondered what he'd told Elizabeth about why he was leaving the office: nothing, she was sure, that would have given away Cora's business here, or her failure, or her desperation. Nonetheless, she burned with those things, just as if Elizabeth knew about them – and everyone knew. She wished Robert had nothing to do with the whole process, and that she could have come by herself, in secret. Wasn't he only consoling her, playing along with one of her whims? She couldn't remember them ever discussing fertility treatments at a point before it would have been a subject charged with importance for her, but as they sat in silence she attributed to him a masculine disdain for them, a stoical preference for letting nature take its course, for the discipline of accepting whatever life sent. His views would be based on a long perspective, taking into account world population growth, viewing the cult of baby-making as a kind of sentimentality only available to those in the advanced economies.

She was in fact quite wrong about what Robert thought, but she seemed to hear these opinions uttered in his reasonable, reluctant, rather growling voice, which never ran on unnecessarily, but chopped and cut to minimise wasted words, always holding something back. The judgements she attributed to him threw her into an agitated dismay, so that she longed to get up and walk around the room, but didn't want to give herself away to the others waiting. Robert fetched her a drink of water from the cooler. Cora had some idea of the humiliations that awaited them, after the doctor had turned his doubtless considerable charm on them, although she wasn't sure whether they would happen today, or at a second appointment. It didn't matter if she was pushed and pulled about like a doll, and probed, she didn't care. But she scalded at the idea of the affront to Robert, shut in a little room, perhaps even a toilet, with magazines, to produce a sample. How could she allow it? This place and everything about it was a mistake, she was suddenly sure. There must be a way out from it, in which she was true to herself, didn't betray her deepest instincts.

She cast around, remembering the last days of her mother's illness. How had she summoned then that strength beyond herself, to act well? She remembered how at a certain point when she might have allowed herself to sink in suffering, the thought had come to her like an instruction: bite on the bitter pill. Bite hard. She had bitten hard, and the flood of strength that came had even had a savage joy in it. Now, too, she was carried away, in a suffering beyond her control. Cora stood up, the receptionist and the strangers in the waiting room looked at her, Robert looked.

– I'm just stepping outside, she said loudly, picking up her mac and her bag. – For a bit of fresh air.

In the street, the rain blowing at her was a balm; she lifted her face into it. Robert came hurrying after her, with the silk scarf she'd forgotten.

– No, she said definitively to him, gripping his forearms. – It isn't what I want.

– Then that's all right, he said. She imagined he was

relieved, although this wasn't in the least true, he was only trying to cover up his regret, so that she didn't feel she'd failed at anything. He was disappointed that what had seemed a way out of Cora's sorrows was a dead end.

– Let's go somewhere and have lunch, he said.

– Do you want to go back and tell them?

He was indifferent to the administrative hiccups at the clinic when they discovered that one set of clients had fled. It must have happened before. – I'll phone them later.

– Don't you have to be back in the office?

– I told them I'd be away for a couple of hours. They won't expect me back till two. We've got till then.

She had wanted him to say that the office didn't matter.

II

Cora, three years ago, on the train from Cardiff to Paddington.

It was a few weeks since she'd run away from the fertility clinic, almost six months since her mother died. Her teaching had more or less finished for the summer, and she was throwing herself furiously into the transformation of the Cardiff house, telling Robert she wanted to do it up to sell it. No matter what difficulties came up, how the builders found dry rot, or messed up the French windows in the extension, she encouraged herself: bite the bitter pill. She had got her force back, even if she didn't know what to do with it, and was only pressing mightily up against an invisible resistance. She had chosen a wood-burning stove, she had scoured the reclamation yards for antique tiles for the bathroom, for lovely old pink bricks. Now, outside the train windows, the afternoon landscape fumed with rain, the green fields and woods were secretive, withdrawn around their own dense history, pressed under a lead-coloured lid of sky. The train wasn't full; she sat at a table by herself. Dark drops rolled sideways along the window glass. For no reason, her heart was beating thickly, as if she was expecting something, though she wasn't, she mustn't look forward, because there was nothing ahead, nothing.

A man stopped beside her, carrying a cardboard cup of coffee from the buffet, a briefcase slung on a strap across his shoulder.

– Do you mind if I sit here? I'm escaping from an idiot with a mobile phone.

– How do you know I'm not one?

He glanced at her, taking her in quickly. – You don't look like an idiot.

– You're safe, she said. – Mine's turned off.

– Good girl.

Half-heartedly she was offended by his calling her a girl. Sitting down in the window seat opposite her, he got out a book from his briefcase and started to read. It was a book of poetry, by someone Cora hadn't heard of. She was embarrassed that she was reading *Vogue* – she knew the man had taken this in, in his quick survey, as a mark against her. She never used to buy magazines, but on her journeys backwards and forwards from Cardiff, not wanting to think too much, she tried to fill her head with ideas for things she might get for the house, or plans for new clothes.

He scowled into his book, gripping it as if he might tear it apart at the spine. Cora always looked at people's hands when she met them (Robert's were huge, with

230

soft hollows in the palms and unexpectedly delicate finger ends). This man's hands were long and tanned and tense, slim as a woman's though he wasn't effeminate, one finger nicotine-stained, the nails naturally almond-shaped; when he took a mouthful of coffee she noticed that they shook. He wore a wedding ring. She thought he might be precious, or pretentious; there was something dissatisfied in his ripe, full mouth, although he was attractive, subtle-looking, only just beginning to lose his hair – which was the colour of silvery washed-out straw – at the temples. Under the hooding curved lids, she seemed to see the quick movements of his eyes as he read; he was a hawk, jabbing into his book for its meanings with an unforgiving beak. Determined not to care what he thought, she returned to her magazine. After a while he dropped the book down on the table. Cora looked up from serious contemplation of a winter coat.

– You didn't like the poems, she said.

She expected his vanity to be gratified by her taking an interest in his opinion, but he only looked surprised that she had spoken, as if they existed in different worlds.

– Do you read poetry?

She supposed he meant: as well as magazines.

– I do. I'm an English teacher.

He wasn't enthusiastic. – Oh, good for you.

– Well, actually, I love what I do. But I don't get to teach much poetry.

– Have you read this?

– No, I've never heard of him. I don't think I'll bother

now. You looked violent. I thought you might have thrown it out of the window, if these windows opened.

– As a matter of fact, I did quite like it, he said. – But not enough.

– Enough for what?

After a pause he added that he wished the windows did open, because he would have enjoyed throwing books out of them, from time to time.

Cora had read that when someone is attracted to you they begin unconsciously imitating your own movements: she noticed that when she sat back in her seat now, he was drawn forward towards her, leaning his elbows on the table, frowning. It was obvious he didn't want to talk with her about poetry, dreading the conventional and gushing opinions she might try to impress him with, reluctant to unpack his own ideas for anyone not likely to appreciate them. He had a high opinion of himself, she thought: his surface as it met the world was obviously touchy, ready with disdain. He asked where she'd got on the train and whether she lived in Cardiff; she replied that she was born there, but lived in London.

– Visiting your parents?

Cora explained that both her parents had died, and how she was doing up their house to sell. She expected him to say something sympathetic, but he only asked her what she felt about Welsh nationalism. She replied that her father had taught her to be suspicious of all nationalisms as parochial.

– Sounds like a good old Trotskyite.

– He made up his own mind about everything.

– You're very Welsh.

She said she hated having any set of qualities foisted on her.

– That's what I mean, he said. – If you accuse anyone of being very English, they accept it apologetically.

His accent was English, neutral rather than distinctly ruling class.

The train drew into the station at Swindon, new passengers got on, someone hesitated in the aisle at their table. They made no effort to move their bags from the seats beside them; both looked studiedly out at the platform, where those who wanted a different train seemed to wait in suspension, in a vague dusty light, cut off from the rain that poured in streams from the ends of the roofs. The person moved on: there were plenty of other places to sit. Neither acknowledged that anything had happened, but by the time the train started up again the atmosphere between them was altered, they were cut off together in their corner.

It turned out he had a house in the Welsh countryside somewhere – her geography was approximate; Robert would have known where it was. He had three daughters, two small ones, one from a first marriage, who didn't live with him and must be about fifteen, maybe sixteen.

– How often do you see her?

– Not often enough. We don't have anything to talk about when we do meet. I find her thoughts impenetrable. No doubt the feeling's mutual. My other girls are darlings, they're my heart's delight. And do you have children?

He looked at her ring.

Something impelled her not to answer him 'not yet' or simply 'no'.

– I can't have them. We tried, but I can't.

– I'm sorry. Should I be sorry? Are you?

She shrugged. – I would have liked it. But there it is.

– Might you think of adopting?

– No.

– OK.

It was a relief, to state the thing with such finality – as if she made it exist as an object to contemplate, stony, with clean lines and hard edges. With the loss of her parents behind her, and the loss of the babies she might have had ahead, she was withdrawn out of the past and future into this moment of herself, like a barren island, or a sealed box. It was easier to lay out this truth for the stranger's penetrating scrutiny, and not in expectation of any kindness. The hawk beak of his interest jabbed at her, as it had at the poetry book.

They could lose one another at Paddington.

She was sitting forward at the table now, and he had fallen back into his seat. He was studying her, half-closing his eyes, as if to get her at a distance, in perspective.

– So you're an English teacher. And what does your partner do? he asked.

– He's a civil servant. Quite a high-up one.

– Oh dear.

– He's an intensely moral, conscientious man, and I love him dearly.

– I can read it in your face, he said.

For a moment, ready to be enraged, she thought he intended a cheap irony; but no, he meant what he said, quite straight.

– Really?

– Yes, he's there in your expression, something settled and steadied.

– That's nonsense. You wouldn't have known if I hadn't told you, you might have thought I was involved with an unstable drunk. Or someone who taught juggling skills. You can never guess other people's partners, they're almost always unexpected.

– I'd never, ever, have believed you were involved with anyone with juggling skills, he promised her solemnly.

– But an unstable drunk . . .

– An unstable drunk, at a stretch. Though you wouldn't put up with him for long. You're not the martyred kind.

Cora didn't ask him about his wife, mother of the little girls, his heart's delight. That corrected the imbalance between them, where he was freighted down on his side with children.

He went to the buffet to get them both coffee. She commented that this was his second cup, and he agreed it probably wasn't good for him – and he smoked too, he confessed, he ought to give that up. To her relief he didn't show much interest in these subjects; some of her colleagues could talk for hours about their diet regimes and health.

– So, are you a poet? she asked him.

– Do I look like one?

– What is this physiognomy thing with you? There's no art, you know, to read the mind's construction in the face.

– Shit! I forgot, you're an English teacher.

– What have you got against English teachers?

– Nothing, he said with exaggerated gloom. – Someone has to do it. A quotation for every occasion.

– Don't you think it's a wonderful thing: opening up young minds to the possibilities of literature?

– Oh, that. Do you really do any of that?

– Not much, she admitted. – I work with young adults with literacy problems. But I do like it. And I do read to them sometimes, good difficult things. You'd be surprised how much they can take in. You see, they're made to stumble, because their reading is stumbling. So everyone gets the wrong idea, that they're not interested in what's in books. But just because they can't read for themselves doesn't necessarily mean their minds aren't capable of following a sophisticated text. Some of them. I mean, I wouldn't want to exaggerate. I wouldn't want to claim I was reading them Henry James.

– No one reads Henry James these days, he said. – Do they? Not after they've been made to at university. The shelves in the bookshops are full of them, people buy them because of the titles and the nice pictures on the covers, they think it's going to be fun like a costume drama on telly, but they don't actually read them, not to the bitter end, surely they don't?

– *The Golden Bowl* is my favourite novel. I reread it every couple of years.

– Well, you're one, he said. – You're the one. You're a rarity. You're the rare, exceptional reader that the book was looking for. It found you, across the years. Rather you than me. I'm not sure I'd want to be found by *The Golden Bowl*.

He wasn't really listening to what she said, he was watching her: or, he saw what she said as if it was an attribute, part of her quality, not an idea separate from herself. She felt herself laid open in the bleaching light of his attention. What he liked, she understood, weren't her liberal ideas on education, but her hardness, which was personal and – newly, after the last two years – had something finished and ruthless in it. He was not taking advantage of her desperation; it met something in him, he reciprocated it. And also, of course, he was drawn by how she looked; he couldn't help it and she couldn't help drawing him after her. She began to feel herself enveloped in that rich oil of sex attraction, so that she moved more fluently, knew there was something gleaming and iridescent in how she turned her head away or smiled at him. The sensation of his physical close-ness mingled with her awareness of herself, as if there'd been brandy in the coffee they drank: the ripe blend in his face of softness – cheeks and skin and mouth – and hard hooded eyes, the deliberate slow changes in his expression, as if each thought she offered dropped into a cave inside him, lit up with ironies. She would not have wanted to belong to any mere club of desperate people, if there hadn't been sex and beauty in it.

In the past, she had always tried to deflect any attention to her looks onto something else, as if in itself it wasn't worthy of her. She had insisted on being loved for her qualities or her ideas; but she might put those aside, for this moment. Dizzy, she was confused about what she was supposed to be arguing for; somehow they had got onto the subject of class. He was insisting that Marx was sentimental, deluded with hope on the subject of the proletariat. When Cora had to get up to use the toilet she looked around dazedly at the other occupants of the carriage, suddenly returned inside herself and self-conscious about their conversation – how loud had they been? – as if instead of coffee they really had been drinking alcohol. Making her way back to him, balancing between the seat ends, after the unnerving swaying toilet and its complicated locking, she saw the cooling towers of Didcot power station float past the windows, the squat, fat pillows of their steam half-quenched in drizzle. The sight lifted her back into the surrounding routines of her life – they would be in London in less than an hour, she needed to shop before she got back to the flat – as if she was surfacing from somewhere underwater. When she reached their seats, he had picked up his book again and was reading as if he was reconciled with it. They had lost their momentum and sat in silence, restored to their separate existences. Cora thought coldly that their little exaltation had all been nothing, a false flurry.

I don't even like him very much, she thought, embracing emptiness with relief. If I saw him talking to someone else, I'd think he was opinionated, and preoccupied with his own inner life, blind to other people. Physically, he's not my type, with that face that will grow into pouches and folds as he ages, like an actor in a Bergman film. I prefer someone with sharper bones, leaner. Not that Robert has sharp bones exactly.

She looked out of the window, repudiating *Vogue*, taking in the pleasure boats disoriented on the flooded upper reaches of the Thames, then the outer sprawl of the capital, its usual intricate mica-glitter extinguished in the rain, stretching out in its flat plain in every direction like a plan of itself, punctuated with green, with the poignant ruins of the old factories. They were swallowed between the backs of office blocks. As they stood up to leave the train at Paddington, they said goodbye.

– It was nice talking to you, he said.

– Yes, wasn't it? she idiotically replied, and then blushed furiously at her mistake, which he obviously noticed and took – so unfairly – for the last word on her vanity and self-satisfaction.

In the crowd hurrying along the platform he was ahead of her, taking long oblivious strides. They were borne forward, apart, in the tide of the combined purposes of so many anonymous others, all moving in uncanny swift unison without speech, only to the sound of their steps.

239

The great station gave out its roaring exhalation of echo. She hadn't even asked him what he was coming up to London for. Dirty pigeons flapped like derision under the vast arch of the roof. Following, faced with his back, Cora was suddenly desperate at the idea of letting this unknown man go into the crowd where she would never find him again; she convinced herself that she might not be the whole of what she could be, without his knowing her. Hurrying behind, she willed him to turn round. And beyond the automatic barrier where they fed in their tickets, he did. He stopped in his tracks.

He was wearing – she noticed properly for the first time – a slightly ridiculous blazer, grey linen with a light stripe, like something a woman might have bought for him but had meant him to wear in the sunshine.

Cora almost fell into him.

– Oh, hello, he said. – It seems a shame, not to see you again. After we got on so well. Didn't we? When are you next in Cardiff?

That was Paul: Paul, although she didn't know his name yet – he forgot to tell her, forgot to ask hers. Or perhaps didn't forget. They didn't exchange phone numbers either. They were bound together, for the moment, only by the slenderest thread of an arrangement, an hour, a place (not her parents' house, but a café near the park).

When the day and the hour came round, Cora was almost too busy putting on white undercoat in the upstairs bathroom. By the time she got all round the window frame she was already late, and then when she changed out of her decorating clothes she realised that she smelled of white spirit and there was paint in her hair and under her nails. This seemed a doomed and desperate condition in which to seek out a love-affair. In the mirror she saw a caricature of herself, lips bloated, eyes bloodshot, charcoal eyeliner smudged. Fatalistically she almost changed her mind again and didn't go, only she couldn't bear the idea of the hours passing after she hadn't. Crossing the park under her resisting, buffeted umbrella, she felt the louring sky and sodden, thrashing trees were her own blemish, a weight she had to carry on her shoulders.

As soon as she came into the busy, noisy, steamy place, putting down the umbrella and shaking it out of the door behind her, he stood up from the table where he'd been waiting and came over and put his hands on her, holding her while she unbuttoned her wet mac, kissing her – right cheek, left – as if they knew each other well. Her mind was still in the chaos of wind and rain in the park. They were both breathing hard. There might be people in the café who recognised her, had known her parents: she didn't care. All the shops and cafés in Cardiff were poignant to her in that moment, suffused with a fond idea of home and the past.

– Oh, he said into her neck, – I thought you wouldn't come.

He smelled of cigarettes.

– I'm sorry I was late. I was painting.

– Pictures?

– No, the bathroom window.

When they had got coffee and were sitting down he brought out a notebook and pen. His hands shook, but she remembered they had shaken on the train, even before he noticed her. – Listen, he said. – I can't ever let you go again, English teacher, Henry James lover. Married to the senior civil servant. What's your name? What's your number?

She had forgotten everything about this man; it was like meeting a stranger all over again. He seemed more compact than she had remembered, more sleek, he might have had his hair cut in between their meetings, he was less like her idea of a poet. His eyes were grey-blue – she hadn't remembered that – and slightly prominent, the sleepy lids lifted as if he were shocked awake. She could hear traces of a Midlands accent now in his voice, which was deliberate, strong, lazy. He contemplated her steadily, drinking her in, swallowing her, so that she had to look away, down into her coffee. Sometimes she thought afterwards of the man on the train as if he had been someone else, whom she'd never seen again after that first time.

Cora had no notebook with her. Paul wrote down his name and mobile number on a scrap of paper he found screwed up in his pocket, and she put it in her purse, still thinking she could throw it away later, or put it through the shredder when she got back to London. He took her hand, hot from nursing her coffee cup, in both of his, unfurled her palm and kissed it, pressed his knees hard against hers under the table. She thought: this works, it's his system, he's done this with women before. It's not a trick or anything, but he's worked out that if you prevaricate too long, you pass a point where you can't get back to the truth of what you really want from the other person, and you wind round and round each other in tedious games, which are for children. So if you want sex, you might as well be plain about it, seize the possibility that's flowering at once, before it passes. That's all this is.

– Cora. I made up names for you. But none of them was as good as that.

– This is ridiculous. We don't know one another.

– I don't want to know you. Not so that you're familiar, filmed with familiarity, so that I forget the shock of you.

– You might not like me if you knew me.

– I like you. But that's the least of it.

What would she think of him, she wondered, if she was watching this from a cold distance, if she wasn't herself? Her nostrils tightened for a moment in disgust. She didn't want to be one of those women with hardened faces, joking about sex, lighting up at the idea of sex like an old, tired torch when the contacts are pressed, expert in techniques and devices.

But then, Paul – Paul, she savoured the name, as though she had always kept it ready, empty, as a mansion prepared for him – Paul wouldn't have wanted one of those women.

She thought: isn't it what I came for? Aren't I glad, that he is shameless? She didn't pull her knees away.

– Where can we go? Paul said.

*   *   *

The house smelled of paint and damp plaster, it was coldly unfriendly. The men had gone home: Mark the plasterer who had been finishing the walls in the new front room, Terry the builder who had been putting in the units in the kitchen. Ladders were propped along the hall, cloths were spread out across the floors, the empty rooms resonated as Paul and Cora walked around them, stepping over the mess. If Terry or Mark had still been in the house, she would have made Paul tea and then sent him away, and she would have shredded his note. Everything they touched was thick with plaster dust; she seemed to feel it coating her tongue.

– I'm an idiot, bringing you home with me like this. Like one of those desperate women who get murdered. I don't know anything about you.

– Cora, he said. – It's all right.

But he must be thinking the same thing, anxious suddenly that she would bore him, or cling to him. Now they were alone together, they must both be full of doubt. She was coldly ready to let him go, and at the same time frantic at the idea of it. After he went, what would she have left?

– Here, there were two poky rooms, she was explaining. – I've knocked through.

He was bored, desperately bored, his eyes slid away from what she showed him. She took him upstairs, but only to show him the paintwork in the bathroom. He must be imagining that under the veneer of her caring for poetry, this was her secret self, devoured by the cult of home improvement.

– There was an awful old suite in here. You know, face-powder pink? Anyway, I ripped that out.

She could not help herself processing round the rooms, explaining the plan of the old house, which was disappearing under the emerging shape of the new. She even showed him the airing cupboard and the new boiler, hearing herself mention constant hot water, knowing she sounded quite mad. They opened the door and went into her parents' bedroom. She had had the fitted wardrobes taken out and the floor sanded, got rid of most of the furniture. The room was a light, white box, rain washing down the curtainless window.

– My mother died in here, Cora said, surprising herself.
– In this bed.

When she had opened the door, the whole scene had been laid out in front of her for a moment like a tableau, shaking her violently: she had seen it in a new perspective from the doorway, herself at a distance standing bent over her mother, the nurse on the other side of the bed, perhaps preparing a syringe, with her back turned. At a certain moment, without warning, something like thick black blood had gushed from her mother's mouth, choking her, flooding over her night-dress and the bedclothes. She had met her mother's eyes, seemed to read full awareness in them, protest and shame and terror. The next moment the nurse had turned round and cried out in surprise. 'Oh, she's gone.'

Cora had run downstairs and out into the garden in the dark, unbelieving.

– How long ago was this? Paul asked. – Were you
with her?

He looked where she was looking, as if he might see
something.

The room was empty.

In Cora's room, he closed the door behind them.

In here too it was almost empty, there was just her
bed and a chair, no curtains at the windows, a few books.
She slept in here when she stayed over.

– At last, I've shut up, she said, lifting her face to be
kissed.

– At last, you've shut up.

– It was funny, when I insisted on showing you the
boiler.

– Sssh.

She remembered his hands holding the book on the
train, as if he might tear it in half. Those same hands,
hard and precise, now took possession of her – the hands
first. They were determined, he knew what he was doing,
he didn't fumble over her buttons or her zip. She gave
herself up to them, to the dangerous sensation of being
possessed. When it came to her skirt, he told her to step
out of it, and laid it on the chair. Her skin as he un-
covered it goosefleshed in the unheated room; her
nakedness was changed, because this stranger saw it with
new eyes. He reached round with both hands behind her
to unhook her bra, without looking; did it easily, and
pulled it free. Her breasts spilled out against his shirt front.

– Oh, he said, and staggered, losing his poise.

246

She staggered too, they fell onto the bed together, then he had to scramble out of his clothes, pushing trousers and boxers down and kicking them off his feet, tearing his half-unbuttoned shirt off over his head. Their love-making was clumsy, this first time, because they didn't know one another yet, they were too desperate for one another. He actually still had his socks on the whole time, which was something people joked about as un-romantic. The violence of Cora's sensations – afterwards she lay unsatisfied against him, too shy to ask, with her wet thigh over his, and then had to finish her climax alone in the bathroom, avoiding the wet paint – was something new. She had only made love with one boyfriend before she married Robert. Both her lovers, before Paul, had been deferential, grateful, careful, eager to please her; she had never shaken off knowing that they found her lovely. She had not known whether to believe in this grabbing, grunting, flaunting, heedless sex, when she had seen it on television and in films.

– I like this rain, Paul said, after the storm of sex had passed.

He didn't seem in a hurry to go anywhere; she didn't know how long he was able to stay. They lay listening to it: spilling over the rim of the gutter, drizzling into the street, bringing the exterior acoustic suggestively inside the room. The tyres of passing cars pressed, hissing, through surface water on the tarmac, footsteps smacked in pools collected in the hollows of the old pavings. This bedroom seemed somewhere Cora had never existed in before, as if she'd gone through the mirror into the reflection of the place she'd known. The veiled grey light, the pearly shadows blooming and moving on the walls, made her think it must be about seven o'clock, evening: but evening as an infinite sea to sink into, not the couple of short hours between afternoon and night. Back from the bathroom, she had not known how to lie down beside Paul, because she didn't know yet what their intimacy was. She arranged herself on her side, not touching him, looking at him lying on his back, smoking a cigarette; she'd brought him a paint-pot lid to use as an ashtray. From where he lay hieratic, thoughtful, outward-borne, he skewed down his glance to take her in, his eyes sliding over her – naked shoulders, breasts slipped sideways, mound of her hip under the duvet – in a slow retrospective satisfaction, which ran like oil over her skin.

– Cora, Paul said, relishing her name. – Cora. Was this your bedroom when you were a child?

She said it was, but hardly believed it as she said it.

– Then where are all your things?

Before she started decorating, she explained, she had put all her old toys and children's books in a skip. She had given away the desk at which she used to do her homework, and her clarinet.

– I'm doing the place up to sell, I had to get rid of all the old junk.

– Commendably unsentimental.

– I'm not sentimental.

– Good, for an English teacher.

She thought that he saw through and through her: to the filthy stricken sessions she had spent clearing the house of her parents' things, dreadful as scrabbling in a mausoleum. Robert had tried to help, and Frankie; they had tried to persuade her to keep stuff, when she had wanted to throw everything out or give it away.

– Are you an only child? Paul asked her.

– How can you tell?

– Me too. That's why we understand one another. Two onlys. We want too much.

She hardly knew how he earned a living, she didn't know where he was born. As they talked, she seemed to perceive the outlines of his character as if they were drawn in ink, in clean lines on the air. He was interested in his own ideas, not very interested in hers, though he wasn't oblivious of her: he addressed himself to her intelligence, so that she moved ahead of him, agile, to meet him. He was anxiously gloomy, disappointed with what he'd done in his life (he wrote critical books, he taught, he had once hoped to write a novel, he had tried and failed). And yet he was springing with energy, much of it negative. He tried to explain a book he was reading, which was filling him up: on commodity and singularity, and the control of knowledge in commerce between the rich and poor nations. She didn't dare tell him that Robert worked in immigration; she could guess what he would think of that. She liked his thick strong chest, not muscled, but not soft with fat. When she put her hand over his heart, on his hot skin, she seemed to feel his personality bounding and burning there.

– I can't leave my little girls, he said. – Can you forgive me for that? I have to tell you right away.

This moment wasn't really right away. But Cora only shook her head as if an insect buzzed; she had not even been sure he would want to see her again, let alone imagining a future in which she might make any claim on him. They agreed they were desperate for a pot of tea. Cora hadn't got any food in the house, only biscuits and bread. Paul said he was ravenous, he would like toast, but then when she made a move to get up from the bed, he put his arm around her and kept her.

– Don't go. I can't part with you yet.

– I'm only going downstairs, I'll come back.

– But not the same. You won't be exactly the same as you are now.

– Don't be ridiculous, she laughed, settling down under his arm, tasting cigarette on his skin, in his mouth, wet sweat in the fine tangle of hair on his breast.

– You're grieving for your mother. Of course you are. Good girl.

– Is your mother alive?

– She's frail, lives in a flat where there's a warden on call. But she's beginning to be confused. She may need full-time care.

– Are you close to her?

– We're friendly, Paul said. – We get on well. We were very close, once, but I changed. I grew away from her.

– I don't know how people go on walking around, after their mother dies. I don't know how they keep getting up in the morning.

– But you're walking around.

– No. Not really, she said. – Really, I'm not.

He only nodded, taking her seriously. Pushing the duvet off onto the floor, he knelt beside her on the bed, taking her in intently where she lay naked on her back on the sheet, as if the grief she had confided in him was dispersed around her body, not her mind. She succumbed, experiencing herself opened out and pressed flat, against the white background, liberated from possession of herself.

Cora kept the scrap of paper with Paul's name and telephone number scribbled on it, though she soon knew it off by heart. The paper grew soft with folding and unfolding. She left it in her address book where Robert could easily have found it, and might have asked whose name it was, although he might not.

– You're wearing more make-up, Robert once commented, and she thought for a moment that he knew.

– Am I? Don't you like it?

He considered carefully. – I think it means you're feeling stronger, which is good.

– But you don't like it.

– I like your real face.

She couldn't answer. She carried these words round with her like a hot coal, hardly knowing how to take hold of them. Did he know about Paul? Had he guessed? He never gave any other sign. How dared he think he knew her, that he could judge what her real face was? She felt contempt for his schoolboy puritanism, disapproving of women wearing make-up. Treasuring them up, she thought of the words Paul used to her, shamelessly, for parts of her body and for what they did together. Robert never used those words, he never even used them for cursing. But then what Robert said about her make-up surprised her again. It wasn't like him. Ordinarily it was in his nature to be vigilant against just such a loaded remark, with its knife-twist of appearing-love. Did that mean he knew? Was he striking at her, to hurt her? But there was never any other sign.

When Cora did her face in her bathroom in the flat – she and Robert had a bathroom each, hers was all mirror glass and white tiles – she painted her eyes elaborately in defiance of him, put on blusher and lipstick. Then she scrubbed it all off and began again. She put together a separate make-up bag to keep in Cardiff, but often didn't bother with it. Paul didn't care what make-up she wore. She asked – calculating carefully so that she didn't sound needy – whether he liked her better with make-up or without, and he said both.

The scrap of paper where Paul had written his number was a compliments slip from the *London Review of Books*. Cora began to buy the *Review*, looking out for articles by him, but never found any. When she asked him about it, he told her some long, complicated story about how he had offered to review something for them, then got stuck and couldn't do it, and now they were offended with him and wouldn't give him anything else to write about. There were a number of such stories about his relationship with various kinds of authorities, fraught with offence and resentment; she wasn't able to judge yet whether his account of them was to be trusted, or whether the feuds were in his imagination. He was relentlessly critical of power. His explanations of politics – of the war in Iraq, for instance, or of the credit boom – were illuminating, he sliced away the slack of lazy language, and always seemed to have access to facts and insights that weren't common knowledge. She found it difficult to argue with him. Sometimes, thinking of the difficulties of Robert's daily work, Cora wanted to ask him: but how would you do it better, if you were them?

– It isn't so easy, she said, – to put everything right.

He said any ambition to put things right was subject to the doom of unintended consequences; she experienced his pessimism as a force, clean of the contaminations of privilege and duty. He came from a working-class family and had studied hard to get into Cambridge, and then been unhappy there; he got away to London to do his PhD, and then spent years in France. He let slip to her once that his wife – his second wife, mother of the little girls – had been to boarding school, and although Cora pretended to hardly notice this, she seized on the information as if it set the two of them apart, connected through their modest backgrounds. When she told him about her grandfather working in a coal mine and going to fight in Spain, she could see it moved him, even though the episode in Spain wasn't particularly edifying: her grandfather had become sick with dysentery as soon as he arrived, then injured his hand in an incident while training, and had to come home. Cora's dad had used to tell it as a funny story.

She never, ever searched for Paul's name on the Internet; it was a superstition with her that everything would be spoiled if she unleashed into their secret intimacy the world's promiscuous noise, its casual judgement of him. Or it might have been worse if she'd not found anything, apart from the listings for his books. He insisted he was no one, he had no public profile, no one cared what he thought: but surely that was disingenuous, as he had a publisher, and readers? She heard him once giving an interval talk on Radio 3: completely by chance, because he hadn't mentioned it, and she never looked at the radio listings. At home in the Regent's Park flat, she had been half-listening to a concert of piano music, half-reading the paper: then suddenly Paul's voice was loud in the room, uninhibited, talking about Georges Sand and Chopin, blasting her with dismay and joy. The traces of his Birmingham accent came over more distinctively in his recorded voice. All the time it was on, Robert was working at his desk, with the door to his study open, so that from the sitting room Cora could see his back bent over his papers, hear the occasional percussion of his biro, jotting notes. If he had only turned around, she thought, he must read the truth in her excruciated stillness. She couldn't move from her chair to turn the radio down, or off, or shut the study door, until Paul's talk was over.

She bought his books, the most recent first, having it

sent to her address in Cardiff; she devoured it eagerly, full of admiration and interest. It was difficult, but her knowledge of him was like a light held up to each page, so that she leaped ahead and understood where he was going even before he explained it. At unexpected moments his ideas went stealing through her like a secret power. That summer, she often stayed over in Cardiff for days at a time during the week, supervising the building work in the house, getting on with the decorating, driving to fetch whatever was needed from Ikea or the DIY store. When Robert asked her when she was putting the house on the market, she explained that it wouldn't be ready for a while yet. Paul came over every evening that he could. He said he told his wife he was visiting a friend who lived nearby, across the park.

– Does this friend know what you're really doing?

– More or less. I haven't spelled out the whole situation.

– What does he think? Does he mind?

– Don't worry. He doesn't mind. It's not sleazy. He's imaginative.

As if light flashed off some jagged glass-shard, Cora guessed: he's covered up for you before. But she didn't say anything, or allow herself to think about this properly. It was good to be busy all day. She got on well with Terry and the other men who came to work in the house. For as long as they were around, she was calm, could lose herself in her plans for each room. She was able to see clearly what effects she wanted: clean and open, unfussy, with bold touches of romance (the ironwork in the conservatory-dining room, the old French mirror she'd found to go above the front-room fireplace; at night in her dreams the little house was a crumbling, burdensome palace). Often she could prolong this calm into the early evening. She would take a bath after the others left. They hadn't done the floor tiles yet in the bathroom, so she stepped out of the water onto gritty bare boards, then dried her hair in her room and made herself something to eat on her new cooker. Consumed in expectation of Paul's arrival, she would hardly be thinking about him consciously. She had given him a key. Then, when she heard his key turn in the lock, for a split second she could even feel panicked; the serene hours of waiting for him drained out of the air, replaced by his complicated real presence, which was almost too much.

Once or twice when she was expecting him Paul phoned at the last minute – sometimes using the flat, subdued voice that meant he was talking where he could be overheard – to say that for some reason he couldn't come. Although she was clever enough to keep her voice steady on the phone – 'OK, I'll miss you' – her reaction afterwards, in the privacy of the empty house, was extreme; she frightened herself. She never told Paul about these times – when they were over, she didn't even like to think about what they meant. She reached inside herself and found nothing there without him, only a void. Once, she stayed crouched for what felt like hours in the dark, downstairs on the floor by the phone where she'd taken the call; when finally she tried to move, she was too cold and stiff to stand up straight, and had to crawl upstairs on her hands and knees. There was no television in the house, and she couldn't read. She would get into bed with the radio on, and try to fall asleep to the sound of voices, so that time would pass, bringing the morning.

He would bang the door behind him, his shoes were loud on the uncarpeted stairs. Then he was in the room with her, already throwing off his coat, which was sometimes a green country waterproof, dripping wet. She'd never seen again the grey-striped blazer of their first meeting on the train. Even while he was still talking, explaining, he would come over to look into her face intently, framing it in his hands. Sitting on the side of the bed to undo the laces in his trainers, he grumbled to her about his journey into the city, or how he was stuck with his writing. She too would be undressing, because she never quite wanted to be waiting for him in her pyjamas, or naked: how terrible, if she was eagerly undressed and he for some reason didn't want to make love to her. Sometimes, depending on how much time they had, they didn't undress right away, but huddled together in their clothes, talking and kissing; or she made him coffee in the kitchen, or got them drinks. She made Manhattans, which he said he'd never had before, although she couldn't believe it; he swore that every Manhattan he drank, for the rest of his life, would be dedicated to her. Although it was their joke that Cora had tried on their first day to put him off by taking him round her home improvements, nonetheless she some-times showed him the latest alterations in the house, and he tried to pretend to take an interest. If she made food, she felt as if she was playing at keeping house, and enjoyed having him watch her. Once, they were over-taken by sex in the kitchen, in the middle of cooking tagliatelle, which was spoiled; afterwards they had to shower, because the newly laid slate floor was still thick with dust, however many times Cora washed it. They were comically concerned together, brushing out his clothes, that he shouldn't be in trouble with his wife for getting his trousers filthy.

Paul reminded her sometimes, carefully, courteously, that he would never leave his little girls; once, when she sat on the side of the bed, and he was kissing her knees. She saw herself at that moment as a tiny figure at a great distance, like an illumination in a manuscript: a naked female with little white, forked, vegetable legs, emblem-atic of the vanity of earthly delights. Pushing her hands into his hair, bending over him, she felt the cup of his skull under her palms, as if she held his thoughts there.

– I know, I know, she said soothingly into his hair.

As if it was all right.

Sometimes the phone rang downstairs while they were in bed together. Cora never answered it, but they had to wait suspended, not moving or speaking, while it went on ringing, sometimes for a long time, because she didn't have any messaging service set up. Once, she forgot to turn her mobile off and it rang in her handbag, in the bedroom with them. Once, Terry the builder came in to get on with the kitchen on a Saturday morning, when Cora was not expecting him (he'd been going away with his wife for the weekend, but they'd cancelled because of the weather). She had to run down to negotiate with him, in her sweater pulled over her pyjamas, elaborately regretful, making up some un-convincing story about friends coming to lunch. She was sure that Terry guessed something; she shouldn't have pulled the bedroom door so carefully shut behind her. Their friendship afterwards, working together in the house, felt strained.

It was the rhythm of this love – love, she named it to herself in the mirror, not to him – that every hour she and Paul spent together existed in a perpetual present, which when they parted would recede in an instant without warning, becoming the irrecoverable past, sealed in itself, not to recur. She longed to have back his pursuit, his desperation for her in the café, when his hands had trembled, writing down her name.

– I read your book, she said to him shyly.

– No, really? Which one? Did you buy it? I could have given you a copy.

Even though it was August, it was cold in the room. He pulled the duvet up around her shoulders; she had begun to notice every sign of his attentiveness outside of the love-making itself, because she had flashes of fear that he was losing concentration, was over the first flush of his passion for her. Trying to give him her responses to the book, about the representation of nature in children's stories, Cora was nervous, not wanting to betray some gross error of understanding, even though while she was reading she had followed his argument confidently enough.

– I can't explain, she said, stumbling. – But you know what I mean.

Animated, Paul pointed out the gaps in how he'd covered his theme, saying he would do everything differently if he could write it again. Cora had hidden away her copy of the book in her bag; she had been afraid – naively, she saw now – that he would be embarrassed by her having sought it out, as if she was smothering him with her devotion. Paul suggested he should sign it. She hesitated before she handed it over, fearing the finality of whatever words he chose.

– What if your husband finds it?

– I'll tell him I queued up for you to sign it at a reading.

Paul laughed, and showed her what he'd written. 'For Cora, wild for to touch'.

– Some reading, he said. – Better keep it on a high shelf. Do you know where it's from? It's a quotation.

The Wyatt poem had been a favourite since she was a girl. – Of course I do.

– Of course you do. You're the English teacher.

In another life, she might have judged his dedication cloying, somehow preening. It fixed her. His power over her sometimes made him clumsy. The rest of the poem fast-forwarded past her awareness – didn't Anne Boleyn belong to Caesar, and it all end badly?

But I have had this, she thought. No matter how it ends.

She already knew that she was pregnant.

Paul went away for a week to Scotland, on holiday with his family (including the teenage daughter from his first marriage). While it rained in the south, they were lucky up there with the weather. Cora flew to Paris for a long weekend with Robert, but afterwards could hardly remember what they did, as if she only existed in connection with Paul. When he came back she held his hands in hers, burying her face in them: felt his calluses from rowing, seemed to taste salt, smell suncream, babies (his smallest girl was only three). She couldn't tell him yet about her pregnancy.

That evening she said that she would like to spend time with him somewhere else apart from in her half-made house. Sitting up against the pillows, drinking coffee, the sheet pulled across his chest, he calculated how he could plausibly get away for a whole night. He would tell his wife he was on a research trip for his new book, about zoos. As he got more used to Cora he relaxed, tolerant and benign, while she stiffened as if a wire was pulling tight around her. She talked less, she shrank from making mistakes that would disgust him intellectually. It was difficult to believe that when she first met Paul on the train she had half-disliked him, thought him pretentious, been ready with her contempt in return if he'd despised her; those judgements only seemed flaws now in her own understanding. She was aware how anyone else would see her abjection, if they looked at it from outside; how she handed him his dangerous power over her. In her life before she met Paul, she had not known about this capacity in herself. When she had heard or read about other women desperate or abased for love, she had passed over the descriptions with puzzlement or pitying distaste, along with a vague sense that she might have missed out on something.

At the end of August Paul drove her to west Somerset, and they stayed one night in a bed-and-breakfast place, a tall grey house on the main street in a little town on the Bristol Channel that had a marina and a paper mill. She was enthusiastic about the house precisely because it wasn't too pretty: it was clean, but the furniture and decor were utilitarian, relics from the 1950s, brown linoleum on the floors and up the spindly high stair-case. In the windows the glass was ancient and distorting. Their bedroom at the top, where the bed was made up with cellular blankets and a candlewick bedspread, overlooked a wet cobbled back yard and a high black wall sprouting ferns and buddleia. The weather was cold and it rained. When they went out she had to wait on the esplanade while Paul walked away from her, crouching over his phone in the wind, pulling his jacket up round his head, talking to his wife; the sailboats' rigging clanged and rattled. They ate fish and chips in a corner café, squalls of rain blowing against the windows, which steamed up on the inside. Cora hardly thought ahead, beyond the end of the night.

When they got back to their room the heating didn't seem to be on, though they fiddled with the knobs on the radiator.

– It's dismal as fuck, he apologised gloomily. – I'm sorry. I thought it was a nice little town when I came before. I expect the sun was shining or something unlikely.

– Don't worry, I love it.

She actually did love the bad weather that seemed to wrap them up together in the room; she had a moment's intense consciousness of the scene, as if it was revealed by a lightning flash, or in a painting. Paul stood at the dark window with his hands in his pockets, irritated, water sluicing down the glass, while she arranged her wet outer clothes along the cold radiator. In the strange surroundings it was as if they had passed through into a different country, might step out next day into the unknown. Cora's new state of pregnancy made her feel unknown to herself. She hadn't had any real morning sickness, but she had been sure she was pregnant even before she did the test: she felt a faint perpetual nausea, not unpleasant, and a floating sensation in her full tender breasts. Her secret hadn't had time yet to accumulate responsibilities or consequences: she couldn't tell anybody about it, only shielded it and tended to it, like a flame lit inside her.

When Paul turned from the window, she was afraid she would see in his expression that he regretted coming there with her, but to her relief he had collected himself finally after his phone call. She should have trusted him to know how to seize their opportunity. He was ambitious: not in his career like Robert, but for himself, his experiences. He wouldn't waste this night by spoiling it. In the veiled light from the beside lamp – chrome, with a little upright press-switch, parchment shade, ancient twisted flex – his tapered male silhouette melted her, wasting from the shoulders to its centre of gravity in the lean hips. She had not known what it was like to make love to a man whose body she worshipped; this had to do fatally with his arrogance, and some cold core of his freedom. Taking his hands out of his pockets, he admired her – she'd bought new underwear in Paris. His look on her skin was like a force, and in it she felt the ends and limits of herself. Their relations were asymmetrical. She was the completed thing he wanted, and had got – he had seen her whole that very first time on the train, her strong particular stamp of personality written for him to read, clear as a hieroglyph; whereas she was absorbed in his life as it streamed forward, lost in him, not able to know everything he was. She couldn't have imagined, in her old self, the pleasure to be had in such abandonment.

– You're so lovely, he reassured her.

Sex each time had its different flavour and character. In the pink cave under the candlewick spread (they were cold, they kept it wrapped around them) it was muddled for Cora, because of the funny room and the rain, with imaginings of austerity, as if their bodies here were thinner and sharper, their sensations acute and poignant. They were the sensational expurgated passages from a

264

black and white Fifties love-affair, in cheap boarding houses, on wrinkled sheets.

She woke in the night from a dream of her mother. It was something trivial – some anxious muddle of arrangements, an appointment to meet Rhian that Cora had missed, or was trying to keep, prevented by the usual stalling sequence of diversions, a bus straining to climb a high hill, students waiting for her in a classroom. Her mind ached with the effort to keep fixed on this goal of a meeting, which moved ahead of her, dissolving; there was not any grief in the dream, only panic and pointless indignation.

Waking and remembering was as terrible as tearing through some restraining membrane; she flooded with sorrow and came to herself bunched up against Paul's curved back, nose and mouth pressed up against the knobs of his vertebrae, his skin wet with her breathing, her knees crooked inside the bend of his. Excising carefully, she separated herself without waking him, pulled his shirt over her head and crept to the bathroom, which was not en suite, but across the top-floor landing, shared with another room. They had been confident this second room was empty, but now she saw a light under the door, and was ashamed they might have made the bed creak, or rocked it against the wall. The house was still cocooned in the hurrying noise of the rain.

The bathroom was crammed into what must have once been a boxroom under the slope of the roof; there was a slanting skylight, more lino, a shower with black mould

265

growing in its corners. Cora stepped squeamishly in her bare feet. Around the toilet pedestal was a pink mat that matched the bedspread; when she tried the cold tap, wanting to wash her face, all the piping in the house shuddered loudly in sympathy, and she turned it off quickly. In the middle of the night the old-fashioned austerity didn't seem quaint but hostile, the setting for a disaster. Doubled up on the loo, she sat hugging her knees, wanting to cry with pity for herself, but rigid with shame and dread. Her parents had adored her, she had been spoiled, their treasured princess, their little star. How hideous this now seemed, what dust and rotten falsity. The pain of missing them was so severe that she expected to see blood when she dabbed at herself with the toilet paper, but there wasn't anything, it was all in her mind.

The door handle rattled, someone was trying to get in: Paul? Surely he would have called her name. Then Cora heard some peremptory and disapproving noise, unmistakably male and close at hand. She kept very still, although it would have made more sense to flush the toilet, or to call out that she was almost finished. Whoever it was waited longer, then padded off across the landing, pulling his door shut: not quite banging it, but loud enough in the middle of the night to convey righteous grievance and reproach. No doubt it wasn't only the locked bathroom she was being reproached for, but also the bed springs earlier. Cora cowered in the bathroom, gambling like a child that, so long as she wasn't seen or heard, she might get away with her invisibility.

What if I was really ill? she justified herself. I'd have a right to stay in here. Anyway, there must be another bathroom the man could use, on the floor below.

Eventually whoever it was came out and tried the door again, rattling hard; then he hung about on the landing until Cora was forced to flush the toilet and open up. Luckily the landing light wasn't on, because she realised that Paul's shirt hardly covered her bottom. Seeing her, the stranger made something like the same subterranean noise of disgust as before – phlegmy and guttural. Their interaction at that hour and under the circumstances seemed stripped of all requirement for courtesy, or even mutual acknowledgement. Cora didn't look towards him or mumble any apology, only fled across to her room; in the light from his door open behind him she took in a tall white-haired man, very upright, with a big choleric face, jowly as a mask. He was wearing pyjamas and one of those striped towelling bathrobes that seemed of a piece with the period effects of the whole place, knotted with a cord around his high, hard stomach.

In the morning she asked Paul if they could go out for breakfast, and he agreed, thinking she was only afraid that the food might be awful. He paid, and they got out of the house without encountering any of their fellow guests. They had a happy day together. He had brought his car; she had never been driven by him before. She didn't know this part of the country well. After the rain the late-summer sunshine was chastened and tentative, and had the first frisson of autumn in it.

They walked on a single-track road so little used that dark moss grew down its middle, and their passing roused washed-pale frail butterflies like dust out of the high hedgerows, which Paul said were ancient field boundaries. He said the soil was red because the rock beneath was red sandstone. The beech hedges were a revelation to Cora. Paul explained how in winter these hedges didn't drop their leaves like the other trees, although they were deciduous; the dead leaves stayed in place until the next spring when the new ones grew, making the hedges an especially effective windbreak. The beech leaves were by now a heavy metallic green, almost bronze. At regular intervals a tree was left to grow whole above the height of the laid hedge, standing up eloquently in the slanting light, grey limbs thick and smooth in the spacious crown, casting its shadow on the dense wheat in the fields.

The following week in an explosion of drama it was all over.

Paul's wife – Elise – found out what had been going on. One morning when Cora was at work in London, in the middle of enrolments for the year's new courses, her mobile rang and a woman's voice asked, 'Who is this, please?'

Cora knew immediately what this meant, and turned the phone off without answering. She finished dealing with a student's query. That was it then. Her whole consciousness quaked, blacked out for one moment imperceptible on the surface – but it was also almost a relief, the onrush of this anticipated smash. Endowed with super-sensory intuition, she seemed to have learned everything about Elise from that momentary snatch of her voice – husky, flattening, contemptuous, capable. She was not fine-grained or clever, but she was powerful. She made fine-grained seem mucky, sickening. Cora believed she could even see from her voice what Elise looked like: stocky, attractive, pugnacious, with sandy fair hair; or had Paul let these details slip? On the way home from work Cora dropped her phone into a waste bin in the street and pretended afterwards that she'd lost it. Everything she did in those last days was worse than cowardly, it was craven and inchoate; she was ashamed to recognise herself. She ought to have had something to say to Elise, if only to concede everything. But instead she fled ahead of trouble.

She called Paul on her landline, fingers so clumsy that she misdialled twice. The story was that Elise had suspected something, found Cora's number on Paul's phone, confronted him. Cora never quite believed that this was really the whole thing: something in the way Paul told it sounded incomplete. There was something else, another story he was keeping from her, involving much, much more confession and concession and preference for Elise and the children on his part; but she would never be able to find out about that, because a door was squeezing shut on her, closing her out from everything in his life. Paul reassured Cora that Elise didn't know her name, or anything about her. This must mean she didn't care to know, because Paul had convinced her Cora didn't really count for much.

He had always warned her that this was what he would choose if he had to.

She didn't tell him about the baby. She held this back, thinking that the right moment might come for spilling out with it. They spent one dreadful final hour together at the Cardiff house, rather decorous. Cora had dreamed that they might make love for the last time, and that she would tell him then that she was pregnant, but knew this was out of the question as soon as Paul came in. He was distracted and embarrassed and after a while, sitting apart at the table in the kitchen, they ran out of things to say. Cora wished she had the strength to send him away; but she was weak, clinging on to her last minutes in his actual presence, however humiliating. All her desire in the world was used up in this one particular body, in his hunched posture at the table, in the frowning way he smoked two cigarettes and ground them out passionately into the saucer she gave him. Even his suffering was exceptional and illuminating, because it belonged to him.

Elise had said: one hour!

When it was time for him to go, Cora clung to his coat sleeve and cried into it, pleading with him for some reprieve. He bent over her head, stroking her hair.

– It's my fault, he said, – it's really all my fault. I didn't know that it would be this bad.

– You'll be relieved to be free of me, I'm sure you will.

– Is that what you think? I won't be free of you. That's the whole trouble. Not so easily.

He was truly unhappy, he pressed her to his heart. She knew he meant it, and it would have to do. If he'd wanted her, he could have asked for her, she would have broken up everything for him. But he didn't ask.

How could something that had filled your life up completely, to the brim, be withdrawn and leave no trace? Sometimes in the days that followed Cora felt as if the huge percussion of an explosion had left her deaf, sucking the noise out of the tranquil, ordinary-seeming days. If she died now, she thought, it would be exactly as if the whole thing had never existed. A body sank into a lake or a quicksand and the lake closed over again behind it, the broken ice healed.

She had not told anyone about him. Perhaps if Frankie hadn't been Robert's sister as well as her best friend she might have confided in her; in the circumstances this had been out of the question. There were no ordinary connections between her life and Paul's, there was no way his name or news of him was going to crop up in conversation among her friends. Only Paul knew what had happened – and Elise, his wife, in whatever travestied version she had it – but he was locked away from her irretrievably now, he might as well not exist in her present. It was true that to begin with she hallucinated meeting with him everywhere. Every step she took, dressing in the morning or teaching her classes, she got through in the delusion that she was performing for him to witness. The hardest thing was the jolting on-off alternation between the delusion of his witnessing presence and the knowledge of his real absence. With some last-ditch instinct for preserving her sanity, she continued her superstitious interdict against searching for his name on the Internet. She bought a notebook to write down what had happened, so that it was real outside her own mind; but when she sat down to begin, she realised she couldn't possibly find the words.

Anyway, a notebook would be too dangerous, it could have consequences: if she was killed, for example, and Robert found it. It seemed quite possible to her, during those first weeks, that she might be killed, or die, at any moment. Infantile, she thought she wanted to die, she wanted to be reunited with her parents, even in nothingness. What kept her afloat, unexpectedly, was the lack of any consequences from her crisis in her daily life. This might have been partly cowardice (she was ready to believe anything low or shameful about herself). She might have simply dreaded too much seeing Robert's face change if he found out about her, feeling his kindness drop to nothing in an instant. In her weakness she depended on his kindness, took advantage of it. She didn't allow herself to think any longer, as she had at the beginning when she was strong, that Robert might have some idea of what she'd done; if he'd ever had any idea, then he must have buried it. Burying was best. The friendly, decent surface of daily intercourse was best. Cora submitted to it, with the remote pale gratitude she could imagine someone feeling who lived with a debilitating illness. Though it was wicked to make comparisons between her suffering and any real illness.

Nothing had happened to her that weighed a feather in the world outside. It was nothing but the clamour and simulated agonies of selfishness.

The baby was the only vivid focus in her present. She clung to the idea of it as the key to another life, growing up out of this collapse; not believing in anything else, she felt this hope inside her body. Although it was the product of what she and Paul had done, it existed now beyond the end of that, and would exact love and responsibility from her on its own new terms, in the time ahead; she could already begin to feel this. If when it was born it looked like Paul, that wouldn't mean anything to anyone except her. There was no one else who could have any reason to recognise him in her child. Her child and Robert's, everyone would think. When it was born she would throw away the scrap of paper with Paul's telephone number, and all his books, including the book with the dedication, so that no clue was left to lead anyone back to him. She hoped it would be a boy, because Paul had only had daughters. She saw those little girls in her mind's eye often, small as if through the wrong end of a telescope, so that she couldn't make out their faces clearly: one was dark, one blonde.

Once in a spasm of longing she rang Paul's number, and got a recorded message saying it was unobtainable: he must have changed his phone, Elise must have made him change it. It seemed extraordinary now that Cora had never asked him for his home address, or his email; she supposed she would have been able to find these out, if she'd really wanted them. Paul did write her one letter, after the end of their affair, which he posted to the Cardiff house: the builder must have picked it up, it was propped waiting for her on the radiator in the hall when she arrived one weekend to show the estate agent round. She had half-expected there might be a letter, and had held off the expectation. Tearing it open with blind fumbling urgency, her heart striking like blows against the cage of her ribs, she felt her fate was in it. It was a wonderful letter. He said extraordinary things about her, in words that were not too smooth or coaxing or clever; he struggled to tell her truthfully how he felt. He said they all had been ill with flu, that family life had not been glamorous, that in his fever he had dreamed horrible dreams of her, in which her skin was hard and cold, or they met in a polluted ruined factory, or she mocked him in a foreign language he didn't recognise (was he dreaming now in Welsh, he asked?). He told her what he was reading, and that his writing was stuck and dead. Cora couldn't forgive him for that letter. Sobbing, she tore it into tiny pieces and then lit them with a match in the sink, washing the soggy cinders down the plughole. She never answered it. She had nowhere to send an answer.

The estate agent thought she would sell the Cardiff house easily, for a good price, but Cora decided that she wasn't ready to part with it, not yet. She didn't tell anyone she was pregnant, not even a doctor. Until one day when at about fifteen weeks (by her estimate) bleeding began while she was at work, and wouldn't stop; her colleagues called an ambulance, and kept the students out of the car park when the paramedics carried Cora out wrapped in a red blanket. She took in for the first time why it needed to be red.

– It's an encouraging sign, Robert said in the hospital when it was all over and she'd come round from her routine dilation and curettage. He sat heavily in his work suit on the plastic chair beside her bed, tie loosened, hands clasped between his knees, weighed down and made inept, inarticulate, by the degree of his upset and pity for her. – It shows something could happen.

III

Cora was weeding the books in the library. This meant she was going through the shelves, taking out any books more than seven years old, or any that had not been borrowed for a year or longer. When she had selected the books for withdrawal she had to scan them and make a note beside their entry on the computer; sometimes there was a flag beside the name of the book, warning that it was the last copy in any of the Cardiff libraries. Weeding was a job that waited for whenever there was nothing else more urgent to do. At first Cora had felt it was an outrage, she had argued indignantly with Annette and Brian that they mustn't get rid of Penelope Fitzgerald, or Colm Toibin. But she had got used to the idea. Everything had its moment in the sun, then must give way. Anyone really interested in the back catalogue of these writers could buy what they wanted online. Books withdrawn from the system were offered for sale at 10p on a shelf beside the checkout, and Cora bought some of them herself.

She had been ruthless when she brought her books from London, getting rid of more than half of them, but now her shelves were filling up again.

She always turned her phone off while she was at work, but today she was checking it every so often. She had made friends with a woman called Valerie at choir practice, and Valerie was trying to get them tickets for the Welsh National Opera's *Orfeo*. Valerie was active in the local Amnesty group and had tried to get Cora to come along to that too, assuring her they were a nice bunch of people. Cora thought she might join, but not yet. Sluggishly, her old conscientious discomfort had begun to prickle her, like something coming slowly awake after a long oblivion; she had been surviving as cautiously and unimaginatively as an animal in its burrow, husbanding her strength. Now, her mind sometimes ached to stretch and flex itself. Was working in the library enough, as the expression of her belonging in the world? There was always a gap between the urge to do something useful and the actuality of what was possible. She was wary of making some gesture of commitment, then having her faith in it collapse, so that she let people down. This distrust of herself, of her capacity to act, was a new element in her personality. Once, she hadn't waited to ask herself what she believed.

She saw Frankie had left an urgent message for Cora to call her back. Cora went outside to make the call in the little garden outside the library entrance. It wasn't raining, but the day was stuffy, dark under a woolly layer of cloud.

– Cora, he's disappeared, said Frankie as soon as she answered. – Is he with you?

– Who's disappeared?

There was a fraction of a second's register of Cora's insensibility, like a coin falling into a deep well: plink!

– Robert.

– Robert's disappeared? How do you mean?

– He isn't with you then?

– Of course not.

Frankie explained that Robert had had Sunday lunch with her and Drum, then apparently had been in work as usual on Monday. On Tuesday his PA – Elizabeth – had called Frankie to ask if she knew where he was. That morning he had been supposed to chair a meeting and hadn't turned up. He never missed anything, even if he was at death's door. Well, he never was at death's door. No one had seen or heard anything from him since; he wasn't responding to phone calls or emails. His office colleagues were cautiously and tactfully alarmed. Frankie had been round to the flat, she had let herself in (she had a key), but there was no sign of him. All his stuff seemed to be around; it looked as if the cleaner had come in as usual on Tuesday morning and nothing had been touched since. She was calling from there now.

Frankie's voice had the elated breathlessness of crisis, although she was trying not to give way to that, to keep up her humorous, sane perspective. Anxious about her brother, she must be tempted to blame Cora for something: only Cora had ever disrupted Robert's equanimity and imperviousness. She would also be squashing this impulse to blame anyone, because she was going to be a vicar and had to hold back from condemnation.

– And that was Tuesday?

It was now Thursday.

There was a horrible man, Frankie said, an Adviser or something, who wanted to borrow her phone in case Robert called her on it, so they could talk to him. And wanted to take his computer.

– A Special Adviser probably. A SPAD.

– I'm not letting him have it. It's Robert's business whether he wants to call anyone. But he came over pretty aggressively.

– Frank, would you like me to come up? I could be there in a couple of hours. Three hours. Perhaps I could help. I could wait there at the flat.

– I don't know why everyone's in such a flap. He could have just thought, you know: bugger this, decided he needed a break from it all. Well, I presume that's what's happened. What else could have happened? He's not the suicidal type. Or the breakdown type. He was fine on Sunday. At least I think he was fine. He doesn't make much noise. We're so noisy collectively, did we drown him out? Will you try ringing him? I know it's awkward.

– Of course I will. And I'll come, Cora said. – It'll be all right.

– It's bedlam here. I've got all the kids with me, it's half-term. I had to bring them on the Tube, Drum's got the car, I've given mine up because of the carbon footprint. It's only funny that Bobs hasn't called us. Wouldn't you have thought he'd call?

Cora told Annette she had to go, something had happened in London involving her husband.

– I expect we'll hold the fort without you, Annette said. – What husband? I thought you were divorced.

In an emergency Cora had natural authority, seeing straight away the best course of action without making an unnecessary drama of it, or using it for any display of herself. She ordered a taxi to the station, asked the driver to wait outside the house while she threw a few things in an overnight bag. She tried ringing Robert's mobile, but he didn't answer.

The train was delayed, and then they were diverted to Waterloo. There was an incident on the line – someone said a suicide – beyond Reading. Cora hadn't really been worried about Robert when Frankie phoned; her idea of him as the rational centre around which other people's chaos whirled wasn't easily dislodged. While they waited motionless in a siding, however, then had to transfer across the station platform into a new train, which trundled at walking pace in a detour past all the back gardens of Surrey, she began to experience the symptoms of panic: her heart raced, her thoughts circled round and round the same vacancy. Restlessly she stood up out of her seat, walking forwards along the train to a gap between compartments, deluding herself that she was getting somewhere, leaning to look out of the window, calling

Frankie with updates. The other passengers, with nothing else to look at, looked at her: tall, commanding, handsome, with straight thick brows, curving cheekbones, clear grey eyes, a concentrated urgency in her face. Men hoped she was a doctor or a lawyer. They tried to draw her in to their resentful outbursts against the train staff; someone joked tastelessly about bodies on the line.

Cora couldn't help thinking of Paul whenever she caught the train to London: although she was skilled now at shutting up the memories of him, as soon as they came, into their casket, turning the key. She imagined a casket like a part of some dangerous, obsolete game, like the gold and silver and lead caskets in *A Merchant of Venice*, with their folklorish trite messages about love. She had seen him once since they separated: not on the train, but driving down a road in Cardiff not far from her home. He hadn't seen her, he wouldn't have been looking for her; she knew that his friend lived nearby. That ordinary glimpse of Paul – sealed inside the completed fullness of his life on its parallel track apart from hers – had made her nauseous, helpless, desperate. She fantasised about meeting him on the train and simply walking past without acknowledging him; in the first year after they parted, it had seemed very possible that she would meet him in her travelling up and down from London. Now, taking in the hundreds of strangers who made that journey, day after day, she had understood that their meeting was improbable – which was a relief and also a flattening loss.

* * *

No one watched her paying off the taxi outside her old home, although she felt conspicuous returning: the street had its usual air of privileged absence, withdrawn and clean behind its railings, flights of worn stone steps, broad Regency front doors. Out of habit she checked for the beloved glimpse of park trees at the road's end: she had seen those trees thrash, but today they stood motionless under the muffling cloud. Their flat – Robert's flat – was on the first, best floor, with a balcony they had never used, because its publicity was too theatrical for the deep discretion of the street. Cora had some- times imagined the Prince and Charlotte sitting out on it in *The Golden Bowl,* watching Maggie bringing her baby from the park, although she knew their house didn't even begin to be grand enough for those charac- ters. She hadn't been back for months. It was odd to ring the bell: there was a door key somewhere in Cardiff, but she hadn't stopped to look for it. Frankie was at first suspicious over the intercom.

– Thank goodness it's you. That SPAD's threatening to come round, he wants to look at Robert's computer. I've said he can't, it's private.

The two women embraced, with more feeling than when they'd last parted in Cardiff: separating, both were faintly tearful, relieved; each had feared that the other might hold out against her.

– Frankie, don't think it's my fault, will you?

– Don't be an idiot. Bobs is a grown-up. He'd never forgive me if I blamed you. It's just awful not knowing whether there's anything to worry about or not.

Frankie was satisfied that Cora was stricken, which was all she needed to see. Walking round, Cora took in how the flat had altered since she had lived in it. Robert hadn't actually changed any of the furniture, but everything was in a subtly altered and less attractive arrangement, probably not moved deliberately, but only having drifted. He must never have shared her vision of how it all worked together – or he hadn't cared about it after she'd gone. She hadn't cared much either, in the months before she left. Cora had found the place before they were married, in the first strange flush of having money (not only Robert's salary, but money he'd inherited – not enough to buy the flat outright, but enough to make mortgage repayments possible); inside its old shell, it had been smart and bright and modern. Twelve years on, it looked used up and dated. Chairs, pulled away from around the table, or from the sociable huddles Cora had used to arrange them into, were piled up with newspapers and papers from work, which the cleaner hadn't touched. Cushions were ranked in straight lines along the sofa back, and everything ornamental on the white marble mantelpiece was pushed to one end for easy dusting: photographs, yellow feathers from the Adirondacks and striped stones from a beach in Angus, a Dresdenware flautist that had been Robert's mother's, a Bangladeshi silver teapot Cora had bought in a junk shop. A suit still in its bag from the dry cleaner's was hung on the open kitchen door. A laptop was open, but switched off, on the glass-topped dining table, where Johnny and Lulu were colouring. The toothbrush and

283

shaving gear weren't gone from Robert's bathroom. Magnus was asleep in the bedroom in his pushchair.

– I tried to ring him, but he didn't answer, Cora said. – I'm glad you're all here. It would seem very empty. Perhaps it seems this empty when he's here on his own.

– Don't let's get soppy, said Frankie. – I'm making soup.

– Soup?

– We'll need to eat. Children are just engines really, running on the fuel parents put in at one end. So I bought vegetables and butter and bread on my way here – at that little organic shop round the corner. He's such a lovely man, and the bread's good, but did you know everything in there costs at least three times as much as it does in the supermarket?

– This is that part of the world. Everybody has three times as much money.

– Ten times as much.

– Probably a hundred times as much, some of them.

– Some of them bathe in asses' milk. The shop probably sells it.

Johnny and Lulu were colouring fanatically, and only glanced up for a moment to recognise Cora. Frankie said she'd set them a competition: to stop them running round the rooms, in case there was a clause against it in Robert's lease. She would have to choose between their pictures eventually, which would be tactically difficult. Lulu, as she chose felt pens, sucked one lock of chestnut hair in absorbed meditation; Johnny, filled with the burden of being better because he was older, stood nervously to work, shifting from foot to foot, grimacing grotesquely at what he'd made.

They touched the keys of the laptop warily.

– Should we turn it on? Cora said. – There might be clues, but we wouldn't know what to look for.

– Anyway, it's none of our business. And we don't have his password.

– We have to trust him.

– He might come in at any moment. He might ring.

Frankie said she'd phoned their sister Oona and was keeping her updated, but they'd decided not to tell their brother in Toronto anything yet. Soup simmered in a pan on the spotless hob. When Cora looked for it, the liquidiser was still in its place in the cupboard where she had left it. The two women sat down in the kitchen at the breakfast bar – the estate agent's awful name had stuck; Cora had never known what else to call it. All the kitchen surfaces were solid oak. Frankie poured them wine out of a bottle from Robert's rack; between them her phone loomed portentously silent. She said she had wanted to call in the police yesterday, Wednesday, but Robert's office said they had already spoken to a Met senior and didn't think the matter needed escalating further. So she hadn't known what else to do. She'd rung everybody she could think of.

– They really, really don't want the press to know. I've picked up that much. I suppose it's embarrassing, losing a senior civil servant.

– You don't think that he could have gone to Bar? Cora said.

– Bar? God, no. To be honest, the idea of her never crossed my mind. Why ever would you imagine ... ?

– Probably nothing. Only that we mentioned her the last time we met.

– Bar was fearsome. Not the sort of person you're involved with twice. Anyway, surely she's married to somebody else by now?

– That's what he thought, Cora said. – If he's just taken off by himself on an impulse, then I'm glad.

– Me too.

– Who couldn't want him to get out – as a human being – from under all this? It's as if he didn't belong to himself.

– Though we have to remember that mostly he likes it. It suits him.

The Special Adviser when he turned up was improbably good-looking, a youth from a Caravaggio painting, long-faced, long-bodied, dead-pale, black hair curling on his collar, thumb-print smudges under fatigued eyes, hollow belly under shirt half-untucked from his jeans, double-jointed fingers. He was carelessly charming, bestowing the favour of himself, wishing he was at a more interesting party. Cora felt with a shock that she was growing old, and would be shut out from beauty. He told them, when they insisted, that his name was Damon.

– Shepherd boy, Frankie said.

Damon agreed without interest. Briskly his observation roved the flat behind them. – Any news?

– I'm Robert's wife, Cora explained.

He took her in. – D'you have any idea where the auld fella's got to?

For a moment she thought he was really Irish, then realised he was putting on an accent. Damon gave off impatient contempt for the nuisance this middle-aged senior was making of himself. This is how it is when someone falls from power, Cora thought, though it was too soon to know if Robert had fallen anywhere. There's a shudder when they hit the ground, then everyone steps over them, humiliating what they were, resentful of their own past subservience.

Frankie said they hadn't heard anything. – We're starting to panic. What's going on? Is it to do with the inquiry about the fire?

– What do you know about that?

– Nothing.

– Is he going to make a scene or something? It doesn't look good for him: he should have stayed to take the flak.

– What flak? What scene?

But he wouldn't tell them. Magnus cried in his pushchair and Frankie brought him into the kitchen to feed him; uneasily Damon ignored her bringing out her breast, which in the same room as him seemed voluminous. Frankie altogether – the curvaceous untidy bulk of her – seemed made on a different scale to Damon's. He asked Cora if she could think of anywhere Robert might have gone, and she said she couldn't; he asked if she'd tried calling him and she said she had, but he wouldn't pick up. She was aware how she stood around

287

awkwardly in Robert's rooms, not wanting to pretend she belonged to them; the SPAD probably knew all about the break-up of her marriage. Frankie was much more at home in the flat. Her brood brought into it the noisy solidity it had needed. When Cora lived there with Robert they had both worked late, they had often hurried out again in the evenings – the place had worn thin and dissolved in their absence. Lulu and Johnny ran into the kitchen with their pictures; Damon graciously adjudicated, knowing how nice it made him look, preferring Lulu's.

– Take it like a man, hey . . . He ruffled Johnny's red hair. Frankie privately thanked God Lulu wasn't sixteen. Lulu draped herself in an attitude anyway against Damon, adoring him.

– Mind if I look around?

– We do rather.

– You can't have the laptop, Cora said.

– I can, he said regretfully. – I'm afraid it's one of ours.

Frankie's phone was beside her on the table where she sat, pulling her blouse across to hide the baby's working head; every so often Magnus twisted round to stare at the interesting intruder, tugging away from the nipple, which sprayed a fine thread of milk after him. When the phone bleeped, she glanced quickly at it, but said it was only Drum calling to see where they were. Damon packed up the laptop into its case and carried it off with him, after a cursory look around the rooms, which Cora begrudged him, following him everywhere.

He eyed the second computer in the study, but couldn't have carried it, even if she'd let him have it. – It really isn't a big deal, he said, not reassuring but diminishing the women. – We aren't really that bothered.

– It was Robert, Frankie said excitedly as soon as he was gone. – The text was from Robert.

– What does he say?

– He says he's all right, that's all. But at least we know he hasn't been kidnapped or knocked down or lost his memory or anything. Text him now on your phone, ask him where he is.

After Cora had texted, they waited for more communication, but none came. They were subdued, as well as relieved, by the assurance that Robert was all right, wherever he was; their crisis had subsided. They ate Frankie's soup with the expensive bread from the organic shop. Cora found coffee, and boiled the kettle. Apart from the coffee, and the milk and butter Frankie had bought, there wasn't much else in Robert's fridge: a tube of tomato purée and a square of Cheddar drying out, ancient jars of mustard and pickle that dated surely from when it was her kitchen. Frankie said she would take the children home in a taxi after supper, there didn't seem much point in staying on any longer; Cora said she would sleep over in the flat, just in case.

– Just in case what? Come back with us. I don't like the idea of you all on your own in here. Although you'll probably get a better night's sleep.

Once she had imagined it, Cora wanted to have time

to herself in the flat: alone, she might be able to find any signs Robert had left behind him. She could sleep in the spare room. Frankie was spooning soup into Magnus in his pushchair; Cora, on her hands and knees under the table, was sweeping breadcrumbs into the dustpan.

– Were you praying that Robert was all right? she asked Frankie, sitting back on her haunches with the brush in her hand. – I mean really praying to God, not just the usual phrase that people use.

Opening her mouth wide and making baby noises to encourage Magnus, Frankie was wary. – Do you hate that idea?

– No, I don't hate it. I'd hate it if I did it, because it would be fake. But I suppose if you believe in it, praying is what you're bound to do.

– Not in the sense of asking for favours, like asking for a bike for Christmas. Otherwise the believers would win all the football matches. Believing would just be a kind of cheating.

These comic-book illustrations – bikes and football matches – made Cora think Frankie sounded like a vicar already, evasive and jollying.

– So you're not allowed to ask God to bring Robert back?

– You can ask God to keep him safe. That's not the same. You know he might not.

– Then what's the point? Johnny demanded reasonably.

– Believing doesn't make everything all right, you know. It just fills out the way things are, it expresses our longings.

290

Frankie was thinking there was something newly intransigent in Cora's expression as she knelt there with the dustpan, tickling Magnus's feet with the brush so that he lifted them delightedly, distracting him from his soup. She was losing her old resplendence – she was restless and too thin. She was wearing more make-up than she ever used to. Cora said that she just didn't feel what Frankie felt. She had used to feel it sometimes, but now when she reached for it, nothing was there. Although she said this as though she regretted it, Frankie could also hear a kind of triumph: who could want false consolations, once you had seen past them?

Then unexpectedly Cora put her head in Frankie's lap for an awkward, odd moment. The gesture was enigmatic – afterwards, Frankie blamed herself terribly that she hadn't responded to it, and she searched in herself for hidden reasons. She had been taken by surprise; but she should have stroked Cora's hair at least. Of course she had been feeding Magnus, holding the bowl in one hand and the spoon in the other. But she could easily have put the bowl down. She had only laughed, disconcerted. It didn't matter how much you thought about charity, and thought you were prepared for the way the requirement for charity would present itself, you missed the occasion when it actually flowered in your own lap, you even recoiled from it. In the next moment, as though it had only been a joke, Cora picked herself up and got on with the sweeping.

* * *

She went downstairs to see them off in their taxi. As soon as it turned a corner and she was left alone in the street, Cora regretted staying, and was reluctant to go back inside. The flat was full with Robert's absence. She took off her shoes so as not to make any sound, walking from room to room as if she might surprise something; for a long time she didn't switch on the lights. From the window of the bedroom they used to sleep in, looking along the gardens to the park, she watched a last brooding storm-light, mauve and silver, drain from behind a magisterial horse chestnut. The night outside completed, she turned back to the interior darkness, asking herself what she was doing here. She had no business trying to find where Robert was, now that they knew he wasn't hurt, or dead. He and she were no longer connected. It was wholly understandable that he had called Frankie, but hadn't wanted to respond to the text that Cora sent. Reluctantly she went round putting on the lamps, hands remembering where to find each switch as easily as if she still lived here. The place flared into visibility. She tidied the mantelpiece, put back the chairs. In the last months of her living here, disenchanted, these remnants of an elegant older London hadn't seemed gentle or nostalgic to her, more like the command centre of an ageing imperium, sclerotic and corrupt. Yet Robert wasn't corrupt.

She turned on the computer in his study and googled his name, but got only the routine link to the department. Letters, opened and unopened, lay around everywhere, but there was nothing personal or even interesting that she could see, only bills and bank statements and junk mail. There were no messages on the answerphone except a couple from Elizabeth, and one from Frankie. Slipping her hands inside Robert's jacket pockets in the wardrobe, she didn't even know what she was looking for; finding nothing, she opened drawers and went through them. He must have been taking his clothes to a laundry, the shirts were beautifully ironed. She couldn't tell whether anything was missing. At the bottom of one drawer, underneath his socks, was the little black-bordered packet of his dead father's rings, and a supermarket bag with her letters inside – the ones she had written from Leeds so many years ago, out of such childish certainty. Even the sight of her own handwriting on the envelopes repelled her, and she shoved them back in their bag and out of sight. She would have liked to throw them away or shred them, but they didn't seem hers to dispose of, she hardly felt connected to the girl who wrote them.

It had occurred to her naturally to wonder whether Robert could be reacting because he'd found out somehow about Paul; but the idea shamed her as soon as it presented itself. Robert wouldn't be overthrown by sex, any more than he cried in restaurants. Anyway, when she thought about it now, she believed that Robert had always known: not all the details, but that there had been something. He might even have worked it out, about the miscarriage. It was part of her character, she thought, grinding upon herself in condemnation, to think of whatever had happened to Robert now as if it must have to do with her. Of course it didn't. She shouldn't even be here, inside his privacy, poking around in it.

Her phone rang and she answered eagerly, but it was only Frankie, checking she was OK. – You could still come over.

– No, I'm really fine here, I'm thinking.

– That's what worries me.

– Constructively. But I haven't found anything.

Cora said she thought she'd go back to Cardiff in the morning, if nothing had happened, and Frankie agreed that now they knew he was all right, there was no point in Cora hanging round. As she talked to Frankie, standing at the dining table, Cora was flicking through Robert's bulging ancient leather address book, which was losing its pages and so fragile it wasn't surprising he hadn't taken it with him wherever he'd gone. If he'd wanted addresses from it he'd have copied them out – he used to do that. Idly she turned the pages over and found Bar: Barbara. An original Norfolk address had been crossed out, who knew when, replaced with one in Tiverton, Devon. Cora said goodbye to Frankie and put Bar's address and number into her own phone, hardly knowing why she did it. Then she poured herself some of Robert's whisky and curled up in his chair to watch the news, smelling his hair on the upholstery.

An item on the report on the removal-centre fire came low down the programme running order; someone from the Refugee Council was asked to comment. Was there any embarrassment for the government in the contents of the report? There ought to be, the woman said, if people read between the lines of the report, if they went inside these places, to see for themselves how men and women had to live, in the midst of plenty in a rich country, deprived of their hope. There ought to be embarrassment for all of us. She spoke about the Iranian who died, and they showed a blurry black and white photograph of someone surely too young: handsome, bearded, the photograph flattening black hair and white flesh into stark contrast, making the eyes black smudges. Cora had remembered that the man was middle-aged; according to Robert, in the last years he had drunk too much and suffered from ill health, he had let himself go. Which could have happened anywhere. Everywhere people grew old, if they didn't die.

Checking to see if there were sheets on the bed in the spare room, Cora saw the same photograph, reproduced on the back cover of a paperback pressed open on the bedside table. The bed was made up; under the cover roughly pulled across, the sheets were rumpled and the pillow dented. Glancing in this room earlier, in her search around the flat, she hadn't taken in that it had been used; it was always the space least stamped with their occupation, carved off the end of the sitting room running across the front of the house, furnished merely for use when they had guests, neutral as a nice hotel. Robert must have been sleeping in here, and he had been reading the Iranian's collection of stories. He could have found the book on AbeBooks, where Cora hadn't thought of looking for it; for the first time she got hold of the writer's name properly, seeing it spelled out. No wonder he had looked too young in his picture on television; weren't these stories published in the Eighties? Picking the book up, she sank down onto the side of the bed, starting in on the page where Robert had left off. Beginning in the middle of the story, it was impossible to pick up what was at stake, except that it wasn't what Cora had expected: not passionate protests over life under tyranny (which tyranny anyway? she had for a moment to mentally run over dates), but a man who seemed to be quarrelling with his wife, about her mother. The writing was on an intimate scale: deadpan and absurd, comic. It was rather dry, in a sparse terse style, without atmospherics, or much description of people or places. Cora was relieved; she had expected the stories to accuse her of her privilege, living in the indifferent west. After reading a couple of pages she put the book down again for later, when she went to bed.

Could she sleep in Robert's sheets, or should she change them? She put her head down experimentally, from her sitting position, on the pillow he had used. From her new position she could see through the window out to where the branches of a lime tree agitated, seemingly without sound, against a street lamp diffusing its cold light mistily. Robert might have watched this; like her, he had preferred to sleep with curtains and blinds not drawn, windows open. It would be comforting to sleep inside his shape, in the untidy bed, and he need never know she'd done it. He must have taken refuge in this room, from their old lives crowding the rest of the flat; he had not wanted to sleep in their marriage bed. Cora understood all that. Her phone bleeped, and she started up to answer it: but it was only a text from her friend Valerie, saying she had got them tickets for *Orfeo*.

Cora hadn't ever met Bar. When first she had fixated on Robert all those years ago, she had interrogated Frankie about her brother and found out that there was a girlfriend, off and on, but that she was not – in his siblings' opinion – satisfactory. Frankie said this before she ever knew Cora wanted him. Bar was a bit of a family joke, she had explained: the daughter of friends of their parents, very county. She rode in point-to-point, drank with the men though she couldn't stand feminists, and sometimes wore a flat cap like a jockey. When they were children, Robert and Bar had apparently always been paired up together, like head boy and head girl, because they were strong and sane and knew how machinery worked.

– I'm afraid of him settling with Bar eventually, Frankie had said, – out of sheer kindness.

Robert at Frankie's graduation had been patiently bored, and at first Cora had watched him because he was unexpected, with his clumsy bear-shamble and courteous, impenetrable reserve. Frankie and her sister Oona were a noisy, clever show, by contrast. Robert was remote, yet a light flared from inside a dark cave when something amused him. He wouldn't even have seen that Cora noticed him: his nature wasn't put on for anyone to watch. When he took the two girls out to dinner after graduation with a few of their friends, and paid for it all, he was the gravitational centre of their shrilling and planning and tearful parting, without saying much himself, except that he had talked at some point to Cora about his own degree in anthropology, and how he couldn't think of a better preparation for politics.

Cora asked what Bar looked like, and Frankie tried to explain how she wasn't pretty, but sexy nonetheless.
– You can see why people like her.
– The flat cap.
– Horsey. No, not horsey, that's cheap. Staggy. Stag at bay: bony head, and rolling eyes, backing off if you get too near her, treading sideways. Not that I've ever seen a stag at bay, except in paintings. She looks like one of those paintings.

Cora had written to Robert the day after she met him at graduation, asking if she could visit him in Whitehall, pretending she was interested in the Civil Service. He had written back helpfully, offering to take her out for lunch. Later, she had seen photographs of Bar, though not many: Robert wasn't the photograph type. He hadn't bothered to get rid of Bar's photos either, only put them away out of decency in the drawers of his desk once he had broken with her: including an old studio portrait of her in a frame, which she must have given him. Cora wasn't exactly jealous of these pictures, but she had searched for them and studied them when Robert wasn't around, to work out what their relationship had been. If she interrogated Robert about it, he wouldn't give her anything to go on ('she was an old friend of the family').

Bar in the photographs was blurry, blonde, lean-jawed, urgent: on a yacht, on a horse, on Robert's arm in an improbably glittering ball gown, slit to the thigh, in which she was somehow more sporting than tarty. If Frankie hadn't suggested it, Cora would never have thought of a stag, but it was true Bar was nervy and leggy, and with a slight cast in one eye, not unattractive. Only in the portrait – done when she was very young – was she revealed as her mythic self, in ardently dreamy profile, gazing into the black of the studio background. Cora had felt about this picture as poignantly as if Bar had been dead.

She didn't sleep well in the spare bed, although the mattress was expensive, better than the one in Cardiff. Her dreams were shallow, and she woke up several times to lights crawling across the ceiling as cars passed in the street. It was strange then to realise where she was, and why she was here. In the dark, Robert's having gone missing seemed less explicable, more ominous; horrible possibilities unravelled in her thoughts until eventually they drifted into dreams again. She was relieved when it was morning and she could get up. After her shower, she poured the milk down the sink and tidied away any signs of her occupation of the flat, dropping rubbish in a bin outside. Then she bought breakfast in a steamy café in Paddington, ringing Annette to tell her she would be back at work on Monday morning.

She had no idea in her head except getting the next train back to Cardiff. Obediently she waited under the oracle of the departure boards, showed her ticket and found her seat when the time came. Rain blew against the train window, and Cora couldn't concentrate on the *Guardian* she had bought. She had the book of Iranian stories with her too: she had put them in her bag at the last minute, thinking she didn't want Damon to find them if he came back. But she couldn't read those either, she couldn't read anything. Travelling away from London on a Friday always had a gravitational inevitability, like machinery winding down into torpor for the weekend: every nerve in her seemed set against this. She imagined the book, with its significance beyond itself, smouldering in the dark, jumbled in among her pyjamas and sponge bag and yesterday's underwear. Then she stood up abruptly when the train pulled into Bristol Parkway, pulling her bag and umbrella from the overhead rack, hurrying off, asking at Information when there was a train to Tiverton.

It matched her mood that Parkway was hardly a real place at all, hardly a building: bolted together out of steel at some point on a map, outside the city. Time wore away in the perfunctory waiting room, or stalking up and down the platform. For some reason she had fixated on the idea that Robert might be wherever Bar was; though it wasn't any business of hers any longer, she told herself, whether he was or not. By the time she arrived in Tiverton it was afternoon and grey, though not actually raining. The station was outside the town. She thought about telephoning Bar to warn her she was coming, then changed her mind. A taxi driver looked at the address and explained that this wasn't in Tiverton at all, but half an hour's ride away; Cora said she didn't care how much it cost, and took out more money from the cash point. En route she involved herself, with genuine sympathy, in the taxi driver's feud with his son-in-law, the tussle over the grandchildren, their wronged mother, the son-in-law's jealousy, indefensible after his own transgression. The taxi burrowed into a countryside thickly green, intricately settled, mostly wealthy. Big fields swept up to woods crowning round, wide hills. They had to stop on several occasions to consult a map, then to ask at a pub.

At the moment of paying and parting, pulled up on the gravel outside the house that was supposed to be Bar's – a shabby early-Victorian box, dark under trees, distinctive in just how blank it was, with half its shutters closed, a muddy concrete forecourt piled with junk, an old bed frame, bikes, a rusting harrow – they were suddenly too intimate, and couldn't look one another in the eye. Cora muddled her percentages, tipping what she thought was generously much, realising too late it was too little. In her flurry, she forgot to ask the driver to wait for her, in case there was no one at home. As the noise of the retreating car subsided, her mood sank and she felt herself absurd. The house was obviously empty. She had imagined finding a thriving stables, or a farm. Even if it wasn't empty, she had no business here. She had penetrated to the heart of nothing. Robert and Bar had been out of touch for years, why had she ever thought he would have her up-to-date address?

Anyway, now that she had come, she might as well try the door: broad, black paint flaking, at the top of a couple of stone steps set with an iron boot scraper muddy with scrapings, flanked by damp pillars. A bell pull yanked on dead air, so she used the knocker. There was an old Vauxhall estate, she noticed then while she waited, parked beside an overgrown yew hedge, stained, spattered with needles and berries, but not derelict, though it was hardly the gleaming four-by-four she had prepared for. Just as she gave up – and prepared to face the idiotic consequences of her impulse, coming here – footsteps sounded beyond the door, and then it swung open. Behind the woman who peered out, hostile, a rectangle of daylight from the doorway was reflected in a gilt-framed mirror at the back of a dim hallway. A weakly lit energy-saving bulb dangled at the end of its flex, unshaded. An old dog plodded out of the dimness, dutifully roused from sleep.

– Barbara?

– Yes.

– It's Cora. Robert's wife. I'm so sorry. I know this is awful, turning up here without warning. Can I talk to you?

She couldn't tell how Bar reacted to her announcing herself. Cora would not have recognised Bar if she hadn't been braced to see her. She looked nothing like her old photographs: she had bulked out, which made her seem shorter, and her long hair, turning grey, had thickened and coarsened. Incongruously girlishly, it was pulled back from her face at the temples and tied on top of her head in a floppy ribbon, like Alice in Wonderland. Only the long nose and disdainful slight squint were traces of the old sporty urgency: around them her face had sagged into ambiguously expressive folds. Swags of flesh under her eyes were thunder-coloured – she looked older than fifty. She was wearing a filthy linen smock over jeans, and held up a piece of toast and marmalade out of the dog's way. Cora had not calculated for her turning out eccentric: her hope wilted, and she wondered if she had energy for any struggle with Bar. She had imagined deflecting a will resilient and bright and impervious.

Bar persisted, planted stubbornly in the doorway. – I haven't even started work yet. You know, I guard my work time very fiercely.

– I should have called from the station. I'm sorry, this was a stupid idea. It's all my fault. And now I've let my taxi go. I'm a complete idiot. If you give me the number for a local firm, I'll call another cab.

She thought that if she could get inside the house she'd know whether Robert was around. Bar sighed theatrically, frowning, taking a bite of toast. – Now you're here, you might as well see the stuff, I suppose. D'you want coffee? I just made a pot. I like it strong, I warn you.

What stuff? Cora wondered.

Following through the house after Bar and the dog – several rooms, then a passage, then a cold kitchen – Cora could only take in that its neglect and chaos were gargan-tuan, and that it was furnished with wonders to match:

a carved sideboard vast as a ship, a glass case of stuffed hummingbirds, a jukebox ('my husband's, it works'), baronial fireplace, stone angel, rotten Union Jack hanging in rags from a ceiling. There were bikes in better condition than the ones outside, a big telly, a PlayStation, child-drawings stuck up with Blu-tack. Walls and shelves were crammed with art, night-dark Victorian oils (cows in a river? horses?) alongside expressionism, collages, a ceramic torso in fetish gear. Cora's own displays of art at home appeared to her at once as what they were, primly bourgeois. Everywhere smelled of dog. On the kitchen table there was an open bottle of brandy alongside a packet of sliced bread and a full cafetière.

– Not as bad as it looks, Barbara said. – Just a swig in my coffee, to get me started. Want some? I ought to work normal hours, but in the day I just stall miserably, I only get going when everybody else is in bed. Afternoons in the studio I tinker around, tidy up, decide whether to scrape off everything I've done the night before. Until my son gets home.

She was cranky and rather barking and abrupt, but her performance of her character was unapologetic as if it was often required of her to produce it, even exaggerate it. Cora said yes to the brandy. Barbara's hands were bleached pink, thick-fingered, with naked nails. The coffee was thick and bitter, Cora spooned sugar into it. – You've got a son? That's nice. How old is he? Do you have any other children?

– Only Noggin – who's Noah really. He's nine. Ten, ten of course. Christ, if you make those sort of mistakes at the school gate, they alert social services. That's why I usually send my husband to pick him up.

– So you're a painter, then.

Puzzling, Barbara peered at her more closely, finishing her toast. – If you're not sure, what are you doing here?

– I'm Robert's wife. I'm looking for him.

– How disappointing. I thought you were going to buy a picture. My agent had mentioned she was sending someone, I assumed you were them. Robert who? You're not a *wronged* wife, are you? She gave a shout of laughter. – I haven't had one of those come calling for a long time. I warn you, Gummo bites, if anything turns nasty. We've had a whole succession of dogs, named after the Marx Brothers. The name's got nothing to do with her missing any teeth.

– I'm not wronged, Cora said.

She explained which Robert she meant.

– God almighty: that Robert! But I haven't seen him in years. So you're *Cora*! But didn't you bugger off? Someone told me you had.

– We're separated, Cora said. The word seemed carping and finicky, as she used it. – But because he's gone missing, I've got involved in trying to find him. I don't know why I thought he might be here.

– Nor do I. What do you mean, 'missing'?

Cora explained. A copy of the *Telegraph* was still in its polythene packet on the breakfast table. Barbara tore it open while Cora was talking, laid it flat while she spread another piece of cold toast, turned through the pages noisily.

– Oh look, here it is, she said. – Poor old Bingo.

– Bingo?

– Robert, Bobby, Bobby Bingo. There's even a picture of him. Calls for his resignation. 'Lax regime,' it says. What nonsense. It's a miracle these places don't go up in flames more often, if they're so full of terrorists. Nothing about him having done a runner.

There was also the usual picture of the dead man. Robert in his photograph was on his way into the inquiry, so it must have been taken within the last few weeks. Cora searched the picture for any signs of distress; but he was remote from her, competent, locked up inside his public role, only glancing accidentally and obliquely towards the camera. Smiling, he was passing some remark to a colleague – it made him look blithely insensible to the seriousness of the case.

– He's kept more hair than some of my old boyfriends, Barbara said. – I used to think he'd get awfully stuffy, if he stayed on in the Service too long. Has he got stuffy? Is that why you're separated?

– No, said Cora stiffly, – nothing like that. Robert's got a very independent mind. I can't imagine why he's disappeared. It's not like him: even if this inquiry's blown things out of all proportion. He takes everything in his stride. What would he be afraid of? He would face things out.

– Anyway, he isn't here.

– I made a stupid mistake.

Bar suggested that Cora might as well see her pictures, now she'd come. Perhaps she hoped she could still make a sale. She was completely stony broke, she said – they

306

were in danger of having the house repossessed. Her husband was a landscape artist, away at present working on a commission on Fair Isle, building a causeway. Photographs of a row of stakes in shallow water, a path of white stones winding round a hill, must be his work. Bar's studio was in a long attic conversion, cleaner and brighter than the rest of the house. Cora was ready to dislike the pictures, but they weren't what she had expected, less forthright, more fantastic: skirts and petticoats of real cloth were dipped in pinkish-yellow plaster and then embedded in a dark paint surface where they dried to caked stiffness. Touches of over-painting added what might have been embroidery, or rusty bloodstains. How surprising that this brusque, barking woman was making art about femininity, which Cora thought of as her prerogative. Bar seemed to forget Cora had only come to the house to look for Robert, and talked about processes as if she must be fascinated.

Cora said she hadn't known Bar was an artist, Robert had never mentioned it.

– For years I mucked around, not doing anything seriously. Then, would you believe, the same month I was signed by Hyman's, I discovered I was up the duff. Hell! Talk about a late developer.

Cora was suffering, she was crushed. This was the world Robert really belonged to; where they all had nicknames for one another – Bingo and Bobs and Bar. Everything they did came to have importance somehow, even if they started out in life caring only for horses and hunt balls. Bar was vague about prices, but found a list from an old exhibition, where they were way out of Cora's reach. If Bar asked her what she did, she thought she wouldn't mention the library, she would say that she taught literature.

With a yelp Barbara remembered Noggin.

– Do I smell of brandy? They think I'm the mother from hell. Also, that I'm old enough to be his grandmother. They've probably already got their eye on a suitable foster family.

She offered to take Cora to the station, if she didn't mind going via the school, which was in the next village. Cora was grateful, wanting only to escape. Gummo curled up behind the front passenger seat, diffusing a bad smell like old cooked vegetables into the close quarters of the car. Bar drove fast, braking violently in the single-lane roads when she met anything coming the other way, cursing and reversing expertly. Cora had to open her window. Then after all they were early, and had to sit waiting outside the school in a queue of parked cars, because Bar couldn't face the playground.

– It's a ghastly microcosm, isn't it?

Cora said she wouldn't know, she didn't have children.

– Well out of it. Other parents look to see if you're using the wrong washing powder, or giving your children laudanum to make them sleep. If only I could get my hands on some. Nog's out of control because his dad's not here. He rampages. I'm lucky if he's in bed before midnight. And I can't get started on my work till he's out of the way.

The school was Victorian, with twin doorways for

Boys and Girls, behind a venerable church; those were the days, Bar said. Then she sat slumped behind the steering wheel with her eyes closed, suggesting the performance of her personality was exhausting. Opening them, she talked about Robert as if they'd never left the subject.

– His cutting out like this isn't so untypical, actually. From what I remember. He's rather an Olympian, you know. Well, I expect you know. High-handed. Like when after he left school he was so absolutely set on going into the army – which I thought lunacy – then something or other happened in the early stages of training to make him change his mind, and he just walked away.

Stonily Cora stared forward through the windscreen, jealous of Bar's claim to prior knowledge of Robert. She hadn't known any story about him wanting to be in the army.

– Literally walked away. Set out on the road, and came home. Well, I expect he caught a bus or something. But straight home. Except they didn't really have a home, of course, after their parents smashed. So to my parents' house in Devon actually, of which he used to be very fond. He was in all kinds of trouble for absconding; people had to run around after him, pulling strings so that he got away with it. I don't remember the details. When he's finished with something, he just drops it, tramples it on his way to the next thing. I should know. Bingo was my dearest, bestest friend when we were kids. It's a shame. We should never have got in the sack together. Fucks everything up, always. Avoid the sack. Too late of course for you. But good advice. And not much of a lover anyway. You won't mind me saying that, as you're separated.

Noggin when he appeared, borne on a tide of children, was small and pale, with swags of shadow under his eyes to match his mother's. Shoving a couple of drawings indifferently at her ('Nog, these are utterly splendid'), he slung his bag across the back seat and announced like a gloomy little prince that he would get car-sick if he wasn't in the front. Cora didn't offer to change places. It was difficult to imagine him rampaging.

– Gummo stinks the place out, he complained.

Barbara dropped Cora off at the station.

– Did you think of looking for him at our old place near Ilfracombe? she suggested at the last minute, leaning out of the car window. – As I said, he used to be fond of it. They stayed there, even before their parents died. My brother and I still keep it up – can't afford it, but you know, it's our childhood. Bing had lots of happy holidays there.

– Where is that?

Bar explained to her how to find it, and then Cora remembered having spent a few days in the house once, when she and Robert were first together. – I hadn't realised it belonged to you.

– It's just like him not to tell you.

But Cora decided not to go to Ilfracombe. If Robert was there, it must mean he didn't want her to find him.

* * *

On the train, when Cora opened the *Guardian* supplement, she found a piece by Paul: a double spread about his childhood reading. Trapped in her window seat – a woman beside her tapped her keyboard inexorably – Cora gasped for a moment for air, crumpling the pages down in her lap, drinking in help from the landscape that was still and cooling beyond the window glass; a green hill, a little stand of birch trees. His picture come upon so unexpectedly was a blow. She'd never had any photograph of him apart from the out-of-date one on the back flap of his books. She looked again. He was in quarter-profile, staring sombrely in black and white, outlined against bookshelves. Painfully, Cora had to begin to supply him with a study in his house somewhere in the Monnow Valley. She couldn't read the blurry titles on the spines of the books. Paul's hair was untidy and she thought that his air of spiritual, troubled absorption was contrived for the camera. He had become already not quite the man she'd known, changed by whatever had happened to him since they parted: the set of the full, pale lips was more definite, the grain of the complexion thicker, the jaw fleshed more heavily. He had never belonged to her.

There was a childhood picture too, which was almost more wounding – the socks pulled tightly up, the skinny chest thrust forward as if at attention, the too-beaming offer of himself to his mother or whoever pointed the camera. Cora didn't know if she could bear to read the article – and then she read it. Paul remembered borrowing books about nature from the Birmingham central library when he was a boy. His idea of nature at that time, he wrote, had been as a Platonic intimation of a more real reality outside the built-up cave of his city present: the lists of bird names and diagrams of animal spoor were symbols of a transcendent elsewhere. That library building had replaced the Victorian reference library, demolished in the Sixties, and had itself been replaced since. He said that since his mother had died, the last link to his past in the old city had been broken.

So his mother had died.

And his oldest daughter must have had a baby; he was a grandfather, which seemed extraordinary. This daughter must be living with them now, or near them, because he implied that he saw his granddaughter every day.

It was as if Cora read these things about a stranger.

Once, Cora had believed that living built a cumulative bank of memories, thickening and deepening as time went on, shoring you against emptiness. She had used to treasure up relics from every phase of her life as it passed, as if they were holy. Now that seemed to her a falsely consoling model of experience. The present was always paramount, in a way that thrust you forward: empty, but also free. Whatever stories you told over to yourself and others, you were in truth exposed and naked in the present, a prow cleaving new waters; your past was insubstantial behind, it fell away, it grew into desuetude, its forms grew obsolete. The problem was, you were always still alive, until the end. You had to do something.

* * *

Robert felt the afternoon outside without looking at it: mildly grey, unimportant. A flossy indefinite light made everything seem to keep still, out of indifference; summer was over, foliage wasn't miraculous any longer, only a plain fact. Footsteps approaching in the street, and passing, didn't rouse him. He was in Cora's house in Cardiff, sitting with his back to the window, at the wooden table in the front room she used as a desk (but didn't use much), writing a letter on her laptop, painstakingly picking out the letters with his right hand because his left (he was left-handed) was bandaged, and in a sling. The air of the house was vaguely stale around him – he had been there now for two days, waiting for her, and he hadn't opened any windows, or got round to washing any of the dishes he'd used, which were piled in the kitchen sink, though he fully intended to attack them sometime soon (his excuse to himself was that the bandage made chores bothersome). He hadn't gone out once since he arrived, in case he missed Cora, but there had been food in her freezer, home-cooked and meticulously labelled in her big clear hand. Defrosting and heating soup and shepherd's pie in her microwave, he had felt himself in a kind of comical, tenuous connection with her, though only through his theft; eating her food alone, the illusion of their connection failed him. He did not know what she would think of his invading here, making himself at home among her things. He had run out of milk this morning and was drinking his tea and coffee black.

Deliberately, Robert hadn't once turned the television

on. He didn't want to know whether they were making any fuss about him – or not, as was more likely (he didn't flatter himself on the subject of his importance). He had not opened up the computer either, before he sat down to write this letter; nor had he spoken on the telephone until twenty minutes ago, when Frankie called him on his mobile. He hardly knew what he had done with all the hours that had passed since he got here. At first, of course, he had expected Cora back at any moment. When he'd arrived yesterday he hadn't had any idea of entering the house without her permission; however, when he turned into the little concreted area in front of the house, he'd seen at once that her keys were hanging from the lock in the closed door. Robert rang the bell and knocked, but no one came; Cora must have opened the door in a hurry and then gone out again later, not noticing that she hadn't retrieved her keys. From her key ring there dangled – as well as an ornamental knot of beads and ribbon, tarnished from being tumbled around in the bottom of her bag – other keys beside the Yale stuck into the lock, including a mortise Robert guessed was for their London flat. It was lucky he had come along before anyone else saw them. He had hesitated before letting himself in. But it would have been too ostentatiously tactful to hover outside, waiting to present the keys when Cora appeared, so that she could open her own door. He hoped she wouldn't imagine that in rescuing them he meant to be reproachful, or gloating.

At first he had wandered round her rooms, picking

up sections of newspapers that were out of date, and then not finishing reading anything in them. He had made a conscious effort, to begin with, not to take anything in: he was not supposed to be inside here, so he mustn't take advantage of it by studying the shape of how Cora lived, or interpreting any traces she had left, as if he was spying. In any case, there were no traces; it was remarkable, he thought, how little mark the tumult of inward experience leaves on the external shells we inhabit. He couldn't tell whether the clean, tidy place, with all its bright, hopeful decoration, meant that Cora was happy in her new life without him, or unhappy. He only allowed himself to notice, because it was relevant to his mission here, that there were no signs of any man living in the house with her, or even visiting it. Anyway, being so acutely attuned to her sensibility – and because she was so conspicuous, incapable of concealment, whatever efforts she made – he had felt sure from their few meetings and conversations recently that there was not another man now; just as he had felt sure when there was. As the hours passed and she did not return, he was less certain. After all, anything could be happening to her, in this very moment. Nothing could be worse, he supposed, than for Cora to come back from the embraces of some new lover and find him waiting.

Nonetheless, stubbornly, against all his best calculations, he waited.

It was even oddly a relief, inhabiting Cora's space, as if it meant he could stop thinking about her. He had a lot of other things to think about. He had to make plans.

On Thursday evening his mood was buoyant, exhilarated, amidst this comical blow-up in his career. Its tone was definitely farce as opposed to tragedy. He even began to be glad that Cora hadn't turned up yet. Where else in his life would he ever come across such a pocket of free time as this one he had stumbled into accidentally: empty hours upon hours, with no external constraints, nothing required of him? Losing his inhibitions, poking round in Cora's cupboards, he found her whisky first, then decided to help himself to food. He turned on his phone, only for long enough to glimpse a backlog of messages and missed calls he didn't check through, and to send one text to his sister, reassuring her he was all right, but not telling her where he was. Then he looked on Cora's shelves for something to read, and took down *Vanity Fair*, which he had loved when he was fifteen for the Battle of Waterloo.

Long past the middle of the night, when he felt sure that Cora wasn't going to come now until morning, he went upstairs to sleep. The spare beds weren't made up, and he didn't know where to find sheets, so he slept in hers, only stalled momentarily by the sight of her pretty white-embroidered pillow cases and duvet. Really, he was suddenly too tired to care whether he desecrated anything. He hadn't bathed for a couple of days; he was still in the crumpled suit he'd dressed in on Monday morning, although he had at least bought clean underwear and shirt on his way to Paddington. He had changed into these – more farce – in the toilets in the first-class lounge. He undressed down to this underwear now, climbed into Cora's bed – only cold at the first shock – and slept that night more deeply than he had for weeks, or months or years, dropping down so far that if he had dreams at all, he carried nothing back from them when he surfaced, only seemed to have dredged some deeply silted ocean-bottom. Waking on Friday, he had no idea what time it was. He'd slept with the blinds up: the stuffy, unsecret daylight outside the window gave no clue whether it was morning or afternoon. Cars droned every so often in the street, the footsteps of passers-by were dawdling and indefinite after London. He heard their dogs' scuffing, or the dogs' nails tip-tapping on the pavement.

By the kitchen clock, it was past one in the afternoon. He hadn't slept as late as that since he was a teenager, even when he'd been ill (he was hardly ever ill), or jet-lagged after a long-haul flight. Some tight-coiled spring wound up in him for years was winding down dramatically. He ran a bath and washed his hair, a strange indulgence in the afternoon; found a new toothbrush in its packet in a cupboard. His bruises hurt less, and he unbound the bandage to check on his sprained wrist, and the gash on his hand. After his bath he had to dress again in the same clothes, and he couldn't shave. Still Cora didn't come. There was no reason to think she would be back today, Robert decided: probably she had gone away for the weekend. But he would wait. His wait had transformed into something beyond its ostensible purpose, weighing him down like the silt from his dreams.

A tabby cat persisted in its efforts to make eye contact through the kitchen window; he let it in, fed it the end of the shepherd's pie. Then he played music. Cora had taken most of the music when they separated, and some of the CDs he recognised as his, from before he knew her: the Amadeus playing Beethoven late quartets, Solomon playing Mozart. These had been his mother's favourites, he liked them for her sake, even though he hadn't been close to her. He had used to dread the scenes she made. Probably he'd been horribly priggish, he thought now. His mother must have thought he was trying to imitate his father's detachment. She must have seen through the stubborn, principled stands that Robert made when he was a boy and a young man, pretending he was the only sane and reasonable one, conforming to some inflexible standard of decency and decorum, while all the time he was burning with a rage like hers, only turned inwards. In Robert's dreamy, sluggish state now, the music penetrated him purely, without distraction.

The letter he wrote late Friday afternoon, on Cora's laptop, wasn't to her. The things he wanted to say to Cora – ask her – couldn't be written, they could only be communicated face to face. That was what he was waiting for. In the meantime, he was writing a letter of resignation. He explained to the Permanent Secretary the whole sequence of events that had led to his absence from work on Tuesday, and in the days following: that on his way to work as usual on Tuesday he had been involved in an accident on the wet steps leading down to the Underground station, sustaining significant bruising down his right side and a sprained wrist, also a deep cut on his hand that had produced a quantity of blood that was not really significant, but alarming enough for someone to call an ambulance. The paramedics had insisted on taking him to UCH, where they had stitched him up and X-rayed his wrist and given him a tetanus injection, keeping him in for observation, because he seemed to be exhibiting some symptoms of mild amnesia, not remembering where he lived or worked. Because of this temporary amnesia he had failed to let the office know where he was, and he apologised for any inconvenience this may have caused. In the meantime, as he recovered, the unexpected interruption to his routines had given him an opportunity to reflect on his deep dissatisfaction with his present work-life balance – entirely his own fault – and he had decided to terminate his relationship with the Civil Service from this point.

It all sounded magnificently unconvincing, although apart from the amnesia it was more or less true. It had not been amnesia, it had been something stranger – a dark tide of malaise, a conviction of disaster – that washed over him as he lay on the filthy floor, where he had been thrown quite accidentally by a boy who'd tripped over an elderly woman's umbrella and then fallen into Robert with all his weight. Everyone had been most concerned, and kind. He had wanted to reassure them, but he had lain silent, as if speech had been knocked out of him, or some ancient rusting machinery in his chest had locked on impact and refused to function. Probably his silence had frightened them more than the blood. He hadn't spoken at the hospital, either – he had only written on a pad whatever they needed to know, and in the end after two nights of broken thin hallucination that was not quite sleep, he had discharged himself, simply walked out. Probably he had not spoken to anyone since his fall (except perhaps the cat). At Paddington he had bought his ticket from a machine.

There were other aspects of the story that had no place in his letter: for instance, that the Underground station where he fell was King's Cross and not his usual one, and that he was there because he hadn't slept at home on Monday night, but had slept alone in a Travelodge in Gray's Inn Road, after an evening with a nice woman, an old friend from work, which probably both of them had meant to end in something more, but which had not. He had never intended, of course, to take this woman friend with him to the Travelodge – he might not be romantic, but he wasn't quite that bad. He had meant to go home with her, after they finished dinner, to where she had a nice little place off Upper Street: he had gone home with her a couple of times before, since Cora left. But when he did not – even though the friend made it clear that he was welcome – then he didn't want to sleep in his own flat, either. He was developing quite a horror of that flat, for a rational man. He'd already moved out of the bedroom he'd shared with Cora into the spare room, because it was less haunted.

Before he began writing, as a token of his re-establishing connection with a world outside, Robert had turned on his phone without checking it. When he was halfway through his letter, Frankie called. He cleared his throat, and talk was easy after all.

– Bobs! I can't believe it's actually you. Where on earth are you? Everybody's going mad here!

– Don't worry about me, I'm absolutely fine. Didn't you get my text?

– Didn't you get ours? Cora sent you one just after we got yours.

– I haven't checked my in-box. Where is Cora?

– Well, that's the strange thing. She came up here, because you were missing and I was sort of holding the fort at your flat. Damon took your laptop, by the way.

– Who is Damon? I don't care about the laptop.

– A ghastly SPAD. Is it all about the inquiry?

– I'm just rethinking my work-life balance.

– I can't believe you've actually said that. That's the kind of thing I'm supposed to say, and you laugh.

– So Cora's at the flat?

– No, that's just it. She slept there last night, in case you came back, but she was supposed to go home to Cardiff today, that's what she said she was going to do. But I've just had the most extraordinary call – from Bar, of all people.

– Bar?

– Exactly. And how did she get my number? I can only think she got in touch with Elizabeth, and she gave it to Bar. Anyway, I'm sure she was drunk, in the middle of the afternoon. Not Elizabeth. Did you know she had a son – and exhibits at a gallery in Savile Row?

– I knew about the paintings. They're rather good.

Frankie explained that apparently Cora had turned up at Bar's house, somewhere in deepest Devon; she had got the address out of Robert's book, and seemed to think Bar might have him stashed away somewhere.

– Probably I shouldn't be telling you this, Frankie said. – But it's all kind of extraordinary.

– Are you sure Bar didn't just get the wrong end of the stick?

– She was definitely pissed.

Cora, outside on the street, was searching in her bag for her keys. It was an awful moment: the street turned its stony face to her, implacable in the hard, dull afternoon light. She was supposed to leave spare keys with her neighbours, but they were often out. Anyway, she had a feeling she hadn't returned those keys since last she'd borrowed them back – they might still be in the pocket of her other coat. She was dog-tired and felt like crying. But what was the point? Sturdily she brought herself around to her new perspective, facing forward. She had better go down to the locksmith.

Then the door swung back, as if under the force of her will, which had pressed at its resistance without hope – and Robert was there, utterly unexpectedly. He looked awful, unshaven and in his socks.

– You left your keys in the door.

Irrationally she was angry, or her anguish sounded like it.

– Where have you been? she protested. – I've been looking for you everywhere.

In the shower an hour later, Cora thought she would confess to him. She would confess everything – that her heart had been fastened by heavy chains for a long miserable time to another man, and now it wasn't. She would confess all this before they consummated their reunion in bed. She would show him Paul's article – she had almost left it on the train, and then at the last moment she had put it in her bag and brought it with her – and she would get out all Paul's books and show them to Robert and then she would throw them all away. Cora was remembering her old, candid, self: unafraid, flinging open all the doors to the rooms of her life. She had put out fresh towels on the heated rail and the pelting hot water streaming off her was a glory. She had forgotten this exulting happiness was possible. In the garden beyond the open bathroom window a blackbird sang out in the intensifying late-afternoon light; the day was lovelier for hiding behind its grey veil. Robert had gone to buy shaving gear and clean underwear and clothes – God only knew what he'd come back with. She had laughed to think he'd have to go to the local Peacocks because there was no time to get into town before the shops shut.

– What's Peacocks?

– Don't you know anything? she'd teased him. – Don't

you know how ordinary people live? Then you'll have to learn. Peacocks is very, very cheap.

They had no idea what they were going to do next.

They weren't going back – not to London, not to Robert's job. For the moment they needn't decide. They had no ties and they could do anything, go anywhere. They had money; they could sell her house, or the flat, or both. They could go to India or America or Scotland. All that was certain was dinner that evening; they were both ravenous. She booked a table at the Italian where she used to go with her parents, warning him it was nothing very wonderful. After her shower she dressed quickly and dried her hair in front of the mirror in her bedroom, sprayed her wrists and behind her ears with Trésor. Then there was a change in the light, tipping between afternoon and evening – air that had been banal and transparent refined to blue, and a bar of dark lying along the floor crossed like a touch over her skin: sobering, admonitory. Cora stood breathing carefully under the spell of the moment.

She wasn't afraid of Robert, only of herself – in case she spoiled anything.

What words were there for what had happened while they were apart?

She wouldn't say anything, unless Robert asked. She would watch and see what he wanted. The night ahead was a brimming dish she had to carry without spilling it.

Acknowledgements

Thanks to Richard Kerridge, whose judgement mattered, and to Alice Bradley and Liz Porter, whose help with certain details was invaluable. The library building is based on a real library in Cardiff, but the staff are entirely imaginary. Thanks to Bath Spa University for teaching relief, and to Academi for a writer's bursary; these gave me precious time and freedom to work on the novel. Thanks of course, for everything, to Dan Franklin and Caroline Dawnay.